THE
NORTHLANDER

⚜

JOHN E. ELIAS

© 2011 John E. Elias
All rights reserved. No part of this publication may be reproduced or transmitted in any form or by any means electronic, mechanical, photocopying, recording or otherwise, without the prior written permission of the author or publisher.

Published by AKA-Publishing
Columbia, Missouri
www.aka-publishing.com

Designed by Yolanda Ciolli
www.yolandaciolli.com

Library of Congress
Elias, John E.
The Northlander

ISBN 978-1-936688-08-1

THE NORTHLANDER

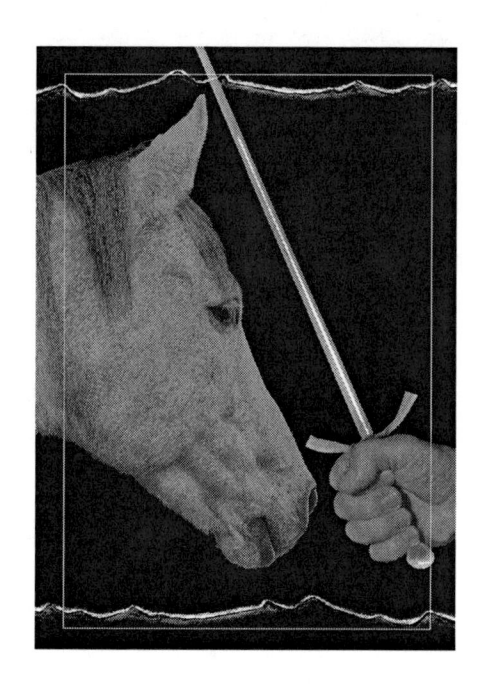

JOHN E. ELIAS

Dedication

This book is dedicated to my four wonderful and loving children: Lisa, Alan, Michael and Paula.

CHAPTER ONE
THE GENTLE PEOPLE

The stranger strolled down the dirt road, followed by a horse slightly behind and to his left. Their steps lifted small clouds of dust that trailed behind them.

The man was average height and slender; some would call him thin. His skin stretched tightly over his face, accenting his high cheekbones, sharp nose, and thin lips. His eyes, a unique dark gray color that was almost black, were the most prominent feature of his face. Though his eyes were focused lazily ahead, they gave the impression that they missed little.

His hair was also dark gray, but that seemed to be its natural color, not from age. It was short and wiry, the cut rough as though he was unconcerned with appearance.

He wore clothes of dark brown hide, and the material rippled and moved with his stride, like cloth instead of leather. His shirt appeared more like a short jacket covering the top of his trousers with a cowl hanging down the back.

His brisk pace exposed the hilt of a short sword hanging at his waist and except for the two long swords that hung on his back his appearance, while unique, would not have drawn more than casual attention. The swords were much longer than most and incredibly thin. The hilts sat above his shoulders on each side of his muscled neck, and the blades hung almost to his ankles. Because of their length, it looked like they might tangle with his legs and trip him at any step, but they swung in rhythm with his stride, as though from long and careful practice. The swords were enclosed in sheaths made from the same material as his clothes.

The horse was dun colored, his body compact with powerful legs, neck and back. A large roll of what looked like an animal hide was thrown across its back and fastened neatly under its belly. A bag was tied to either side of the horse, and attached to one of the bags was a bow as long as an average man was tall, and wraps containing many long lethal-looking arrows. Like the man, the horse appeared unconcerned with his surroundings. Both walked steadily, their pace purposeful, as though they had a specific destination in mind.

Steep mountains lay in the distance in all four directions. Between the mountains, the land rolled with gentle hills, meadows, slow-moving streams, and a river. While most of the land was open, forests and groves of trees were scattered throughout. The countryside was peaceful; birds sang, small animals strayed in and around buildings, and people went about their tasks intent upon their work.

Homesteads with cabins and barns dotted the landscape, and the farmland was divided into small fields by rock walls. It was spring planting time. Men, women, and children worked the fields. The men plowed furrows in the earth, using horses, oxen and, in some cases, donkeys. The plows ranged all the way from sturdy metal to wood. Women and children sowed the seed, while older children followed, employing a variety of implements—from flat boards with handles to limbs with branches—to cover the seeds. If any of the farmers noticed the pair on the road, they did so covertly.

The river ran lazily through the land bordering the road. It was relatively wide, shallow, and slow-moving, but at a few points it narrowed and speeded up, running noisily over rapids.

Farm work was underway on both sides of the river. When the river was quiet, sounds carried clearly over the water, and the man could hear families talking as they went about their work.

Across the river, a young boy working with an older man threw down his hoe angrily. His voice carried clearly across the water as though he were beside the road.

"Why do we have to work so hard when they take everything?" he shouted. "We go to bed hungry at night while they feast on what we grow and on the animals we raise."

The older man spoke softly, but his voice still carried. "Be careful, my son. We do not know who is listening."

"I do not care, Father. We just buried Londa. If there had been enough to eat, she would still be alive. And mother just stays in the cabin and cries. I wish we could leave this place."

"Please, my son, your mother cannot travel. And where would we go? Our families have lived here as long as any of us can remember. I have no idea where to take us."

"Anywhere would be better than here," the boy said bitterly.

The father's sigh could be heard clearly across the water. "Please, my son, we must get this field planted and let me think about it."

The traveler murmured softly to the horse, "Jago, it may be that this will be an interesting place."

A small village appeared ahead of them. It was laid out haphazardly as though it had simply grown over the years rather than being the result of a plan. The buildings were constructed from rough-hewn lumber of varying sizes, and the roofs were thatch. There were few windows and the doors were small. From the coloration and aging of the wood, the cabins were obviously of different ages; few were new. The others varied so greatly in age that they seemed to be from separate eras.

A short distance apart from the village, on a small hill, stood a tiny church, very different from the other buildings. While the buildings in the village were in good repair and showed the effects of care, the church was neglected. Weeds and shrubs grew high around it. Windows were broken, and the door hung off its hinges. Part of it had been damaged by fire.

Six children played a game with smooth, round stones in the road. To the traveler, it seemed that the purpose of the game was for one player to cast a large stone a short distance ahead, and for the rest of the players to attempt to hit it with smaller stones they tossed. The four boys and two girls were engrossed in their play, squealing gleefully when a small stone struck the large one.

Suddenly, an argument broke out and one of the boys grabbed the stone of the smallest girl and tossed it away from the playing area. The stone skipped down the road, striking the traveler's boot. The children grew silent except for the small girl, who cried softly.

The man stopped, reached down, and picked up the stone. The stone and the children at play cracked through the normal tight control of his emotions and brought back a painful memory.

As a small boy, he had watched other children playing. They took turns tossing little, round vertebrae from a marlot, a large rodent, toward a line they had drawn on a rock. The purpose of the game was to see whose cast came closest to the line. When each player had made a cast, the game began anew. Björn the boy watched.

"Come, Björn, that is not for you," a tall man said to the boy. The man turned and walked up the path. When the boy did not follow, he spoke again. "Come, Björn," he repeated. The boy reluctantly followed.

One of the players teased the boy. In a falsetto voice, he mimicked, "Come, Björn. Come, Björn." The memory was still alive for the traveler.

"Mister, can I have my stone?" the small girl asked. When he did not respond, she repeated, "Mister, can I have my stone?"

The traveler started as his mind was yanked back to the present. Squatting, he held out the stone to the child, who took it with a small "Thank you." As they resumed their game, the traveler stayed in a crouch, watching them for several long moments. The long-forgotten memory brought with it strange feelings, feelings he found disturbing. He stood, shook himself like a dog shaking water from its coat, and continued down the road into the village.

Except for the children playing in their strange fashion, the only people to be seen in the village were two elderly women sitting on a log in front of a small cabin built into the side of a hill. One of the women smoked a long pipe while she stripped husks from a basket of corn, and the other worked on a small piece of material in her lap. From the look of it, she was creating a small garment. Neither woman spoke, each working diligently at her task, one smoking with small streams of smoke coming from both her mouth and the bowl of the pipe while the other sewed. With downcast eyes, they furtively watched the stranger.

The traveler and his horse stopped in front of a building

different from the rest. While built in the same casual style with the same rough-hewn wood, and obviously ancient; it had two stories rather than one, and was wider than the other buildings. It looked like some sort of community building, and it squatted as though it had been built and then dropped into place rather than being built where it stood. Its heavy door hung open, as if the last person in had forgotten to close it.

The man gave a small movement of his left hand to the horse. The horse stopped and stood still, and the man moved through the large door and stepped quickly to the left against the wall.

The room was huge. To the traveler's left was a store with items displayed ranging from clothing to farm equipment to produce. Ahead and to his right, a massive bar ran to the right wall, and rough tables and matching chairs were scattered aimlessly on the dirt floor in front of it. Seven men sat at a round table in front of the bar, several drinking from large mugs. They stared at the stranger expectantly.

A giant of a man with his back to the bar rose slowly and deliberately to his feet, as if the movement pained him. His heavily muscled arms hung loosely at his sides. His large head and its blunt features matched his body. A shaggy thatch of black hair hung to his shoulders, but it was not quite enough to hide the fact that he had no ears, which appeared to have been severed from his head. There were numerous scars on his face, hands, and arms. Even though he was an extremely big-boned man, he was almost emaciated.

"Can we help you, stranger?" he said.

"You sent for me."

"You are the Northlander?"

"Yes, I am Björn."

"I am Thane. Can I get you something?"

"No," Björn said tersely. "Tell me what you want."

"Do you want to sit?"

"No."

Thane dropped back into his chair painfully. The other men stared at the stranger, and one of them blurted, "You do not look like much."

Thane raised a threatening fist in front of the man, and he cringed and was silent.

"We have long been a happy people," Thane said. "Because the mountains cut us off from the outside world, we are not involved in the wars or intrigues of that world. Occasionally, travelers and peddlers stop here, and they keep us aware of what is going on beyond the mountains. That is the way our people have lived as long as anyone can remember peacefully with each other and with few troubles.

"This is good land," he continued. "While there are sometimes poor crop years, we have always lived well. We have never bothered anyone else and because of where we are, few have ever bothered us.

"There is a castle near here that has long been abandoned. According to legend, it was the home of a great king, but it was so long ago none of us remember. Some years ago, a cult of cruel people moved there. We know not from where they came, but they worship gods that are foreign to us. These gods are evil, as are the intruders; they took control of our village and the countryside. Some of us fought back, but it was hopeless." Thane's voice became angry. "We are not soldiers and we have no real weapons. The newcomers are armed warriors. They forced some of our people to make repairs on the castle, while from others they took furniture and other goods. Most of the grain and animals we raise they take for their food. They have taken some of our children, who have not returned.

"They have also taken many of our women over the years. Many have returned, but some have not. Those who return tell stories of being raped and beaten. We live in terror of these monsters, and we now live in poverty. Over the years, we have been able to save a little that we hid from them, and when we heard about you, we sent you money we had saved and asked you to come."

One of the drinking men said belligerently, "I do not see what one man can do. There are at least two hundred of them in the castle."

Björn ignored him. "Do they have leaders?"

"There are a few among them, perhaps ten or twelve, whom they call priests. These are the ones who give orders and are the most cruel of all."

"Tell me where they are."

"The castle is in the mountains at the edge of a valley shaped like a bowl. Let me show you." Thane began to draw with his finger in the dust on the table. "Here is our village and here is the castle. You can reach it in half a day. Would you like to rest and eat before you go?"

"No." Without another word, the Northlander slipped sideways through the doorway and backed into the road to the horse. Without looking back, man and beast walked down the road, out of the village in the direction of the castle.

The seven men emerged from the tavern and watched them walk away. The villager who had spoken first repeated, "I still do not think he looks like much. We have wasted our money."

Thane looked at him and sardonically asked, "You can

go after him and tell him that again. He will surely still be patient with you. Of course, those long swords and the knife are just for show."

The first man blushed and slunk back into the tavern.

Another man spoke slowly. "You know we have no more to pay him. You have heard the stories about him. When he returns he will kill us all."

Thane responded, almost as though he was talking to himself. "It is unlikely that he will return, but if he does, at least the rest of our people will be free. Do not worry about yourselves; I will tell the Northlander this plan was all my doing."

The other men drifted away—some into the tavern, others to their homes. Thane, left alone with his thoughts, watched the man and horse until they disappeared in the distance.

Thane could still visualize Netta as well as when she were alive. She was not a pretty woman, tall and angular, with a strong face with prominent features, but when combined with her lively personality, Thane found her beautiful. He had always been amazed that she had picked him out to love, and he was always proud that everyone knew she was his woman. He loved to just watch her; no matter what she was doing, it always gave him a thrill.

He had loved her since they were children. They had often played together with the other children and then later with the youth their age. He had always been bashful around her.

When other young men began to court her, he was jealous, but he could not bring himself to tell her how he felt. He watched her covertly, fantasizing often about them being together. When she rejected all of the suitors, what little resolve he had disappeared. If she will not pick one of them, she surely will not pick me, he thought. He knew he was big, clumsy, and not at all good-looking, and his older brother had inherited the family land so Thane had limited prospects.

He still remembered the day as clearly as though it were yesterday, even though it was many years ago. Working in the tavern and general store, he was loading bags of seed grain for a customer. Out of the corner of his eye, he saw her walking down the road toward him. Placing a bag in the wagon, he turned to find her standing in front of him, hands on her hips and a stern look on her face. Thane feared no man, but he was terrified of this woman, and his huge body trembled.

Netta looked at him for several minutes, then said, "Everyone says you are the bravest man in the village. Are you?"

All he could do was look at the ground because he didn't know what to say.

She continued, "If you are so brave, why are you so afraid to court me?"

"Are you making fun of me?" he blurted because he could think of nothing else to say.

He vividly remembered what she said next. "I have grown tired of waiting for you, Thane. I will expect you this evening after dinner. We will walk by the river, and we will be married next month."

He stared dumbly at her. He tried to answer, but could only stutter. She smiled, and he felt that his heart would leap from his body, and when she said, "I have always loved you, you know," he thought his whole body would melt into the ground.

But he managed to present himself for dinner, and they strolled by the river that evening and the evenings that followed. True to her word, they were married the following month, and they had a great life together. It took awhile, but at last he was able to talk to her. The only disappointment in their lives was that they could not have children.

Then came the awful day when the warrior intruders kidnapped her as they did other females from the village. They took her when Thane was away helping a farmer rebuild a barn that was destroyed by a storm. Two young boys came running from the village, gasping that men from the castle had taken Netta and three other women. By the time Thane returned, two of the women had already stumbled back to the village, but not Netta.

Thane used his great strength to break a massive limb from a tree before he made the trek to the castle, where he was met by armed members of the cult. While they had swords and knew how to use them, and even though he had only the club and had never fought in his life, he killed several and injured a number of others. But they were too many and too skillful, even for his great courage and even greater rage. Cruelly, they did not kill him, but left him crippled, lying in the dirt in front of the castle. He managed to crawl to a small stream where he drank, then immersed himself in the water to clean the blood from his body. He told himself that his strength would return and he would be able to attack the castle and rescue Netta, he forced himself not to think of what they must be doing to her.

The next day he was able to stand with the aid of his club they had arrogantly let him keep. As he hobbled toward the castle, he saw Netta emerge. She was completely bare, her body bloody and bruised. Stumbling to her, he took her arm. She didn't look at him; she only stared straight ahead with glassy eyes that saw nothing.

Reaching into himself, he drew strength he didn't know he had and held her cold body, but she did not respond. Leading her back to their home, he washed her, dressed her, then sat her in a chair at the table. He tried to give her food and water, but she simply sat at the table with a vacant look in her eyes.

All that day, that night, and the next day, she sat like that, neither moving nor speaking. She didn't seem to hear him when he spoke to her. The following day, when he returned with water from the community well, he found her on the floor in blood that had spewed from the gash in her throat. She had killed herself with a kitchen knife.

He had never before cried, but he dropped to the floor, held her body tenderly, and sobbed. A woman from the village found them later that day. She called others, and they took Thane and Netta to the well to wash them clean of blood. Two of the women went to their cabin and brought clothes for them. All Thane could do was stand numbly as they dressed him. Then they took Netta's body, the women supporting him as the men placed her in a coffin and carried her to the cemetery. They placed a small wooden marker on the grave and cut her name in it.

For days he sat lifelessly in the tavern, eating and drinking little, because he couldn't bring himself to return to their home. The day he did return, he torched their cabin and watched it burn to the ground. Then he returned to his duties at the tavern, going through the motions of running the tavern and general store, but his thoughts were almost constantly on Netta.

Now Thane continued to stare in the direction taken by the Northlander and his horse. For perhaps the first time in his life he prayed, "Lord, I have never asked you for anything, and perhaps this is not the right thing to ask for, but if you can see your way to it, please help the Northlander. Please help him destroy those evil men and keep them from hurting others as they hurt my Netta." He spoke again to himself. "I hope the Northlander is all that we have heard him to be."

He turned and walked slowly and painfully into the tavern.

The valley lay in the midst of sharp mountain peaks. The castle had been built into the steep cliffs at one end so that it appeared to be part of the mountain. Most of the castle had fallen into ruin, and the stones that had made up the upper rooms and spires had either tumbled into the rooms below or toppled into the valley.

There were only two approaches to the castle that Björn could see. One was a natural winding, but wide road through passes in the mountains to the north; the other was a steep, narrow road that had been hacked into the mountains on the opposite side of the valley. As the road climbed the mountain, the edge dropped off abruptly into the valley. Stones, rocks, and debris from the mountain lay on the valley floor next to the cliff.

Björn and Jago stood unmoving on the narrow road. They had spent several days circling the valley, learning the land, and watching the fortress. They had come to know the land but had learned little of the castle or its inhabitants. Dark-robed figures moved about the castle grounds, evidently going about chores. Beyond that there had been little activity.

Björn and his companion, Jago had been standing there since the sun had risen above the mountain peaks, illuminating the valley floor and the semi-ruined structure. The sun was directly overhead when three robed figures with deep hoods hiding their faces left the castle and walked across the valley to the bottom of the road. Wide sashes encircled their waists, and short, heavy swords hung from the sashes.

"What do you want?" one of them shouted from the valley floor. Björn did not answer. The man repeated his question and still Björn did not respond. Neither he nor the horse moved.

The three figures climbed the road and when they stood in front of the pair, the man in the center repeated his question. "What do you want?"

After a tense silence, the Northlander answered. "If all of you leave now, taking only the clothes you wear, we will let you live."

The robed men started, and the man on the right blurted, "Where is your army?"

"We are the army," Björn replied.

The men stared at him, then the one in the center signaled the other two with his head and they drew their swords. Showing they were well trained, they lunged at him in unison, but before any of them could land a blow, Björn caught the wrist of the center man, preventing his weapon from doing damage. Still holding the man's arm firmly, Björn whirled and planted a violent kick in the stomach of the man nearest the edge of the road, sending him flying to the rocks below. Lifting the man into the air and using his body like a club, he struck the third man with such force that he was knocked from the road to join his partner on the rocks.

Björn returned the man to his feet, but still held him fast.

"I will let you live for now," he said. "Return to the castle and give your priests my message. Leave the castle with only the clothes on your backs before the sun sets and you will live. If not, you will all die here."

Björn released the man with a shove that sent him staggering down the road. Recovering his balance, the man turned and ran across the valley to the castle.

A short time later, a dozen men in the same dark cloaks marched out of the castle and stood under the trees on a small plateau next to the castle, watching the man and horse. Björn was still for a few moments, then he stepped to the horse and removed the long bow and two arrows. Notching an arrow in the bow, he took aim and let the arrow fly. One man fell, kicked for a few moments, and then lay still. The others looked at him for a few seconds, and then turned to flee into the castle. Another man was felled by an arrow before they reached shelter. Then all was silent.

Björn and Jago stood as before, watching the castle. Later that afternoon, thirty dark-robed men emerged from the castle. They trotted three abreast down the steep slope from the castle, across the valley, and up the road toward Björn. They marched silently, swords raised. Without breaking stride, they approached at a trot in perfect unison. Up the road they came to within thirty yards of Björn and the horse. Only then did Björn move.

He drew his two swords and grunted a rough short sound. "Jago." The horse flew past him and charged the armed men. Leaping into the air, Jago executed a perfect capriole, striking with his hind hooves. Two men fell instantly from the blows, and then another toppled under strikes from its front hooves before the horse hit the ground. The horse charged into the center of the men, his feet again leaving the ground and striking two men with his front hooves. Twisting in mid-air, he struck two others with his rear hooves. The sound of bones shattering almost drowned out the screams of terror.

The tightly grouped men broke into total disarray. Struggling to escape the horse, the men violently jostled each other, and some on the outside were knocked off the road to fall screaming to the rocks below, ending their screams abruptly.

Björn charged into the disorganized mass. His swords flashed, and heads flew from bodies while torsos were impaled. Jago continued his savage assault, and the robed men attempting to flee were trapped in the chaos. A few attempted to fight back, but they were helplessly off balance. The attack was over in moments. Bodies were strewn on the road and others were broken on the rocks in the valley. Screams, groans, pleas for help, and struggling movements came from those still alive.

The two victors ignored their victims, passing through the gore to the bottom of the road. There they resumed their silent vigil.

The sun passed behind the mountains, and darkness fell quickly. There was no moon and, as night took control of the valley, it grew dark, so dark a person might reach out to touch the blackness.

The two figures moved silently across the valley to the outer walls of the castle and listened, sensing sounds and movements within the castle. Björn touched Jago's neck, and the horse trotted away toward the entrance of the castle, moving unnoticed and stood motionless near the massive front door.

Björn headed stealthily in the opposite direction to the ruined section of the rambling structure. Picking his way carefully through the destroyed walls, he moved like an invisible spirit. Coming to a corridor still open, he entered cautiously. Once inside, he carefully leaned his bow and arrows against the wall and, drawing one sword, he moved warily into the castle.

The interior of the fortress was darker even than the complete darkness outside, but Björn, eyes trained to maneuver in any environment, moved as if he were in broad daylight. The corridor was long and straight, but it was filled and in some places almost blocked by fallen stones, but the Northlander made his way with little difficulty.

The corridor led into the portion of the castle that had suffered least from the years and weather. This part was apparently occupied by the intruders. The passageway ended at a thick door that effectively blocked further progress. Björn studied it, then felt gingerly over the entire surface with his hands.

Finally, he grasped one section of the door that was broken by the weight of a stone that had shifted above it, and gave it a gradual pull. At first it did not move, so Björn braced one foot against the door frame and pulled again. The door groaned loudly and the broken section began to move. Exerting even more pressure, Björn opened the cracked section of the door until the cleared space was large enough for him to pass through.

Twisting his body, he slipped into another passageway. A flickering light appeared in the distance, but Björn continued his forward progress exactly as he had in the darkness.

After advancing a distance, he heard voices and paused to peer around a corner. Three guards a short span away from him were arguing. They appeared spooked, and

Björn guessed that they had heard his attack on the door. One wanted to investigate, another claimed it was only the sound of a rock falling, and the third could not decide what they should do. Björn crept noiselessly toward them.

The discussion eventually abated and the decision became one of doing nothing. The guards remained at their posts with occasional short conversation. While it appeared they took their guarding seriously, they were not on high alert.

Björn waited. He was very good at waiting.

The guards grew quiet, and Björn heard snoring. One of the guards kicked the snoring one, and a second short argument ensued. Then it was quiet again.

Björn continued to wait in silence. The snoring resumed and this time was not interrupted. Björn moved warily down the corridor, a shadow. When he reached the sleeping guards, there was a short struggle and the sound of throats gasping for air. Then Björn moved on, and the bloody scenario was repeated throughout the night. Björn detected men before they were aware of him and then quietly and efficiently dispatched them.

He found a room where many men slept, concluding it was some type of dormitory. Passing it by, he twice more came upon rooms filled with sleeping men, and again crept silently past them.

Discovering a small room dimly lit by a flickering torch, he found three females huddled on the floor. When the two women and a young girl saw him, they clutched each other in terror and drew as far from him as possible. Both women were without clothing and the girl was clothed only in wisps of fabric.

Björn crouched just inside the door and spoke to them softly, reassuring them until they were calm. He moved slowly to them and held out his hand. After a time, one woman took his hand. Motioning to the others, he led them from the room, guiding them down the halls to the place where he had entered the castle. Standing outside in the darkness with only light coming from the stars overhead, he pointed the way for them to take to reach their village. As they moved away, the girl turned to look at him, then turned and walked toward the village with the others. Björn watched until the captives disappeared in the darkness.

"Those are the last females they will take," he muttered to himself. "This world will be a much better place when these monsters are gone from it." He re-entered the castle and continued his careful exploration.

It was early morning when he reached the upper chambers of the inhabited section of the castle. The rooms were lit by sunlight filtering through large windows, in sharp contrast to the lower floors that received no external light and remained in the same darkness both night and day, lighted only by torches placed in wall brackets or carried by patrol squads.

Reaching an area that was richly furnished compared to the Spartan layouts of the rooms he had seen below, he heard voices. He drew into the shadows and waited. The voices came from a chamber beyond where Björn had penetrated. He crept through the outer room to a door at the opposite end. The voices came from within. They were muffled, but Björn determined that there were three men talking. He returned his swords to their scabbards and crouched in front of the door.

Slowly, with efficient movements, he moved the latch, which was locked. Under his slow and precise pressure, the latch opened soundlessly. Applying pressure to the door to open it, he stepped back, drew his swords and kicked the door in. It flew open to reveal three black-robed men, hoods thrown back as they lounged on luxurious chairs in front of a roaring fire. They were tall gaunt men with narrow pinched faces.

As Björn launched himself into the room, they rushed to their feet, scrambling for weapons arranged on a table behind them. Before they could arm themselves, Björn drove a sword through the chest of one and beheaded the second with his other sword. But the third man moved with extraordinary quickness, scooping up a sword as he turned to meet Björn's attack. He wielded the sword expertly and held Björn at bay long enough to shout an alarm, but he was at a severe disadvantage against the two swirling swords.

Focused tightly on his task despite the potential attack the shout might bring, Björn speared the man's midsection with one sword, and with the other sheared his head from his shoulders. Then he fled across the room and down the hall, running into a spacious room he had explored earlier. Like a rabbit in its warren, he had established three escape routes. He sped down one of them. He was confident the room would still be unoccupied, but whether it was or not did not matter; this was his preferred escape route.

He slipped quickly behind a large tapestry hiding a large window. He had opened the window when he first checked the room, and now stepped through it, placing his feet carefully on a narrow ledge running along the castle wall outside. He edged along until he reached a sharp corner. Here the ledge ended, but the corner was actually a deep V and the ledge resumed on the other side. Björn eased into the V, bracing himself against the sides with his feet and arms.

Pandemonium broke loose in the castle. Sleeping men

were abruptly awakened, and Björn heard them as they spread out searching. Cries of alarm and terror sounded as the searchers discovered bodies. By the time the search sounded more organized, the sun had risen over the far mountains.

Björn was still braced against the walls in the V. An ordinary man's muscles would have long ago become cramped from the strain, forcing him to give up the effort, but Björn was unaffected.

He heard rooms and corridors being searched and windows and doors being flung open. The searchers became more quiet. Björn assumed they were frustrated from the hours they had spent trying to find him. He heard the leaders barking commands, ordering the men not to overlook any possible hiding place.

The window from which Björn had exited was opened. It remained open for a short time, and he could hear a man breathing heavily. Then the window closed.

Hanging on his precarious perch, Björn reflected on what he had seen in his clandestine survey of the castle. A few men, most probably the priests, lived in luxury. The rest lived in regimented sparse quarters. There had been one large room with no furniture other than a flat rectangular stone slab set on short stone columns. Four chains were anchored to each side of the slab, and a dark red, and in some areas black, substance that Björn recognized as dried blood covered the slab, the column, and the floor around the slab.

Behind the slab, an enormous tapestry covered the entire wall. Painted on the tapestry was a huge face, long and narrow with prominent eyes, nose, mouth, and protruding teeth. In all his travels, Björn had never seen anything so repulsive and hideous. He guessed the tapestry to be ancient because of many creases and cracks in a few places where it appeared to have been rolled up like a rug. He presumed this was the cult's place of worship, with live sacrifices taking place on the altar, and he could make a good guess as to what type of living creatures were sacrificed there.

Björn estimated that he had killed a few more than forty men in his furtive sortie through the castle. According to the estimate of the man in the village, there were at least two hundred men in the sect. This left considerably more to do.

The search extended to the grounds outside. From his perch, Björn saw small groups of men walking the open spaces, checking the woods carefully, poking spears and sometimes swords into thickets. They found nothing but small animals and birds. He thought it significant that they hunted in groups, none searching individually or even in groups of less than five.

He wondered where Jago was, but he was unconcerned, as Jago would be found when he wanted to be.

Björn thought there was little chance he would be seen. The hunters didn't look up, and even if they had, he was hidden in shadow, in his dark clothing blending into the castle wall.

The sun grew high in the heavens, and the search dwindled. The men searching the grounds returned to the castle, which grew quiet.

The Northlander contemplated his strategy, specifically his next move. From his years as a mercenary, he knew fear was his major ally. He also was aware that fear was greatest in the dark of night. While the interior of the castle was as dark at night as it was in the day, the night hours would be best for his work.

First he had to find a place to hide for the remainder of the day. While he could remain on the ledge, he didn't want his muscles to lock up, making him less effective than he knew he would need to be. He could slip back to the window and into the room and remain there, or move into the hall to try to locate a better hiding place. He decided to move into the room and stay behind the heavy drapes, which would shield him completely from anyone entering the room.

His mind made up, Björn moved along the ledge until he reached the window. As he expected, it was locked, but he had prepared for this when he chose this course as a potential retreat. He had snapped off the catch holding the window closed. Now he opened it quietly and, entering the room, closed the window behind him. Then he made himself as comfortable as possible behind the drapes.

Night came early to the valley as the sun dropped behind the high peaks. The blackness of the castle was interrupted by torches set in the walls. Björn slipped out of the room, noting a brightly burning torch stuck in a holder in the wall immediately to the right of the door. He moved away from the light and continuing his silent movements, returned to the lower floors. Sensing the presence of a small group of men ahead of him, he crept over the rough uneven floor.

As he turned a corner, he saw seven men on guard crowded under a flickering torch. They stood in a circle with their backs inward, on guard against an enemy coming from any direction. Their swords faced the floor, but the men's posture showed they were ready to swing the weapons into action. They were talking, sounding confused about the nature of their enemy. As he listened, Björn determined that they were experienced warriors who had never been bested in all their years of conquest, even by larger groups of armed men. And this was only one man.

Questions buzzed around the small circle. How could this one man be a serious threat? What manner of being was he? Many of their companions had been slain easily. How could one man do this? Why was he doing it?

Björn edged toward them. He moved in fractions of inches, freezing frequently, then moving forward. Like a ghost, he approached unseen.

Time passed. The men on guard gradually relaxed as their muscles grew tired.

Suddenly a whirlwind with two flashing sabers exploded from the darkness into the soldiers. Two fell silently, their heads simultaneously cleaved from their bodies. Before the rest could react, two more died, one by a sword driven through his heart, the point of the sword emerging through his back. The other had his body split from between his neck and shoulder all the way to his groin. Of the remaining three, one stood stunned by surprise and fear, one raised his sword to the ready position and waited, and the third lunged at Björn, slashing with his sword.

Björn's sword impaled the neck of the attacking man and then, moving in a blur, he drove the sword in his right hand across another man's body at the waist, almost splitting him in two. At the same time, the sword in his left hand drove into the midriff of the last man. The unequal battle was over in seconds. The robed men had not had time to cry a warning; the only sounds had been two short screams and the gurgles of dying men. Björn moved on silently.

Throughout the night, a wraith appeared unseen and unheard out of the darkness. In his wake, Björn left more dead men.

The remaining men drew into larger groups for security and tried to calm their fear by sharing it. A group of twenty-eight men stood in a circle in one of the dormitory rooms lit by many torches. Two large doors on each of the walls were closed.

A door exploded inward and Björn was in their midst, swords slashing. Then he was gone through the door he had entered so unexpectedly, leaving five bodies on the floor. Three men bravely pursued him into the corridor. The sounds of a brief scuffle came, then silence.

The remaining twenty men fled through a door in the wall opposite where Björn had entered. Fleeing in disarray down that corridor, they entered the next dormitory. There they huddled with the men from that room. With no apparent leadership, men gradually passed through the corridors to stairwells and gathered in the upper rooms and halls.

Their leaders found them there. At first they ordered the soldiers to find this silent enemy. When that did not work, they argued with the warriors, and finally began shrieking at them to return to the lower areas and find the intruder. Despite those efforts, the men were resolute and refused to leave the lighted upper area.

Even bunched together, the soldiers' fear grew. Their fear of the deadly specter eventually overruled their fear of the priests. As dawn came, they opened the high entrance doors and began to move into the daylight. In groups, they walked apprehensively away from the castle, constantly looking over their shoulders. From an upstairs window, Björn watched their departure. The men left with only their swords in their hands. They divided into a number of groups and marched up the broad road. Of the more than two hundred men originally in the cult, less than one hundred fifty were alive. After a short time the priests, laden with all they could carry, followed.

Björn placed an arrow in his bow, drew the string and missile back, and released. A priest fell. A second arrow pierced another. The remaining seven priests stood paralyzed, looking at the bodies on the ground. Then they dropped their treasures and fled for their lives.

Jago burst from a grove of trees and charged into the priests. His initial charge broke the bodies of two priests. Leaping into a capriole, he lashed out with his back hooves and struck others down. He chased those who attempted to flee and trampled them. Then he returned to the original battle place and dispatched the survivors. Within moments, all nine clerics were dead. The horse turned and looked up at Björn, who still stood in the window with a small satisfied smile on his lips.

Björn turned back into the room and into the hall. Exiting the castle, he strode to where the priests lay. Looking at the carnage for several long moments, he stooped and picked up a small pouch dropped by one of them. Opening it, he examined the contents, then placed it in one of his pockets. He moved through the remaining bodies and retrieved his arrows. Carefully cleaning the bolts, he inserted them into his quiver. Signaling Jago with a head gesture, he moved at a fast trot up the road in the direction taken by the men.

Numerous times during the day, they overtook stragglers. Without remorse, they dispatched them. When the road divided, Björn and Jago turned in the direction of the village, leaving the remainder of the men to their destiny.

Thane was alone in the tavern when Björn returned. Looking at Björn without expression, Thane said, "The women returned. Thank you for rescuing them." Still expressionless, he continued, "I assume the evil ones are gone."

"They will not trouble you again," responded Björn.

Thane rose from his seat. "We asked you to come because of what a traveler told us about you. From what you have done, at least most of what he said must be true. But he warned us that you insisted on your pay and that, if you were not paid, those who had employed you would pay even more dearly. Well, we have nothing more to pay you. I cheated you, and I am ready to pay the price."

Björn smiled cynically. "I thought that was all you had. With those men robbing you blind, I knew there could not be much left."

He pulled out the pouch he had removed from the body of the priest. "This is more than you promised me; we can consider ourselves even. There is much more left, and I would advise you to get the villagers together and collect it. Who knows, perhaps you will reclaim even more than they took from you."

"We can never reclaim as much as they took from us."

Björn looked at him for a long moment. "I am sorry. That was stupid of me. Nothing, not even death, can ever make up for the evil men like that do. But perhaps it will be some solace to you to know that most of them died in fear."

"That was still too easy for them," Thane said. "But I am complaining when I should be thanking you. I thank you, Northlander. If you will wait, the others will come and add their thanks."

"That will not be necessary."

After looking at Thane intently for a time, Björn bounced the pouch in his hand. "This is more than we agreed upon. I still owe you. If you ever have need of me again, and I hope you do not, please send for me. I will come."

"Thank you. I hope we never need you, but you will always be welcome here."

The cynical smile returned to Björn's lips. "I know you mean that honestly. But I have learned the hard way that after I have completed my task, those I have worked for are glad to see me go and hope never to see me again."

Raising his hand in salute, he turned and left the tavern. He and Jago left the way they had come, dust rising from their footsteps and following them down the road.

CHAPTER TWO
THE PRINCESS

"So," the fat man laughed as he continued to wipe the already spotless bar. "Did you create a lot of mischief?"

Björn responded somewhat wearily. "Gibbons, why do I tolerate you? How about I just put a sword through you and make Wudo owner of this decrepit tavern?" While speaking, he gestured toward a slow-moving young man sweeping the worn wood floor.

Gibbons colored a bit, showing he was at least a little taken aback, but pressed on, "I guess it is because you find me so lovable, Northlander. Or perhaps it is because everyone passes here at some time and I know all of them."

The tavern keeper reached behind him and brought forth a sheaf of papers. Some were full sheets of clean, quality paper; some where on dirty and wrinkled scraps. "What would you do without me, Northlander? I am the only person you know who enjoys your company!"

Gibbons handed the papers to Björn, who dropped a gold piece into his waiting palm. "You must be popular. So many messages and so many people wanting you. You must be more likable than I realized." He laughed loudly at his own humor. "Or is it that you have friends other than me and Wudo?"

Wudo looked up from his sweeping and grinned broadly.

Björn weaved his way through the tables crowded into the room until he came to a bench at a far table. Sitting with his back to the wall, he began reading his messages.

Gibbons, knowing that Björn never drank alcohol, shouted across the room with pseudo generosity, "Can I get you a drink?" Being ignored did not faze him. "The fancy leather pouch is from a king. He wants you to guard his daughter! You have never worked for a princess before. Choose that one and I will give you instructions on how to behave around royalty." He stepped from behind the bar and skipping nimbly gave a sweeping swing of his arms. "This way, your Björn-ess." Gibbons guffawed at his own joke.

"Perhaps someone should teach you not to open other people's messages," scowled Björn, pulling a long letter from the already opened, ornately adorned leather pouch. Before looking at the message, he examined the pouch.

"Never saw anything so fancy, have you?" Gibbons exclaimed. "He should be able to pay a lot if he can spend that much on the message pouch. Maybe there will be enough gold for the two of us. Anyone who works for a princess must have a manservant, and I will happily be your manservant if the price is right."

The Northlander tried without success to suppress a grin. "You had best bring along that big club you stash behind the bar for quieting rowdies. Since I am to be a gentlemen mingling with royalty, I will leave it to you to fight the warlocks, ogres, wild beasts and monsters. It would be unbecoming for a dandy like me to engage in such mundane activities."

Gibbons flexed his muscles jokingly as he straightened his big frame. "So long as those warlocks, ogres, wild beasts and monsters are small and weak, and the pay is right, I think I can handle the job. So, is that the job you are going to take?"

"I will have to look at the rest of these messages before I decide." Björn sighed. "Perhaps I should stay here for awhile and keep Wudo entertained."

The young man gave Björn a broad, vacant smile and replied, "Wudo be glad to play with you, Mr. Northlander."

Giving a visible shudder at the thought, Gibbons said sarcastically, "With you sitting around here with your happy face, I would not have a single customer left within a week. Pick one of those jobs and go somewhere—wreck the countryside!"

Ignoring Gibbons, Björn continued reading through the messages. One was from a wealthy merchant wanting his protection during a long and dangerous trading journey. In another, a baron was requesting him to serve as his bodyguard. There was a plea from a mother asking him to bring back her only son who had been conscripted into an army. A rich landowner wanted him to evict unlawful homesteaders from his land. Some monks were desperate to retrieve the gold, silver and jeweled religious icons stolen by brigands who had stormed and plundered their monastery.

Björn glanced away from the messages, picking up the pouch from the king. It jingled, and he turned the pouch upside down, dropping five gold pieces onto the table. Looking up at Gibbons with his eyes twinkling, he said, "I wonder where the rest of them are."

"I knew you would say that so I added three to the pouch," Gibbons said.

Björn laughed at the thought of the barkeeper giving money away, but he also knew Gibbons would not steal from him.

Reading the message, Björn was even more intrigued. King Brewster reigned over the kingdom of Kallthom. He had promised his daughter's hand in marriage to the elderly king of Carigo. Carigo was a far distance across the plains from Kallthom, and between Kallthom and Carigo was the kingdom of Delph, a kingdom Kallthom had been at war with for centuries. The marriage of King Brewster's daughter to Carigo's king would form an alliance between the two kingdoms that would give Kallthom the upper hand so Kallthom could finally defeat the Delphs. King Brewster proposed to send his army to surround the princess and Björn, keeping the Delphs away from them all through the journey. He needed Björn to act as the princess' personal protector.

While not sympathetic to the purpose of the request, Björn was fascinated by the thought of working for a king. He had never even met a king. Speculating about the young princess, he wondered why she would agree to a marriage that would take her so many miles from her home, especially marriage to an elderly king.

He tapped the edge of the message pouch on the table, musing, "At least I can meet these proud people before deciding." He imagined he would most likely refuse, for he had no interest in helping them win a centuries-old war.

Rising, he walked to the bar and dropped all but the ornate pouch in front of Gibbons, along with another gold piece.

"Wudo," he asked, "Do you think you can find the king of Kallthom for me?"

The lad trotted to him, nodding his head vigorously. "Yes," he said enthusiastically, "yes, I find him, Mr. Björn."

Björn wrote quickly on the back of the king's letter, stuffed it back into the pouch and handed it to Wudo, placing two gold coins in his outstretched hand. "Find him as fast as you can, and do not get lost!"

Wudo raced up the stairs to his sleeping quarters to begin packing.

Watching Wudo charge up the stairs, Gibbons said, "I know the lad is simple, Björn, but he is a good reliable boy. He will deliver your message." He broke into a wide grin. "So! You are going to work for a king! I promise we will treat you with the respect you deserve when you return. We will clean up this tavern and even whitewash the outside! We will have the ground in front swept clean. Wudo and I will even wear fancy uniforms!"

Björn smiled ever so slightly and slipped silently through the door without responding.

In Kallthom, King Brewster paced the floor with heavy, jerky steps. His typically florid face was redder than usual, and anger radiated from every movement of his large body. While given to fits of quick anger and sudden violence, he rarely maintained that anger. Usually, his mood was boisterous and full of humor. To him, life was to be embraced, lived, loved and enjoyed. Otherwise, what was it worth? But he did not enjoy this kind of anger, which promised to be slow in passing.

Rathe, King Brewster's son, was alone in the opulent study with his father. Lounging in an overstuffed chair, Rathe regarded his father with love and trust, but primarily with silent laughter, somewhat as a loving, indulgent parent might look upon a beautiful spoiled child throwing a tantrum.

King Brewster crashed his huge fist down on the massive desk. "This man should have been here at least three weeks ago—where is he? His man said he would be here soon. Before he arrives, that old king in Carigo could be dead! How can Aleanna marry a corpse?" He continued his frustrated pacing.

Despite King Brewster's behavior, his mood was more than anger it was fear. He had never been fearful in battle; on the contrary, he reveled in fighting. With his big body, incredible strength and considerable fighting skills, he had often led his men into victorious battle. But this was different; he had decisions to make, and decisions that involved the safety of his daughter frightened him. Even though he was still a powerful man, his once heavily muscled body had deteriorated somewhat with age. He feared he might not live many more years, and death seemed nearer. He had never contemplated his own death—in reality, he rarely contemplated anything. He was a man of action, not a man of thought. Now, at this time in his life, when he needed to depend on his wits, he felt unprepared.

King Brewster dearly loved his two children. He loved them more than hunting—which was his passion—and even more than battle. Their mother died when they were very young, and even though governesses, nurses, and later servants were the primary caregivers of Prince Rathe and Princess Aleanna, the three were very close. Their relationship was more as siblings than father and children. Certainly, he had spoiled them, but he devoted a great deal of time to them. Either because of—or in spite of—his parenting, both grew into fine young adults of whom he was enormously proud. His fear now was that, when his children needed him most, he would be least prepared to help them. At his age, it was even possible he might not be alive to protect them. It never occurred to him that their roles had reversed in recent years. Now it was they who looked after and protected him, usually from himself.

Smashing the table again, sending reverberations around the room, the king shouted, "Why not simply fight and be done with it as we have always done?" His coarse voice betrayed his anguish and frustration.

Rathe was taller than his father but without the bulk. He was quick-witted; both children took after their mother in that respect. Rathe assumed his father's rare bad mood was out of concern for his sister. He soothed, "Surely he will be here soon, Father. It is a long journey. We have heard the Northlander always keeps his word."

Only slightly soothed, but at least a decibel quieter, his father whined, "But he should be here. We should be on the road."

Shouts from the courtyard below propelled Rathe to the window. After observing the activity for a moment, he announced with his usual calm, "I believe the Northlander has arrived."

Despite his age, physical condition and faltering agility, King Brewster took the steps down to the courtyard two and three at a time, Rathe following at his normal quick pace. With a flushed face, the king burst breathlessly into the courtyard. The crowd gathered around the stranger and his horse immediately parted to make way for their ruler.

The Northlander watered Jago at the well, seemingly unaware of the excited crowd. With little fanfare, he turned to Brewster and said, "I am Björn, the Northlander. This is my friend Jago. You sent for me?"

The king's red face, made redder by his race down the stairs, turned a deep shade of rose. He tried to talk, but only sputtered. The stranger before him was average height and slender, barely more than half the size of the king.

Rathe, far more perceptive than most people, saw immediately that this was no ordinary man. There was nothing overtly unique about him except his dark eyes and his charcoal gray hair. But Rathe sensed something extraordinary about him. The man seemed to radiate danger, similar to a coiled snake that is motionless but prepared to strike.

When Brewster finally recovered his voice, he shouted, "I sent for a warrior, not a boy-sized man!"

The townspeople laughed. The king moved closer until he was towering over the stranger. "Is this a trick? A joke? Well, I tell you right now that this is not funny!" He moved menacingly toward the stranger.

Rathe caught his father by the arm and halted him. "Let us hear what he has to say, Father. There is no harm in talking to him." Rathe's instincts told him that while his father was an extremely formidable fighter, he would be less than a match against this hawk-faced stranger with his penetrating eyes.

Björn spoke in common language, but with an unusual accent. "Southlanders frequently fail to accept me as a warrior on first sight. Do you wish me to demonstrate that I am the Northlander for whom you sent? Do you require me to prove that I am capable of doing the job you brought me here to do?"

Brewster bellowed, "And how do you think you might prove that?"

Softly, Björn asked, "Do you have a sword?"

"Of course," snarled the king, even more loudly.

"Will you please have your sword brought forward?"

Brewster turned to his son, saying gruffly, "Rathe, get my sword."

It was apparent Rathe did not want to get the sword,

especially to confront this stranger. But he shrugged, knowing it was useless to argue with his father, who was obviously determined to make a fool of this man.

Rathe took his time about returning with his father's huge sword. The sword was almost five feet long, five inches wide, and two inches thick in the middle, with extremely sharp edges. It took a man of Brewster's size and strength to wield such a sword. In fact, his sword smith had custom-made this sword for him years ago.

Grabbing the heavy sword from Rathe, Brewster swung it lightly into the air and asked Björn, "Now, do we fight to prove you are a warrior? I guess it will not cost me anything if I kill you here and now!"

The familiar cynical smile barely creased Björn's lips as he turned from the king and walked slowly to his horse. Sliding a long, thin sword from its sheath, he returned with the sword in one hand and a black cloth in the other.

The king laughed. "A shrimp of a warrior comes with a shrimp of a sword! And to think I waited a month for you!"

Björn stepped up to Rathe and handed him the cloth. "Blindfold me," he said.

Rathe did as instructed and tied the cloth tightly over the stranger's eyes.

"Not over my ears. I must be able to hear," said Björn, adjusting the blindfold away from his ears, "Are you satisfied that I cannot see?"

"Is this some kind of foolish trick?" the king roared.

Interjecting, Rathe said to his father, "I do not think it is a trick. I am satisfied that he cannot see."

Taking several steps toward Brewster, Björn stopped directly in front of him. "Now, try to touch me with your sword."

The king seemed reluctant to play such a game, but

then he extended his sword quickly in an attempt to touch the stranger on the ankle. Before the sword touched his ankle, Björn casually brushed it away with his own sword.

"Surely that was not your best thrust?" mocked Björn.

Even though Brewster was angry, it wasn't his nature to hurt another person without reason. He slowly and gently raised his sword, extending it to attempt to touch Björn's shoulder. Again, with no apparent effort, Björn flicked the sword away at the last moment. He teased again, "How can I show you what a real warrior can do if you paw at me like a baby?"

Sputtering, Brewster fought harder, getting the same result. He began to put serious energy into his attempts.

Björn continued to knock his sword away. The king began to rain blows on his opponent and each time, Björn flicked his sword away at the last moment. Brewster finally grabbed his sword with both hands and began to swing in arcs parallel to the ground. Björn swept them harmlessly away.

Brewster's breath came faster until he was furiously panting. He hurled himself forward and attacked with all his strength, swinging blows from every direction, aiming at any and every part of Björn's body. Try as he might, he could not touch him with his sword. Finally, he stopped, sword upraised.

Björn took the initiative in the uneven duel. Faster than an eye could follow, his sword struck the king's sword slightly above the hilt. Björn's thin sword cut cleanly through Brewster's heavy weapon, and the blade fell to the ground with a clatter.

Björn removed the blindfold.

Between gasping breaths, the king demanded, "How did you do that?" Then with more sincerity, "No matter.

You have proved your point. You have proven you are the man I sent for." Crestfallen, he muttered, "Why did you have to ruin my favorite sword?"

Björn wasn't finished. "If you do not mind, I would like to show you one more trick." Pointing into the courtyard, he asked, "Of the three bowmen standing guard across the way, which is your best bowman?"

"Strom, the one in the middle," muttered the king.

"Strom!" shouted Björn, "do you think you could hit me with an arrow from that distance? You may move closer if you must."

"I can hit you in the gizzard from here if that is what you want," responded the bowman.

Björn turned directly toward the bowman, touching his chest near his heart. "Try to hit me here if you can."

Strom turned his open hands to the king and silently expressed his refusal.

"Do it!" commanded Björn. "I promise you will have no better luck than did the king with his sword."

"Do it!" shouted Brewster.

Strom drew his bow and notched an arrow.

"Wait a moment," said Björn, holding up his hand. He asked Rathe to bring over the blindfold. "You know what to do."

Again Rathe placed the blindfold over his eyes. Björn stepped away from everyone, faced the bowman and shouted, "Now, Strom, do your very best!"

Strom bent the bow, aimed and released the arrow in one expert motion. The arrow flew true, directly at Björn's heart. Björn caught the arrow in flight just before it reached him. He removed the blindfold and handed the arrow to Brewster.

With no emotion showing on his face, Björn said slowly,

"Now, Sir Brewster, King of Kallthom, am I fit to do your job?"

The king nodded with a loud guffaw and wrapped his long arm around Björn's shoulder. "You will do, I suppose," he said.

At his father's direction, Rathe gave Björn a tour of the castle. The Northlander noted that it was old but well maintained. Its dual purpose was to provide living quarters for the royal family and their court, and to defend them while they were in residence.

The castle sat in the middle of a village. It was square and surrounded by a towering rock wall as tall as six men. The wall was about one-half as wide at the base as it was tall. At the top was a walkway wide enough for four men to walk abreast. The walkway had a wall on the outside slightly taller than a man and about the width of two men. Along the wall were broken intervals, or ports, for guards to observe anyone approaching. Two towers with open windows rose from the corners and in the center of each side. Sloping staircases of stone, wide enough for at least twenty soldiers marching abreast, reached from the courtyard to the center of the adjacent wall. Björn found it quite impressive.

Later, they ate in a small intimate dining room. Björn was pleased that Brewster saw no need to impress him by dining in one of the great halls he had seen earlier. He thought it showed the down-to-earth attitude of the man.

Dinner was very informal. Brewster sat at the head of the elegant table in a high-backed chair that would have dwarfed an ordinary man. As their guest, Björn sat at the opposite end of the table in a chair of equal magnitude. Prince Rathe, Princess Aleanna and three of the king's advisors were at the table.

Princess Aleanna had been briefly introduced to Björn prior to dinner. Björn thought her to be very mature for her age. Having no previous experience with royalty, he had expected a spoiled and pampered child. What he met was a tall, slender, attractive self-confident young woman. His original feelings were that she might be too much of a handicap on the trip and had that been the case, he would have rejected the job. He idly wondered what Brewster's reaction would have been if he had.

Among the meats served from heavy, finely hewn wooden bowls were beef, pork, mutton, and wild game, along with a variety of fresh vegetables and fruits. Dining was a boisterous affair; the guests all talked at once, but Brewster was the loudest. Björn, quiet by nature, observed that Rathe joined in some of the revelry, but the princess did not.

Princess Aleanna demurely studied Björn. Very perceptive, she was perplexed by the affinity she felt for this man. He was like no one she had ever met. Even while he ate, she noticed that he had not a wasted motion. He did not initiate any conversation and spoke only briefly when spoken to. At the same time, she noticed that he seemed to be aware of everything around him.

She decided he was not a handsome man. His hawk-like features precluded that, but she found him oddly attractive. Part of it, she thought, was the contrast between his gray hair and his youthful face. While not young, he certainly wasn't old; in fact, he seemed to be in the prime of life.

Occasionally he returned her gaze, and she found herself blushing and looking away. But when she thought his attention had moved on, she continued to stare at him, fascinated by his dark, penetrating eyes and the way they changed color. They changed from charcoal to blue to green and back to dark gray. She didn't know if it was the light, his mood or if he did it on purpose. Whatever the reason, she felt captivated by them. Fleetingly, she was afraid she was making a fool of herself by staring, but she couldn't help it. She was also afraid of what she must be communicating to this stranger.

While the king roared, even with food in his mouth, Björn noticed that the prince and princess showed better manners. He wondered if that was from the influence of their mother, whom he learned had died when they were young; it was certainly not from the king. The kitchen maids brought in more filled bowls as the food disappeared. As was his custom, Björn ate sparingly, sampling the meat dishes and consuming some of each of the vegetables and fruits offered.

At the conclusion of the meal, the king ordered the servants to clear the table. Björn noticed that while they acted quickly to remove the remnants of the meal, they did not seem to be at all intimidated by the bark of their king. It was apparent that there was great rapport between the royalty and the servants. Shortly, the kitchen maids returned with mugs of ale and a plate of cheeses.

"Well, Northlander," Brewster began, "we should be ready to leave in a few days, as it will take some time to assemble our army again." With a scowling voice, he berated his guest, "We tried to be ready for your arrival, but had to send our men home to work their farms when you took so long to get here."

Björn gave no indication that he noticed the implied criticism. He watched wordlessly as the King arose and picked up some clean ale mugs from the sideboard.

"Here we are," he said, placing a mug in front of him,

"and this is Carigo." He indicated its location with another mug. "And here is Delph." He placed a mug between the other two. "We will have to fight our way through Delph's army to get to Carigo. Your job is to stay with Aleanna at all times. We will have our best men close to her also, but you will be responsible for her safety." He frowned. "I do not like taking our army into the plains against the Delphs, but we do not have a choice. We will group soldiers into an arrow formation with Aleanna and you in the center. When you have a chance to get through, you will go on. When we see you are safe, we will withdraw."

Brewster looked expectantly at Björn, who sat quietly, his hands clasped in front of him and his eyes staring down at the table in front of him.

The king couldn't take the silence. "Well, what do you think of our plan? Can you protect Aleanna? Of course, we will have to choose a horse for you. That pony of yours cannot keep up."

Björn ignored the comment about Jago, and finally looked up at Brewster. "I can see that you have given this a great deal of thought. Have you also considered how many men you will lose in the battle? Do you realize how much this will weaken your defenses, leaving the Kallthom castle vulnerable to the Delphs if they defeat you on the plains?"

Hitting the table and bouncing the mugs, Brewster bellowed, "They will not defeat us!"

"Perhaps not," replied Björn, "but you will suffer severe losses. That will leave your army weakened if the Delphs decide to attack your castle."

Brewster responded quickly. "We have thought of that. Of course we do not like the possibility of that happening, but uniting with Carigo will enable us to easily defeat the Delphs. It is worth the risk. Anyway, that is not your concern. Your job is to escort my daughter safely to Carigo, not to protect our castle."

The two men glared at one another, measuring each other's resolve. It was painfully quiet for several moments.

When Björn spoke again, shoulders forward and eyes probing into Brewster's, it was with disapproval. "The reason I took longer than you expected to get to Kallthom was because I was exploring the safest and best options for getting Aleanna to Carigo," he said. "I will not take the risk of trying to guard your daughter in the midst of a battle because too many things can happen—we cannot be sure she and I would not get separated. I cannot accept the responsibility for her safety when events along the way are out of my control."

The king stared open-mouthed at the Northlander, and Rathe seemed puzzled. Aleanna surprisingly looked disappointed, and Brewster's advisors all began shouting accusations.

"Why did you bother to come here if you were not going to take the job we offered?" shouted one of the them.

When they had quieted, Björn spoke again, "I was not simply wasting my time while you were waiting for me. I traveled through the plains from Kallthom to Carigo, studying the layout of the land carefully."

"So do you have a better plan?" asked Rathe.

"I have a plan that I believe gives us a better chance of getting Aleanna safely to Carigo. We will cross the mountains you call the Ice Mountains and travel behind the Delph plains."

The king drew an audible gasped, then yelled, "You are insane! No one can cross those mountains!"

An advisor added loudly, "Even if you could, there are monsters on the other side!"

Confidently, Björn spoke again. "You are mistaken about crossing the mountains, because I crossed them, and here I am. You are correct about the monsters; they do exist in the mountains, plains and forests on the other side. In addition to the monsters, there are brigands and other dangers, but I found nothing that would stop us from reaching Carigo."

Astonished silence met Björn's statement, then the king and his advisors all began to shout at once. Rathe and Aleanna did not say a word. They studied Björn in silence.

Rathe finally asked, "How many soldiers do you plan to accompany you?"

Björn answered, knowing that his answer would not be well accepted, "Soldiers will not be necessary. The Princess and I will travel alone."

"You are absolutely insane," Brewster wailed. "There is no way I will allow you to take my daughter unescorted by our army."

Again, silence reigned, and everyone looked at the Northlander.

Finally Rathe spoke. "Are you certain you can reach Carigo safely by crossing the mountains?"

The Northlander replied forcefully, "Nothing is ever certain. There are grave dangers involved in taking this route around the mountains and passing behind Delph, but I still believe it is far less dangerous than attempting to take the princess through a battle on the plains. I am more than willing to escort the princess to Carigo, but not through a pitched battle between your soldiers and the Delphs."

Again the room resounded with shouted objections. Rathe finally quieted his father and his advisors by saying, "We know the Northlander's reputation. He is renowned as the best. By demonstrating what he did outside in the courtyard, I am convinced that he is the man to direct this expedition. I am convinced that he should take the back route, over the mountains. I only insist on one change in the plan. I will accompany Björn and Aleanna. However, the final decision is yours to make, Father."

Everyone looked toward Brewster. He looked anguished and in emotional turmoil, his eyes on his daughter as he attempted to absorb Rathe's suggestion. Finally he said, "I left it to you to decide upon the marriage, but I cannot leave this decision to you, Aleanna."

Aleanna replied calmly, "I have complete faith in the Northlander, Father. We should follow his advice."

In a much softer tone, Brewster said, "We shall rest on this. It may look different in the morning."

The meeting broke up, and Aleanna showed Björn to his room. It was large and most pleasant, with a blazing fire in a huge fireplace that warmed the room. Björn was not aware that Aleanna had prepared the room herself. For reasons not apparent even to her, she had wanted to make a good impression on him.

As she prepared to leave the room, setting a small lamp on the table beside the bed, she asked, "Will this be satisfactory?"

Björn gave an appreciative glance around the room. "This is real luxury for me. I usually sleep on the ground!" Then, with penetrating eyes, he said softly, "As a princess, you are not anything like I expected."

Aleanna, blushing, answered, "How many daughters of kings have you known? How would you know what to expect of a princess?"

He brightened with an elusive smile and barely audible chuckle. "You are the first princess I have ever known, but from what I have heard about royal families, I expected a spoiled young girl, weak and frail."

"So," she teased, "do you naturally assume that I am just a spoiled princess who is weak and frail?"

"No," Björn assured her. "You seem to be a mature and confident young woman, capable of taking care of yourself. I honestly expected you to be a burden. Your brother also impresses me as a formidable warrior, which is more than I expected of a prince."

Feeling that propriety demanded that she make her exit, a blushing Aleanna bid him good night. While seldom concerned with propriety, she did not want Björn to think ill of her.

Later, at her dressing table, Aleanna brushed her hair, something she rarely asked her personal maid to do. She preferred attending to her personal needs because it allowed her rare private time to think. As she brushed slowly through her hair, she thought of the Northlander. What a unique man! She recalled blushing in his presence, and she couldn't recall blushing since she was a very young girl. Why did she find him so fascinating? She really knew very little about him, yet she trusted him instinctively. Were the tales she heard about him true? One tale said he prevailed in battle against twenty soldiers. Why did she have this sense of security that she would be safe with him in any situation and any circumstance? Why did she feel his respect when they had first met?

Finally putting her brush aside, she slipped into bed, still thinking of this unusual man, the Northlander Björn. She decided she would have time to learn more about him in the days ahead. Turning on her side, she pulled the down-filled blanket around her and fell into a peaceful sleep.

In the morning, after Aleanna had bathed and dressed herself, again without the attendance of her personal maid, she walked to the stables and found Björn grooming his horse. She walked up casually and commented, "You are up early."

"I need little sleep," said Björn, "I came here to spend some time with Jago. He is not accustomed to confinement and is not very comfortable in a stable. I keep telling him it will not be long and we will be out in the open again."

Aleanna asked, "His name is Jago?"

"Yes," Björn answered, "I named him when we were very young—shortly after we first met."

"What do you mean?" she asked. "How do you meet a horse?"

"I think we were looking for each other." Smiling, he continued, "We were both much younger, in the Northland. We were both learning to survive pretty much on our own."

She started to touch Jago, who stood quite still and tense. "You trained him well."

"Do not try to touch him," Björn cautioned, and she drew back. "He does not know you. And I did not train him. Rather I won his trust and confidence. He seems to just enjoy my company."

Björn smoothed his hand over Jago's back. "This horse probably is much different to me than your animals are to you. We are more like partners. He does what I ask only because he wants to, not because I could ever force him to perform. And, of course, I usually do what he wants."

Aleanna leaned against a stall. "He must be very intelligent.

"I think Jago is much smarter than me," Björn responded.

Aleanna continued to study Jago. "He seems small for

a warrior's horse, but very muscular. I imagine this horse can run all day long without tiring," she said. She glanced at Björn. "We should go up and have some breakfast, then while my father and his advisors are arguing about the plan to get me to Carigo, let us come back and I will give you a tour of the castle lands. Would you like that?"

Enthusiastically, Björn replied, "I would like that very much."

When they entered the castle for breakfast, they heard the king and his advisors continuing their loud discussion about the plan to escort the princess to Carigo. Aleanna placed her hand softly on Björn's shoulder and said, "We must not allow them to ruin our morning." She led him into a small dining area, where she addressed one lone servant. "Please bring in some breakfast for Björn and me." As she led him to a small table, she said, "We can have our breakfast here in peace." A servant almost immediately brought fresh coffee, breads, eggs and an assortment of breakfast meats and fresh fruits.

When the princess and Björn finished eating, Aleanna asked him to go on to the stables and wait for her while she donned her riding apparel.

When Björn arrived at the stables, there were two castle horses saddled and waiting. He wanted to take Jago out because he had been confined in the stable since their arrival, but would do as Aleanna wished. When she arrived, dressed in knee-high black boots, black trousers and a tan man's shirt, she walked to the sleek gray mare. Stroking the mare's neck, she said, "I selected this mare as my own because I was there at her birth."

Jago's head was reaching out over the stable gates. Björn took the reins of the horse the stable boy had selected for him to ride and finally, with an apologetic tone asked,

"Can Jago come with us? I mentioned before how he hates to be confined."

Aleanna, with true understanding, said, "Yes, of course. I am sure you would prefer to give him some freedom. You may ride your own horse if you like."

Björn answered, "No. I rarely ride Jago; he prefers to walk beside me."

Björn and Aleanna rode out side by side, and she began pointing out distinct things about the village as they rode into the countryside. Small unique homes and outbuildings dotted the landscape, with wood and stone fencing marking off homesteads and pastures.

After they rode a small distance, Björn stopped and turned back to study the castle.

"Is there something wrong?" Aleanna followed his gaze, as if expecting to see some attacker coming at them.

"No, nothing is wrong," Björn answered, "I was noting how similar Kallthom Castle is to others I have seen. Almost all of the defenses are at the front of the castle where the rolling land comes up from the plains. There are few defense areas at the back of the castle. Your father counts on those rough hills to keep it protected. If I were to attack your castle, I would feint at the front, but send my major forces around and attack from the back."

In a worried tone, Aleanna asked, "Do you really believe an army could get close enough to the castle to attack from the rear undetected?"

Björn didn't want to cause her anxiety but felt compelled to reply. "By moving at night and with the distraction of a fake attack from the front, I think it is very possible."

"I will definitely tell my father of this possibility," she said, "but, as usual, I doubt he will listen."

As they continued their leisurely ride through the

countryside, Aleanna pointed out the numerous small hamlets, where small stores, sawmills and other businesses provided inhabitants with jobs and made the hamlets as self-sufficient as possible. She explained that the people were all free to own their own land, as long as they paid their taxes and served in the Kallthom army when necessary. She explained that the kingdom's inhabitants had the usual complaints, but she thought, in general, that they were a fairly happy and contented community.

As they passed through one small hamlet, a handsome young man at the sawmill gave Aleanna a big smile and a knowing wink. Blushing, she tried to avoid his glance, remembering an afternoon when the two of them rolled in the hay in the young man's family barn. She knew Björn was probably a man who rarely missed anything, and she was sure he noticed the byplay between the two of them. Her cheeks colored even more at what he must be thinking. Here she barely knew the man and he was assuming a place of importance in her thoughts.

The riders and Jago topped a hill that provided a back view to the castle and a forward view of the hamlets upcoming. As they paused to enjoy the view, Aleanna asked, "Why did you leave your home in the Northland?"

Björn hesitated a moment before replying. "I had no real home there. The land is hard and unforgiving, and the soil is poor for growing food and crops. The land can only provide for a certain number of people, so some of us must go and make our way in other lands. I am only one of many who left."

"Why does a man become a mercenary?" she asked.

"When we leave the Northland, we are highly skilled warriors, as you saw. I am as equally skilled with a bow as with a sword. It is the most appropriate occupation available to us."

"But I have heard such horrible things about mercenaries."

Björn looked into her eyes for such a long moment that she became uncomfortable. Finally, he looked away and answered, "It is a profession for honorable individuals. Mercenaries are in great need, but there are too few honorable ones. I consider myself a mercenary who behaves honorably."

Considering his reply, she ventured on, "You must lead a very exciting life."

Taking some time again to think on her statement, Björn said, "For the most part, it is not so exciting. There are times of battle and fighting, but they are few and far between. Most of it is rather boring."

"Well, if it is so boring," she uttered with amazement, "why do you do it?"

"Oh," he said with a half-smile, "There is some excitement, it pays well, and I am very good at it, but it is not as adventuresome as you would think." He turned to face her squarely. "But what about you, Princess? As I told you before, you are not what I expected."

Demurely lowering her eyes, she asked, "And how am I so different?" She raised her eyes to meet his.

"I do not know." He gazed at her intently, and she was caught up in his look. "I thought that a young princess with numerous servants to attend her every need would not be quite like you. You do so many things for yourself. Most surprising is the way you ride." He didn't want to make her uncomfortable, so he averted his eyes and looked out over the castle lands. "You are truly an excellent horsewoman and you carry a sword and bow. While I have not observed your use of these weapons, you are obviously no stranger to them. I did not expect the daughter of a king to be a woman warrior!"

"Of course you know," she said, "my mother died when I was born. I was wet-nursed by a servant and she lovingly mothered me until I could walk. My father did not know much about raising a girl. I tagged along after him and Rathe until they got so tired of me falling off horses and cutting myself on the weapons that they began teaching me how to ride and use the sword." She laughed. "It was much more fun than doing women's things!"

Björn asked, "Does he let you go into battle?"

"We have not had any real battles since I was born. There are skirmishes in the countryside occasionally, but no real fighting. If there was a battle, I am sure the old fogies would try to keep me out of it," she teased, tossing her head and sending her black hair flying. "What do you think of women fighting?"

Björn hesitated. "For my people, there are no distinctions made between men and women when it comes to fighting. I have been among other people of other lands where it is also common. In most countries, though, the men go out fighting and hunting while the women stay home cooking and having babies."

"The women of Kallthom stay home cooking and having babies. But that is not for me," Aleanna said forcefully. "What about those lands where the women fight? Who looks after the children?"

"The old men and women. They also do the cooking and cleaning. In these cultures, the women are treated equal to the men."

"How about other cultures?"

"I guess they are pretty much like they are here."

"You mean the man is the boss and takes a switch to

the woman's backside if she does not do what he says."

"I am afraid that is the way it is."

They were quiet for a bit as they walked their horses, but Björn had to ask, "If you will pardon me for asking, why are you marrying an old man?"

"You have to understand that Delph is constantly absorbing more and more of the nomadic tribes of the desert," Aleanna said, her brow furrowing. "They grow stronger and have been instigating more and more skirmishes. When they feel they are strong enough, they will attack us. When I marry the king of Carigo, we will have an alliance, then Delph will leave us alone."

Frowning, he asked, "But you are personally sacrificing a great deal. Surely there are other ways to protect Kallthom. You might employ a mercenary army, or increase the defenses of the village and the castle. I am sure there are a number of other things that could be done. It seems you are paying a very high price."

"What are you trying to do, Northlander," she said with a smile, "get out of earning your fee? Are you sorry you contracted with us and are stuck with me?" She continued more seriously, "Both Rathe and I were raised to believe we had a responsibility and duty to the people of our kingdom. This is my duty—to do what I can to make the kingdom safe for our people. No one asked me or forced me to undertake this. It is my idea." She paused, leaning against her mare. "Yes, I do have some regrets. I am giving up marrying and raising children in my own land, and I will be a stranger in Carigo, never seeing those I love again. But I believe the benefits will be worth much more than my sacrifices."

Björn shook his head. "I do not know if I can agree with you, but I certainly respect you for what you are doing. It is extremely brave of you." He threw his reins over his horse's head and mounted, then waited for Aleanna to follow suit.

When she was seated securely in her saddle, she said, "Enough about me. Tell me about your homeland, that place you call the Northland."

They urged their horses into a gentle walk. Björn closed his eyes for a moment, as if gathering up his memories of home. "We call it by a different name, but 'Northland' is what people who speak about it call it. It is far to the north and west of here. The mountains are high and cold, and the ice and snow never melt from their peaks. Spring and summer only last for a few months, so we have to grow a great deal during that time. It is a hard and unforgiving land for men, beasts and vegetation, but the land makes us what we are."

"And what," she asked, "is that?"

"Strong, lean and medium-sized," he responded. "And very alert and quick. We became what was necessary to survive in our environment."

Aleanna thought about his reply, then asked, "How old were you when you left the Northland?"

"Oh, I was in my twenties, I guess. Most children of the Northlanders leave home about that age," he said.

"Tell me about your life. What was it like?"

Grinning, Björn said, "You ask too many questions, young lady. Be patient and I will attempt to answer all your questions in time. What about you, Princess? How do you spend your time?"

"I wish you would stop calling me princess. Please call me Aleanna. And what shall I call you, Mr. Bodyguard?"

"Call me Björn."

"Is Björn your first or last name?"

"I guess it is both since it is my only name. I was taken from my parents at a very early age and my trainer named me. But tell me, since it appears you are being evasive, Aleanna, what do you do to fill your time?"

"Are you making fun of me again?"

"No. Knowing you, I am sure it is something important and useful, and I am sure it will be unusual for a girl."

"I suppose you are right about that. I noticed, as I got older, there was little order in the land. The largest landowners did pretty much as they chose. But at least there was a form of peace in that the landowners rarely fought with each other. They knew my father would stop that," she said, looking out over the countryside. "I convinced my father to let me organize and be in charge of a legal system. I think he thought it was only a girlish whim and I would tire of it quickly without doing too much harm.

"I selected twelve good, honest men and trained them to be judges. Their job was to travel the kingdom and settle disputes and punish miscreants. I divided the kingdom into twelve units with one judge for each unit, and convinced my father to pay them well so they could be professionals. They met with me in the castle for several days and we went over their jobs, how they would judge lawbreakers and how they would settle disputes."

Her face was intent as she explained her tasks to Björn. "Initially, I sent soldiers with the judges and had them build jails in central locations, then I went from hamlet to hamlet explaining the legal system we were developing. I had to call out soldiers a few times at first, but it has been some time since I have had to do that. Everyone seems to have adapted to the system and accepted it. I travel a great deal meeting with the judges, checking to see what is happening in each village and overseeing the system. The only real problems I have are with the people in the hills.

They are scattered and fiercely independent. We get along fine on a personal level but I have had to call out soldiers numerous times to enforce a judge's decision. This is a full-time job for me."

"That is how you know people by name in the village we just passed through. Is that the same throughout the kingdom?" Björn asked.

"Pretty much. I have made sure that I am highly visible. I want everyone to know me and know that I care about them. I try to present myself as the head of a fair and just legal system, and I think I can say I have done that."

They entered another hamlet. Recognizing Aleanna, people enthusiastically stopped what they were doing and rushed out to greet them calling, "Princess Aleanna!" Aleanna seemed to know them all by name.

One woman insisted they dine with her for lunch, or dinner as she called it, and would not take no for an answer. The cottage they entered was small but well constructed, with a few bright rag rugs scattered about on a wooden floor. Colorful curtains covered the windows. It had one large room with a kitchen, a dining area containing a large wooden table and benches, a sleeping area for the parents in one corner piled with bear rugs for both warmth and comfort, and a large fireplace for cooking and heating. Bear rugs were also piled in front of the fireplace.

"The children sleep up there," the woman said, pointing to a loft area.

They had mutton stew with slabs of bread and cold milk with vegetables from the woman's garden. It was a fine meal, especially for Björn. The two children talked excitedly to Aleanna until their mother quieted them. She explained that she was particularly pleased to have company, as her husband and some of the other men were in the far pastures and would not return until evening. Then she and Aleanna talked about the livestock, the crops, the affairs of the village and the woman related the latest gossip. When they were finished eating, the children rose and without being asked, gathered the utensils from the table and took them outside. Björn had seen a spring as they approached the woman's home, and he assumed the children were taking the dishes and utensils to wash them in the nearby water.

The woman who had hosted their dinner led the way out of the cottage to find villagers gathered. Björn noticed a number of young women gathered together looking at him and laughing.

"What is it about me that the girls find so funny?" he asked Aleanna.

"They are wondering if you are my boyfriend."

"What will you tell them?" He grinned impishly.

"I will tell them you are my bodyguard hired by my father to protect me and I am showing you around the kingdom." She glanced up at him coyly. "Or perhaps I will simply smile and tell them nothing. That will get their tongues wagging!"

The villagers started to gather around six people who began to play musical instruments. A man and a woman played flutes, one man played a drum, another woman was blowing into a long curved horn, and two men played rectangular wooden-box like instruments with heavy strings.

As soon as he saw Aleanna, an old man approached her, took her hands and led her into the middle of the street. The musicians started to play, and the music started slowly. The couple began to dance with their arms raised over their heads. The music grew faster and louder, and the old man and Aleanna danced faster to the beat. The music grew faster and even louder, and the dancers moved to keep the rhythm. The old man was amazingly quick on his feet; as fast as she moved, the old man kept up with Aleanna. His feet stomped the ground so fast they were a blur.

But Björn's eyes were on Aleanna. He thought she was quite sensuous. The music rose to a crescendo and stopped abruptly. The absolute silence in the village was astounding, then the people began to clap vigorously. When the music started again, they paired off and began dancing.

Aleanna returned to Björn with her face flushed and her breasts heaving.

"You were magnificent," he told her.

"Thank you," she said. "I love to dance."

"I can tell."

Taking his hand, she led him toward the center of the street. "If you are my boyfriend, we must dance. We do not want to disappoint all those young ladies."

"I have never danced," he said, refusing to move even though she was dancing up and down to the music.

"Oh, come on," she said. "The people will be so disappointed, and so will I."

With a twinkle in his eye, he began to dance in rhythm with her.

"You said you had never danced!" she said.

"I have not. I have learned from watching you and the old man."

Just as before, the music grew louder and faster. The music continued its frenetic pattern, and the dancers danced faster. Some couples started dropping out, but Aleanna and Björn continued dancing. Finally it was down to only the two of them.

The music stopped, and the villagers' applause was deafening.

Aleanna wondered if there was anything this man couldn't do.

The music started again and a middle-aged woman grabbed Björn and started to dance. He grinned back at Aleanna and let himself be caught up in the fun. The music and dancing went on for several hours. Finally the dancers stopped. Aleanna and Björn, dancing together again, were among the last to stop. The musicians began to play a softer tune.

Catching her breath, Aleanna announced that it was drawing late. Despite pleas to stay, she asked for their horses.

Saying their good-byes, they mounted their horses and rode out of the village with the people shouting good wishes after them and children running beside them shouting," Goodbye! Goodbye!"

As they left the hamlet and children behind, Aleanna turned her mare in the direction of the castle. "We should be getting back. Perhaps they have finished their discussion."

Rathe took a walk around the castle grounds. He was capable of being quite introspective, and he wondered if his reason for supporting Björn's plan was truly because he believed it was the better plan or that he selfishly wanted to spend that time with Aleanna, They had never been separated since she was born. She was his beloved sister, his best friend and playmate. He remembered when she was young how she would try to follow him everywhere. He was constantly afraid she would hurt herself or be hurt.

She was a tomboy and by the time she was a teenager, she could win fights with boys her age, and he taught her to use a sword and bow until she became as good as most soldiers. Because she wore her hair cut short, visitors to the castle sometimes mistook her for a boy. It wasn't until she was nineteen or twenty that she began to let it grow long.

But what he remembered most were the talks they had. From the time she was able to play with him, they shared almost everything. At first, it was children chatter, but as they grew older, the talks grew more serious. He told her of his plans for when he was king, that they would conquer Delph, not to subjugate it, but to stop the centuries-old war, and the Delphs would have the same individual freedoms as the citizens in Kallthom.

Rathe was different from his father. Although skilled in the arts of war, he did not like fighting and thought fighting and war should only be a last resort when negotiation failed. As a boy, he did not enjoy fighting with other boys and even used his authority as prince to avoid them.

Aleanna was the opposite. He was always having to pull her out of fights with boys. She wouldn't fight with girls; she said they were no fun because they couldn't fight. It wasn't until her late teens or perhaps as late as twenty that she gave up her competitive tendencies and started to become a lady, but her independence grew stronger. She was envious of Rathe as he had his future planned out for him and would do great things while she had no such future. She also wanted to do great things. He smiled, remembering when she had first come up with the idea of a legal system. They were on one of their many trips through the kingdom when Aleanna became offended because the peasants and their families had no power against the large landowners and no recourse against their actions. She was also frustrated with the people and the way they bickered, fought and tried to take advantage of each other. Like her brother, she had a keen sense of justice and fairness and the wisdom to know that they were not always the same thing. They discussed and planned her system in detail and, when they were satisfied with it, together presented it to their father. They knew that he most likely would have refused if Aleanna alone had presented it. The king still had delusions that his daughter would marry, settle down and give him grandchildren. Even though he humored her current behavior, he assumed she would correct it as soon as she grew up.

Rathe realized he had made three trips around the courtyard and people were beginning to stare at him. He knew walking helped him think better and was tempted to go to his room, but he knew he would simply pace the floor so he decided to leave the courtyard and go into the countryside.

Rathe's only weakness was women. His conquests started with women in the court but quickly spread to women in the countryside. Aleanna was extremely critical of his behavior when he confided in her, but he defended it by stating truthfully that he never used his position to take advantage of a woman and his relationships were limited to single women and widows. Her rejoinder was that no woman, especially those who were not of royal birth, could refuse a prince for fear of repercussions. Thinking that over, he gave some credence to what she said and told her that in the future he would be as careful as possible to ensure that any encounter was mutual.

He was both pleased and offended when Aleanna told him of an adventure she had one afternoon with a boy from a village—pleased that she was open enough with him to confide such intimate behavior, but offended and infuriated that a young man had taken advantage of his sister. His anger made him demand who the man was so he could beat him to a pulp. Her response was that she had initiated the encounter and did not see how this was any different from his behavior. She had enjoyed it so much that she intended to continue the same as her brother.

Her attitude stunned him. He remembered his little sister was no longer little and how she always followed him, and he suddenly realized what a responsibility he had. He promised her that he would be celibate until he married as long as she would not repeat her adventure. They both agreed and as far as Rathe knew both upheld the bargain.

They discussed their ideas for significant ways to improve life for the inhabitants of the kingdom. In the process, they developed a sense of great responsibility for the kingdom and its people.

Rathe was convinced that his first duty was to end the war with Delph. First he would attempt negotiation and, if that provided no hope, war was the answer. Then he would work with his sister to make life better for both the people in their kingdom and the people in Delph.

Aleanna and Björn rode leisurely side by side back to the castle, even though dusk was approaching. It was dark when they arrived at the stable.

"Your father and Rathe took some men and went out looking for you," a stable boy told them.

"Those old fuddy duddies," Aleanna exclaimed in disgust, "when will they realize I am an adult and can take care of myself. Besides," she smiled at Björn, "you were with me."

They left their horses with the boy and entered the quiet castle. Aleanna asked a servant if her father and Rathe had eaten and was told they had not, so she told the servant to have the kitchen staff bring dinner for them to the dining room where they had eaten the first night.

"We should wash up and meet in the dining room in about a quarter of an hour," she said to Björn.

"I will be delighted to dine with you, Princess," Björn said with a courtly bow that made Aleanna smile.

They had just begun to eat when they heard the sound of her father and his men arrive in the courtyard. There was no mistaking Brewster's voice as he vaulted up the stairs.

Charging into the dining room, he said, "Where have you been and why did you go off like that without letting anyone know?"

Aleanna smiled sweetly up at him. "And why are you charging about the countryside like an old fool when you know I do that all of the time," she cooed. "Besides, Björn was with me."

Brewster hung his head, a bit embarrassed. "I was worried about you. You know how much I love you."

Getting up, she went to him, planting a kiss on his cheek and giving him a tight hug. "I know, Father. What will you do when I am gone and married in Carigo? Now let us sit down and eat."

CHAPTER THREE
THE MOUNTAINS

Three days later Björn, Rathe and Aleanna rode away toward the Ice Mountains. Rathe rode a heavily muscled golden stallion with a white mane and tail. Aleanna rode her beautiful gray mare. They rode along side by side while Björn, ahead of them, was afoot leading the packhorse with Jago trotting along beside him.

By the second day, Rathe and Aleanna were amazed that Björn had stopped only to rest the horses. He never mounted his own horse, running beside Jago tirelessly. Apparently, the stops were more for the needs of the royal pair and their horses.

The mountains seemed close, but Björn said it would take weeks to reach them. The scenery changed gradually from lush meadows and groves of trees to a desolate plain with only occasional trees. Scrub brush grew profusely, but travel was easy because wild game had beaten down the brush. The party found watering holes where they could drink and refill their water vessels.

Approaching the second watering hole of the day, Aleanna rode up next to Björn. "How do you know where the water holes are?" she asked. "You never seem to search for them."

"Remember," he said, "I have been through here before, but even if I had not, Jago always finds water."

Later, as the sun began to set, Björn announced, "We will stop here to eat and get some sleep because we must start very early tomorrow before the sun rises. Jago and I will keep watch."

Rathe and Aleanna followed Björn into a grove of thick trees.

"We should have stopped at the last water hole so we could bathe and wash our clothes," Aleanna said.

"Animals come to the water hole at night to take advantage of the darkness to drink. Predators come to hunt the animals, and I would not want us to be mistaken for prey." Björn grinned at the horrified look on her face, and she glared at him.

After eating some of the food packed in the leather pouches on the pack horse, they spread out their bedding. Rathe crawled into his bedroll, and Aleanna walked to the edge of the grove where Björn stood guard.

"Do you ever sleep?"

"I need little sleep, but I can sleep and still be alert and on guard. You are not like Jago and me, so you must get some sleep."

Aleanna lingered. "How far will we travel tomorrow?"

"A similar distance to today's span," Björn answered. "Now you must get some sleep."

Aleanna smiled at Björn and strolled slowly to her bedroll. She burrowed deep into its warmth, but she did not sleep right away. Her mind raced with thoughts of this stranger and how he was becoming more and more important to her, but she also noticed he had changed. He did not banter or smile; he was always serious and she determined to ask him about it the next time they talked.

They left before the sun rose the next morning, nibbling on cold meat and biscuits as they rode. It was a long, hard day for Aleanna and Rathe. When they arrived at the next night camp, they were both exhausted; they ate quickly and fell into their bedrolls immediately. Aleanna turned her head toward Björn where he stood guard at the edge of the campsite until she fell asleep.

The days were monotonously alike. The mountains towered above them to the north but seemed to get no closer, and Aleanna felt they would never reach them. It was frustrating to travel so long and get no nearer to their goal.

She galloped to Björn's side. "Are we ever going to get there?" she asked.

He slowed to a walk. "I know it is discouraging, but do not worry, Aleanna, we will reach them in a few weeks if everything goes as planned. You should relish this part of the journey because when we get to the mountains, we will be climbing and in places it will be extremely difficult. Then we will get to the snow and cold. So I advise you to enjoy the journey now, as it is the easiest leg of our trip."

"It may be the easiest but it is so boring," she said petulantly. "The landscape never changes, the days blend into each other and seem to lull me to sleep."

"Please do not go to sleep, little one. While it may not appear so, there is danger here. We cannot afford to relax even for a moment." He glanced around him. "Have you occasionally noticed the claw tracks of large animals? Those are signs of large predators, and some of them pose a danger to us. We must be on guard for that."

"Is that why you have changed?" she asked. "When we were traveling our lands, you were kind and gentle, and you teased and bantered with me. Now you seem detached and you do not talk with me much."

"I did not realize I had changed," he said. "Now that I

recall, I relaxed when we were traveling together in your kingdom. Now I cannot afford to relax. It is my job to keep you safe, and to do that I must stay on guard."

She said nothing for a short distance, as he had hurt her feelings with his words.

"Is that all I am," she asked, "a job?"

He mulled her question around in his mind, sensing that he had to choose his response carefully. "Do you recall me telling you that if you had been the spoiled and helpless young woman I was expecting, I would have declined your father's offer. But I realized immediately that you were anything but that," he said. "And the more I have gotten to know you, the more respect I have for you. But it is still a job because I must get you to your destination safely. I daresay it is the most important job I have ever had."

"Well, that makes me feel a little better," she said, pouting a bit. "So I am not simply a piece of baggage to you. At least I am an important piece of baggage."

"No, you are far from a piece of baggage..." he started. But she had wheeled her mare and galloped back to Rathe, and Björn didn't think she had heard him. Sighing, he reminded himself that, while he might know a great deal about men, he knew almost nothing about women.

The days dragged on. The only difference for Björn was that now Aleanna ignored him. He would have tried to talk with her again, but he had no idea what to say. He intuitively knew that no matter what he said, he would probably only offend her more.

One day in mid-morning, Björn stopped abruptly with Jago beside him still as a statue. Björn motioned Rathe and Aleanna to dismount, leave their hoses and come to him with swords drawn. He signaled for them to stand back to back while he removed his swords from Jago's back, placing them into the sheaths on his back. Then he took his bow and a handful of arrows, notched one and waited.

"What is it?" whispered Rathe.

"Huge mean bipeds of some sort," Björn whispered back, "they are hairy and they stink. You can tell when they are near by their odor."

"Is that what I smell?" asked Rathe, wrinkling his nose. Aleanna covered her mouth with the scarf she wore.

"That is what you smell." Björn readied his bow.

Suddenly, not twenty paces away, a black furry monster leapt straight into the air above the brush, roaring and beating its chest. Before it could fall back into the brush, Björn placed an arrow in the center of its chest. Immediately, two others beasts leapt into the air in different spots but all too near to them. Björn had time to shoot one of them but the other returned to hiding in the underbrush.

"How many are there?" gasped Aleanna

"Four or five, I think."

Three took that moment to leap into the air, but instead of leaping straight up, they charged the party, beating their chests and howling wildly. Björn shot an arrow into one, then dropped the bow and immediately drew his swords. He quickly jumped in front of one that was almost on Rathe and Aleanna.

Jago charged the third monster. Whirling into a capriole, the horse shot both hind legs out into the abdomen of the other beast, doubling it over. Almost before the beast hit the ground, Jago was on top of him, hooves driving like pistons.

At the same time, Björn slashed at the charging beast's throat but it tucked its head into its chest. Björn laid the animal's face open, but even that did not slow it as it continued its assault.

Ducking under the swinging arms, Björn shoved one sword through its chest and cut deeply into its stomach with the other. Rathe leapt around Björn and brought his sword down from over his head with both hands, laying the monster's head open to its chest.

Just like that, the fight was over. Björn walked to the three beasts he shot with arrows and retrieved them. Jago had stopped pounding his victim, and the remaining two lay lifeless on the ground.

Aleanna went to look at one of the beings. The first thing she noticed was its very long hair; it was dirty and the source of the terrible odor. The thing was tall, probably at least a foot taller than Rathe, who was a tall man. Its head was in proportion to the rest of its body, and it had hair on the top and sides of its head but none on its face. Its wide mouth had large, sharp teeth, its paws were huge with lethal claws, and its body was broad and heavily muscled.

"It is an ugly beast," remarked Björn, who had finished his clean-up to come stand by her.

"They are predators but with that strong odor how do they ever get any prey?" Aleanna wondered.

"I think they hunt in packs, surround a large area and close the circle, trapping everything within it."

Rathe strolled up, and Björn thanked him for his help.

"I did very little," Rathe said. "You did most of the work."

"On the contrary," Björn said. "You probably saved the lives of Aleanna and me. I had wounded this one severely but it was far from dead. It could have done some damage to me and could have killed your sister. As you saw, they are monstrous things and are very difficult to put down." He moved toward the horses which, with the exception of

Jago, were crowded together. "Let us get away from here quickly. Dangerous scavengers follow these killers to pick up the scraps, and some of them also hunt in packs so they could be dangerous to us."

As they moved away, Aleanna asked, "Why did they attack us instead of trying for our horses?"

"I do not know. Perhaps they thought to get us out of the way and then have both us and the horses, or perhaps they thought they would like the taste of us better than horses."

"I do not like the thought of being a meal of some wild animal." Aleanna shuddered.

"That is the way wild creatures live and die, little Sister," said Rathe. "The strong always pick on the weak."

"Thank goodness we were the stronger."

They moved quickly, Björn leading the way at a hard pace. Finally he drew them to a halt. "I think it is safe to rest now. I do not think there is anything following us at this point."

Aleanna threw herself to the ground. "You were familiar with those creatures. You must have met them on your trip to us."

"Yes, Jago and I met them."

"How many were there?" asked Rathe.

"Nine."

"What did you do?" gasped Aleanna.

"We killed them."

Silence reigned until Björn called them to their feet and started off toward the mountains.

The following day, the mountains towered over them. Still, it would be miles before they came to their base. Aleanna dismounted and stood gazing at the peaks rising majestically out of sight into the clouds. She had seen the mountains from a distance but had never seen them up so close. They were so huge and awesome that she imagined they surely reached all the way to heaven, and she couldn't imagine a way to travel over them.

She shivered at the thought of what lay ahead for them. But, she thought, I have faith in my brother and Björn. After all, Björn had crossed these mountains from the other side on his way to the castle. Still, she felt uneasy. Holding back a shudder, she walked to where Rathe was brushing his stallion.

Taking a brush from her own gear, she began to groom her mare, looking over her shoulder at the rock giants. "Do you really think we can cross them safely, Rathe?"

Rathe continued to brush his horse. "They are scary. Remember, though, that Björn crossed them alone, so surely the three of us can do the same."

He paused as he walked under the neck of his horse to its other side. "He is something. I have heard the stories about him the same as you have and, like me, you probably thought they were wild exaggerations. But he certainly inspires confidence, and I really think we have done the right thing to come this way rather than try to fight our way across the plain with an army." He examined a spot on the stallion's flank, then ran the brush over the area. "I too am anxious about the other side of the mountains. Since we were wee children, we have heard stories about the monsters over there."

Aleanna lovingly brushed her mare's mane. "I feel very safe with the two of you, no matter what we face," she said in a strong voice. She finished grooming the mare and put her brush back into its leather pouch.

Björn took up his place as guard and after he had moved away out of earshot, Aleanna turned toward Rathe, who was already in his blankets. "Tell me, really, what do you think of him?"

Rathe thought before replying. "I will not worry about your safety while you are in his care, but he is a mysterious man. Do you notice how his eyes are seldom still and how he is constantly listening? And did you take a good look at his horse? I think we all misjudged that one. He had no trouble keeping up with us and he was not even breathing hard while our horses were gasping for air." Rathe's eyes gleamed as he recalled the fight. "And the way he took care of that one beast all by himself was amazing. Jago and Björn are much alike, alert all the time. They are both predators!" he exclaimed.

"Is that bad?"

"Not when they are protecting you, little Sister. Now get some sleep. Björn has warned us of the long and difficult days ahead of us and we do not want a little girl holding us back!"

Laughing, Aleanna kicked a handful of sticks and dried leaves toward Rathe's blankets and retired to her bedroll.

Later, Björn woke them from their sleep with a soft call.

"What is it?" asked Aleanna.

"A large cat is nearby. I hoped it would pass us by, but it is stalking us. Gather some dried brush together and start a fire; perhaps that will frighten it away."

They soon had a large fire throwing sparks into the black sky, then stood on guard ready for action. Moving in his silent way, Björn came closer to the horses, Jago following him.

Suddenly grabbing Rathe's arm, Aleanna pointed at two large red eyes glowing in the darkness. "Look," she whispered.

"I know." Rathe was staring at the eyes.

The Northlander

"What should we do?" She looked at him with frightened eyes.

"Stay here and be on guard."

Aleanna noticed that Björn had moved cautiously to stand between them and the eyes. For what seemed like hours, they stared at the eyes and the eyes stared back. Suddenly the red orbs disappeared, then reappeared further to their left, closer to the horses. Björn and Jago started shadowing the eyes, always staying between the royal pair and the horses. Aleanna felt hypnotized.

The eyes again disappeared, but Björn and Jago moved further to their left until they were barely visible on the other side of the horses. The cat-and-mouse game continued, with Björn and Jago duplicating every move of the big cat.

Aleanna felt Rathe take her hand and say, "We should put more wood on the fire." Hurrying to the fire, they began throwing brush on it again. In minutes, it was blazing as the dry wood caught fire, and sparks flew into the night.

Suddenly a monstrous cat exploded from the darkness, snarling its rage. It had short tawny hair and incredibly long claws and teeth, and its upper teeth looked like knives that curved out over the lower teeth. It was more than fifteen feet long from the tip of its nose to the tip of its tail.

Björn met it with both swords upraised to puncture the beast in the chest. Jago landed two hard blows with his hind hoofs into its midsection. Releasing the swords, Björn threw himself to the ground out of the cat's charge and rolled away. The cat turned toward Jago, who again pounded it with his hooves. The nimble cat partially dodged the blows and leapt on the horse. At the same time, Björn jumped up on the monster and began stabbing it with his knife. In his fury and pain, Jago bucked Björn and the cat off his back. The cat flew one way and Björn the other, but both were up immediately squaring off. For several seconds, they stood facing each other, but when the beast charged, Björn was not where the cat expected him to be. Instead he had rolled underneath the animal, slashing upward into its chest with his knife. Jago lunged forward, striking with his front hooves. The cat rolled over onto its back and convulsed in its death throes.

Aleanna raced to Björn, grabbing him by the arm. "Are you hurt?"

"No, but I am afraid I may be if you squeeze any harder. Come, we must check Jago."

Racing to Jago, they saw that his back was bleeding from a number of wounds. Leading him into the firelight, Björn ran his hands over Jago's body. "Some of these wounds are quite deep and must be tended." Walking to the pack horse, he took a jar from a saddle bag. First he cleaned the wounds, then opened the jar to scoop out some ointment that he spread on the cuts. He stepped back.

"He is all right, but I would like to stay here a day or so to let him heal." Rubbing Jago on the neck, Björn turned to the cat, which Rathe was examining.

"I have seen big cats but never anything like this!" the prince exclaimed.

"You will probably never see one this size again," commented Björn.

Aleanna came to them and holding onto Rathe, shuddered at the sight of the beast.

"It is such a monster. How did you defeat it?"

"With a great deal of luck," Björn answered.

Björn announced that Jago was able to travel a day later. At the next day's camp, after a hard trek, Aleanna was already in her blankets, still staring up at the mountains in awe when Björn and Jago returned from scouting.

"Is this where we will begin our climb?" she asked.

Björn's eyes flirted with a grin. "This is as good a place as any. You seem eager to begin, but do you mind waiting until tomorrow? Jago and I are a little tired tonight."

She stuck out her tongue and rolled over so she was facing into the darkness.

The following morning, in full light, Aleanna realized they were at the base of the mountain. It was both terrifying and awe-inspiring.

Rathe moved to her side. "Do not be afraid, little one. We will make it."

"I know, but it is still scary," she said. "I knew it was huge, but from here it looks bigger and taller than ever. It is almost impossible to believe we can climb it. We cannot even see the top, and we have no idea what is up there in the clouds."

"Perhaps not, but remember that Björn does," Rathe said confidently. "He would not have brought us this way if he had any doubts that we could make it over."

Björn came over and told them his plan. They would climb, leading their horses, with him leading the pack horse. He and Jago would help the prince and princess when necessary. "We will not be able to travel in a straight line up the mountain because I plan to take the easiest routes, which wind around the mountain.

"I made sure that when I climbed down, I did not necessarily take the routes that were the easiest to descend, but those that were the best to climb." Björn glanced over at the horses. "There are some places where we will have to take one horse at a time because of the terrain. It will be slow going, but much of it is not difficult." As he talked, he knelt and drew a rough map for them. "When we reach the snow line, it will become easier because the wind blows most of the snow off the pass, and it hardens the snow it leaves so climbing is not too difficult except for some places where the snow has hardened into ice." He looked up. "It will be a challenge, but I am confident that with your athletic abilities and your character, we will make it safely."

The first day was as Björn predicted. Some areas required little climbing where there were pleasant meadows, but in other areas it was more difficult. Most of the climbing was not difficult, but some parts were very steep.

At times, Rathe and Aleanna had to hold on to their horse's tails as their mounts followed Björn and Jago. Aleanna noted with envy that Björn had no difficulty, at times almost skipping up the steep slopes and waiting for them. Then she remembered that he had been born and raised in mountains probably more treacherous than these.

In the most difficult places, they had to take the horses one at a time. Both Björn and Jago helped—Björn by helping them push and pull the animals and Jago being tied to the neck of the horse and pulling. Both Rathe and Aleanna were constantly amazed at the horse's agility and strength.

At the end of each day, Rathe and Aleanna dropped when they stopped and Björn took care of their mounts over their protests. Then he fixed dinner, usually from their stores, but occasionally he returned from a hunting foray with some small animal to eat. This was a welcome treat from dried beef and cured pork and mutton.

One evening after dinner, Aleanna approached Björn and asked him if he ever got tired.

"Sometimes I do, but it does not take me long to recover."

"How much further to the top?"

"Did you see the snow today?" Björn asked. "We should be at the snow line in a few days and then it is only a few days to the pass."

In the dark of one early morning, Björn awakened Rathe. "Wake your sister. I want to be mounted and ready to start as soon as possible."

"Why so darned early?" asked Aleanna, stretching in her blankets.

"We need to make camp at the snow line tomorrow," Björn explained. "Then we will attack the peak. We all need to be fresh when we start up the mountain."

Aleanna muttered as she rose, "You mean Rathe, me and our horses, I guess. It does not look as though you or Jago ever get tired."

Hearing her softly spoken comment, Björn turned his head toward her without missing a pace, "Oh, we get a little winded from time to time." She caught a glimpse of that rare, cryptic smile.

For the first part of the morning, they rode. When it became too steep to ride the horses, they dismounted and climbed on foot. At places where it was extremely steep, they took the horses one at a time.

Long after Aleanna thought she was absolutely exhausted, Björn called a halt. Again she and Rathe fell into their bedrolls after a quick meal while Björn and Jago stood watch.

When they came to the first snow, Björn directed them to put on their bulky winter hides. By mid-afternoon, they were trudging in snow that reached their knees. Up ahead, Björn had stepped away from the pass into deeper snow, and he and Jago were stomping down the snow, making a small round circle. When they finally caught up with him, he said, "We will stop here."

Rathe, Aleanna and their horses were winded, and even Björn and Jago appeared to feel the stress of the climb. They were almost in the midst of the clouds that obscured the mountaintops. The wind sounded like a giant horn, blowing in different tones, first in a high-pitched whistle, then in a low moaning.

After they had a chance to catch their breath, Björn said enthusiastically, "Believe it or not, the worst is over. Not far ahead, the winds blow the snow away and the climbing is much easier, but the winds will make it seem much colder. I thought it best that we be at this point today and cross the peak in a few days. The peak is high but not as steep as we what we have been traveling over, but we will have to go slowly because of the altitude. For now, we have plenty of time to rest before we go on."

Björn instructed them to get their bedding and crawl into the small circle he and Jago stomped out so the snow piled up around them would shelter them from the winds. The horses stood nearby with their heads turned away from the wind, moisture and steam streaming from their nostrils. Björn and Jago took up their guard positions a few feet away.

Aleanna snuggled deep into her blankets, but before Rathe pulled up his furs next to her, he asked Björn, "Do you think there is any life in these mountains?"

"There may be, but Jago and I encountered no signs of life as we came through earlier and, if there is, it is few and far between. We are not going to be on the mountain long, so we should not have to worry about it."

"How did you locate the pass on your first trip?"

"It took some time," Björn said. "Jago and I prowled across the mountains and almost gave up before finding the pass. There are other ways over the mountains, but they are very difficult."

Rathe gave up his questioning, curling up beside Aleanna in the snow shelter, and slept.

For the first time, Björn and Jago stretched out. Jago curled his nose under Björn's chin, sharing his warm breath and protecting his friend from the chilling night winds. But the brief rest was interrupted so they could go back on watch.

The further they journeyed and the higher they got, they found less snow as the howling winds blew it clear. This was the easiest travel since they had first encountered the snow; only the icy wind made it difficult.

At the end of the day, Björn led them to the snow immediately off the pass. There the three of them and their horses tramped down the snow to make a break from the wind. Aleanna was warm inside her furs, glad they could rest for a few hours.

Morning came all too soon. When Rathe woke Aleanna, Björn was already preparing a cold breakfast, but somehow he had built a small fire from the firewood they had brought on the pack horse. Rathe and Aleanna gathered as close as possible to the fire and each other.

Björn was checking the load on the pack horse when he turned to them and said, "You had better get up and get your blood moving before you freeze."

Reluctantly, they rose and started stomping, then went to their horses, who seemed as reluctant to begin the day as they were. Mounting, they followed Björn and Jago as they made their way back to the open pass and continued their trek up the mountain.

The days continued with little change. Aleanna agreed with Björn that this was easier climbing than the strenuous ascent to the snow line. There was just enough snow to provide traction to walk, but the stress of the howling wind, the cold and the unchanging terrain was hard on them. The clouds hovered near the ground so their vision was limited to only a few yards.

Aleanna had no idea how Björn know where they were going but, for some reason, she realized they were going down. Quickly moving ahead to Björn, she shouted over the wind. "Have we passed the crest?"

He turned, and again she saw the creased lips that served him for a smile. "We did a while ago. I wondered when you would notice it."

"But we are still in the clouds."

"And we will be for some time."

"You did not you tell us," she retorted.

"I guess I was waiting for you to notice it."

"That is just like a man," she said.

He chuckled. "Perhaps it is. Still, even though the going will be easier for a while, we have a long way to travel."

"It makes me feel we are getting closer, though, and I need to feel that." She pulled her wrap around her. "I regret that I am not as strong as you and Rathe."

Björn stopped and looked her in the eye, grasping her shoulder.

"You are very strong and if I had not believed in your strength, I would not have come this way."

"You said you were expecting a pampered and spoiled girl. When did you decide I was strong enough?"

"Almost immediately. You do not realize how impressive you are." He turned away so she would not see him blush under his tanned skin.

"Thank you for the compliment," she said. "But what would you have done if you had found the other girl?"

"Like I said, I would have refused the job."

"Well, I am glad you did not. I am afraid my father would have tried to force you." She paused and continued, "Since you do not strike me as a man who can be forced, you could have hurt him and his men."

"No, I would not hurt him. On the contrary, I like him," Björn said. "I would have found another way, even if it was simply sneaking away." He smiled again. "Now we must move before we freeze."

They continued their journey down the mountain. Except for the occasional realization that they were going downward, there was no change from the previous days.

Suddenly, Aleanna noticed that Jago had gone some distance and was standing absolutely still, looking ahead and to the left. Björn had left the pack horse and was also standing at attention, turned toward the same spot. Hurrying to him, she grabbed his arm and asked, "What is it?"

He didn't respond so she gripped his arm even more tightly, and then she heard the most terrifying sound she had ever heard. She heard it even above the sound of the howling wind. It started out very low and continued rising in pitch until it ended in a screech.

"What is it?" she gasped.

"I do not know but I do not like the sound of it." His body tensed as he tried to discern the source of the noise.

The howling continued and it was coming closer. He leaned close to her ear. "Take the pack horse and go back to Rathe. Jago and I will take care of this." He gave her a gentle push as she grabbed the pack horse's reins, and then hurried to Jago. Drawing the two long swords, he stood beside the horse.

When Aleanna got to Rathe, he grasped her arm, starting toward the two sentinels. He had pulled his sword from its scabbard.

"No," she said firmly. "He wants us to stay here out of harm's way."

"But we should be helping him," Rathe protested.

"Do you really think that if he needs our help that there is any hope for us?"

"Of course, you are right. If he wants us to stay here, we will, but I still think I should be there. But I do have my little sister to think of."

"You do not have to protect me. You know I can take care of myself." She drew her sword from its scabbard as Rathe had done. "But we should hold our horses so they do not run away." She grabbed the reins of her horse, who was skittish and nervous-acting.

With the horses secured, they continued to watch Björn and Jago. They had not moved but were still alert. The bellowing continued, drawing ever closer.

A huge beast covered with white fur erupted from the clouds. It walked upright, had two gigantic arms and hands, and a square face with a wide mouth full of fierce-looking teeth. It appeared to be as surprised as they were, and abruptly stopped roaring. It stood there glaring at them.

Aleanna gripped Rathe fiercely in her terror, and she realized her demise was only moments away. There was no way a man, even Björn, could prevail against such a monster.

The beast roared and charged Björn and Jago. Björn leapt onto the back of Jago, remaining erect with his feet planted on Jago's neck. With swords raised, he awaited the huge being and, as the beast reached them, Jago reared up on his hind legs. At their full height, the two fighters were almost as tall as their terrible adversary.

The royal pair saw Björn's sword flash at the throat of his opponent as the beast's huge paw swung into him. Spewing blood from the terrible slash that lay its throat open, it thrashed about as it died. Aleanna and Rathe were fortunate to have stayed as far away as they did because it kept them safe from the monster's death agonies.

They had seen Björn fly through the air more than one hundred feet into a snow bank off the bare ground of the pass. With a scream, Aleanna charged to where she thought he had landed but Jago beat her there. When she got to them, Jago was standing over the body and would not let her come close to him. Then Björn groaned, and Aleanna knelt to take his arm.

"Do not be quite so glad to see me, girl. I am afraid the little fellow beat me up a bit."

"Where are you hurt?" she asked.

"It is probably a case of where I do not hurt." Checking his body with his hands, he reported that he was sure he had cracked ribs, a broken left arm and a separated left shoulder.

"Oh, I was sure you were dead," she said softly.

By then, Rathe had reached them. "How can I help?" he asked anxiously.

"You will have to help me up so I can get somewhere level and you can patch me up," Björn told them. "But first, I am afraid he dislocated my shoulder. Rathe, can you pull it back into position?"

"I can try," Rathe said dubiously.

Björn gave the prince instructions, and Rathe moved into place and grasped the Northlander's injured shoulder.

There was a pop as the shoulder moved back into its normal place.

"Where else does it hurt?" Aleanna asked.

"The worst are my ribs. At least a few are broken and I hope none were driven inside where they could hurt something else. My arm is also broken, but I do not think it is too bad. All in all, I think I am fortunate to be alive."

"We will carry you," Aleanna said.

"No, that will not be necessary, but I can certainly use some help."

Supported by Rathe, Björn made it back to the cleared pass, where they helped Björn lower himself to the snow-covered trail.

"Tell us what to do," Aleanna said as she fussed around her patient.

"Get some wraps from the packs first," he told her.

Aleanna hurried to their pack animal, which was still standing where she had left him despite the melee, and collected wraps and bandages. Returning to where Björn sat cradling his arm, she noticed he was sweating.

"What now?" she asked.

"About all you can do is protect my arm. We can leave the ribs alone as they are best left to heal on their own," Björn said.

He explained to Aleanna and Rathe how to set his arm for best healing results, and his mouth tightened as they set the arm and wrapped it immobile. Aleanna added a sling.

"That is all we can do for now. Our concern now is for infection," said Rathe.

"Nicely done, and you do not have to worry about infection," said Björn. "Get me the bag from Jago."

When Rathe brought it to him, he rummaged through

it and brought out a small packet. Spilling some powder into his palm, he mixed it with some snow and swallowed it.

"That will take care of any infection. Could you get me some furs? I must rest now."

"How long will you need?" Rathe asked.

"Perhaps until as late as tomorrow. I suggest you go into the deeper snow and pack it down and make walls to protect us from the wind. A fire would be nice, as I will not be able to move much to keep my blood moving."

The royal pair moved into deeper snow, making a makeshift shelter as directed, then Rathe got some wood from the pack horse and made a fire. They helped Björn to the fire and Aleanna made him a bed.

Tucking the furs around him, Aleanna asked "Will that be all right for now?"

"I am fine. I simply need to rest."

Taking Aleanna aside, Rathe spoke softly, "I would love to see the beast. I have not seen it up close."

"Are you sure it is dead?" she asked fearfully.

"If it was not, I am afraid we would be."

"But I do not want to leave him."

"Look at Jago," Rathe said. "Do you think he will let anything get close to Björn?"

"I guess not." She sounded hesitant, but she agreed to go with him to take a look at the beast Björn and Jago had killed.

They walked warily to where the giant had fallen. Up close, he looked even bigger than he had earlier.

"He is all of fifteen feet tall!" exclaimed Rathe.

"How in the world did Björn kill him?" wondered Aleanna.

"Do not forget that he had some help from Jago."

"I know, but it is still incredible. Do you think he will be all right?" she asked anxiously.

"I think he is the most durable man we have ever encountered," said Rathe. "He has to be to have lived through half the adventures we have heard of. Yes, I think he will recover in time but we, with Jago's help, will have to take over for him." He turned toward her. "When we start again, we will take turns watching Jago to see if he shows us any sign of danger."

"I did not think of that. We are on our own now, but that is nothing new."

"Yes, but not in terrain like this and not with whatever we may encounter," responded Rathe.

"We will have to be as careful as possible," she said. "I am sure we can handle it."

Returning to camp, Aleanna checked on Björn, who was sleeping fitfully. Rathe dug into his travel bag and extracted a curved skinning knife.

"I knew this would come in handy," he said. Returning to the fallen beast, he cut off a huge patch of fur, large enough to make a large blanket.

While Rathe was gone, Aleanna prepared their evening meal. Removing a cooking pot from the pack horse, she made a hot stew, thankful that Björn had insisted that they have one hot meal a day whenever possible to keep their bodies from surrendering to the cold.

Retuning to camp, Rathe proudly showed the fur to his sister and then laid it on the snow to soak up the blood from it. By then, Aleanna had managed to get a little of the stew's liquid into Björn and they were ready to eat.

"When do you think we can travel?" asked Aleanna.

"Honestly, I do not know. You heard him say he wanted to move tomorrow, but I am not sure. If we hurry, we may kill him, and if we stay here, we may all die. I think the best we can do is wait until morning to see how he has fared the night."

They wrapped in their furs and settled for the night. Soon Rathe was snoring quietly, but Aleanna lay awake for some time. She was contemplating their situation and thinking of Björn. Where would they be without him? Even more troubling was where would she be without him? She thought back to the first time she had seen him, standing alone in a crowd, and realized with a start that her vision of him was standing alone, stalwart, strong and dependent upon no one nor anything. Try as she might, she couldn't visualize herself standing next to him. At the thought, she felt tears form in her eyes, and she quickly swiped them away out of embarrassment and for fear they might freeze.

In the morning Björn was awake first, even though he stayed in his furs. Rathe was the next to awaken and after he dressed, he woke Aleanna.

"How is Björn?" she asked.

"I am fine considering I had to wrestle with a big bear yesterday," she heard him say from deep in his furs.

"How are you really?" she asked, moving to him.

"If Rathe will help me get up and move around, I think I will feel better. And if you could make some more of that stew of yours, I believe I will be ready to travel."

She beat Rathe to Björn's side and let him lean on her as they moved to the fire.

"Honestly, when do you really think we can move?"

"Today," he repeated, "if you and Rathe will help me mount Jago. I may not be able to travel as far as I would like, but we have to get off the mountain. Even a few hours could make a difference. If we do not move, we will freeze because our firewood will not last, and we do not know if there are any more of those animals around here. Surely it is not the only one of its kind in these mountains, but I am hoping they stay apart except to mate occasionally and cannot live close to each other because of the scarcity of game. If we are fortunate, we will not encounter another one. Remember that Jago and I did not see a sign of them when we came through."

Aleanna took the pot containing the left-over stew and set it over the fire. Within minutes, the food was hot enough to eat. She took him a portion and noticed with satisfaction that he took the bowl away from her and fed himself despite her protests. When he asked for a second bowl, she was pleased.

Balancing the second bowl of stew in his lap, Björn talked between mouthfuls. "We should break camp as soon as you have eaten, then try to get as far away from here as we can," he said. "I am much stronger now after a good night's sleep and after eating that fine meal of yours, Aleanna. Now go eat and we will be off."

Björn waited patiently as they wolfed down some of the stew. As Aleanna tidied up and got things packed up, Rathe loaded everything on the pack horse.

"We are ready," Rathe told Björn.

"If you help me get aboard Jago and if you two will lead your horses and the pack horse, we can get started."

"Do you think I should lead Jago?" asked Aleanna.

"I am afraid he would not let you, and he will take good care of me."

They got Björn up and walked him to Jago, where they helped him mount. Aleanna wanted to tie him on so he wouldn't fall.

"That is not necessary," he said. "I will hold onto Jago's mane, and I am certain I will be able to keep my seat."

He demonstrated by nudging the horse gently, and he and Jago started off, followed by Aleanna and Rathe.

It was smooth going for most of the daylight hours, but eventually they came to a place where they would have to climb.

"We should stop here and rest," Björn said. "Tomorrow we will climb down this cliff."

"But how will you get down?" asked Aleanna. "It is too steep for Jago to carry you."

"I will think about that overnight," he teased her. "Come help me down please."

In the morning, Björn seemed stronger; at least his attitude was cheerful and he was getting about by himself. He checked all the horses, including Jago, to see that the loads were securely fastened. He went from one to another adjusting here and tightening there.

"You should let me do that," Rathe objected. "I can do it as well as you, and you should save your strength.

Björn replied, "I know you could, perhaps better than I. But you are my responsibility and I must see that everything is ready. If something went wrong and I had not checked, think of how I would feel. Now let us get the animals ready."

They finished getting all in order, then went to take a look at the cliff. It was at least thirty feet down to the next level.

"How did you climb this?" asked Aleanna.

"I climbed it over there." Björn pointed to a section of the cliff that was jagged and rough but not nearly as steep. "There are handholds and footholds there. Both Jago and I climbed it, and that is where we will make our climb."

"But how are we going to get you down?" asked Rathe.

"Lower me by rope," Björn said. "I will use the handholds

and footholds to help. When I am down, Jago will find his own way down. Then lower the horses and the pack horse. They should be able to find enough footholds to make it. Now, tie the rope under my shoulders and lower me."

Rathe tied him securely under the arms and Björn walked to the edge of the cliff.

"Are you sure you are up to this?" Aleanna asked.

"I have to be," he answered. "Do not worry, Princess."

He asked them if they were ready and, when they nodded, he eased himself off to where he was hanging in the air supported only by the rope. Using his feet and good arm, he stabilized himself so he was facing the cliff so he could use the handholds and footholds on the cliff face. He urged them to lower the rope faster, and soon he was on the ground. He shook the rope loose and sent it back up to the top.

Aleanna went to put the rope on Jago, but he snorted and went down the cliff on his own. The three others were roped in the harness one at a time, then Rathe looped the rope around a tree at the top of the cliff for leverage, and each horse was lowered. The mare was a little troublesome, but the pack horse and stallion gave them a great deal of trouble. They thought several times they were going to lose the stallion, but finally all the animals were on the ground with Björn.

Next it was Aleanna's turn and she made the descent with little difficulty. Rathe did so very impressively after untying the rope and looping it around the tree so he could retrieve it by pulling on one end when he reached the ground.

Aleanna remembered that, in the not-so-distant past, she and Rathe had climbed rock faces for fun. While today's experience was too difficult and dangerous to be fun, she realized it had been exhilarating.

"This is the last cliff of this type we will face," Björn told them. "Some terrain ahead is still difficult, but this is the only place where we will have to lower the horses by rope. We will have some difficult climbing, but now the worst is behind us."

The trek down the mountain wound circuitously, and sometimes it seemed that they were reversing themselves and actually going back up the mountain. When Aleanna asked Björn about this, he agreed.

"I spent a great deal of time finding the best route, even though it is the longest and most time-consuming," he explained.

In most places, Björn was able to stay on Jago, but in some spots he had to be lowered by rope. Aleanna couldn't believe that he had not once expressed a sign of pain when she knew that his injuries had to hurt terribly.

Finally they reached a spot in a meadow where they set up camp and Björn asked them to look at the mountains in front as compared to the ones behind them.

"Do you mean we are really over the mountain?" Aleanna asked.

"Yes, we have conquered it. You should feel quite proud of yourselves." He grinned at them. "Not many could have done it, especially having to drag me for so much of it."

"We will camp here until you are well," Aleanna ordered.

"You will be surprised at how rapidly I heal," Björn chuckled. "In the Northland, one has to heal quickly or perish. I told you what an unforgiving land it was. But it was the land that made us what we are, and mending quickly is one of the things we learned."

"Realistically," Rathe asked, "how long do you think it

will take?"

"I should be almost back to myself in several weeks, but I do not want to leave here until I am completely well. You will note that is a secluded valley. I selected it deliberately because we will be relatively hidden here, and to stay hidden, we must limit ourselves to small fires. I know we are tired of eating our stores and they have become limited anyway, but game abounds here and I will have no trouble getting us fresh meat." Björn looked at the royal pair.

"Do you think Aleanna and I are helpless?" Rathe's tone was tense, almost harsh.

"I apologize. I did not mean that to insult you, Rathe," Björn said softly. "Rather it is because I have been charged with your safety. I thought I would take my bow and leave Jago here to guard you and your sister."

"You have been charged with the responsibility only for my sister," Rathe retorted. "Besides, you are still in bad shape."

Björn realized he had insulted Rathe badly. Choosing his next words with great care, he said, "Of course, you are correct; I was not thinking. You are the one to take care of us now."

Mollified, Rathe took his bow and sword and departed.

As soon as he was out of earshot, Aleanna said, "I am afraid he is still angry."

"I am afraid you are right; that was stupid of me. I forgot that he came to be an additional guard for you, and he is not a child. Perhaps he will get over it while concentrating on his hunting. Come," he said, "help me make our camp as comfortable as possible, as it will be our home for a period."

When they finished, Aleanna insisted on checking Björn's injuries. She unwrapped them, and was astonished to see how well they were doing. Satisfied, she re-wrapped them.

"You are right about that medicine of yours; there is no sign of infection. Or perhaps that is another attribute of you Northlanders. We know it is one or the other, or maybe a bit of both."

"Healing has never been a problem for me, despite all of the wounds I have suffered through the years, and I have had a few. I give credit to the Northland more than anything else, even though living was difficult. However, not knowing anything else, I did not realize how difficult."

With everything taken care of, Aleanna had time to look around their little glen. "You selected a good spot. It is secluded but does not close in on a person. I think I will enjoy our stay."

Rathe returned shortly with two rabbits. As Björn had predicted, he was now in a good mood. He surveyed the camp.

"You two have done a fine job with this," he said.

Björn in turn complimented Rathe on providing meat for a good meal. He reached for the rabbits to clean, but Aleanna beat him to it.

"You both do so much, and this is something I can do," she said, "so from now on count on me to clean the game and prepare the meals." With that, she flounced away to dress the rabbits.

"Well, I guess she told us," remarked Rathe.

"Yes, she did and does so regularly," Björn laughed. "I am not used to that in a woman. In my experience, most are subservient to men and rarely assert themselves. That is one of the things I respect about your sister."

"She has been this way since she was a child, so different from the other women in our kingdom. But as you get to know her better, you will see many more things to respect."

They settled into a pleasant routine at their little camp. Except for Jago, the horses grazed while being tethered. Jago, of course, went his own way. Rathe asked Björn about this.

"He is both protecting us and grazing for himself. I am sorry to say that he considers himself to be one of us or even our superior, rather than one of the horses." Björn looked over at Jago and smiled. "That is only one of the things that makes him so special."

Each day, Björn performed exercises and one day proclaimed himself ready to proceed. However, Aleanna's keen eyes had seen him favor his arm, and she refused to budge.

"The longer we stay here, the more vulnerable we become," Björn argued. "We must move as soon as possible before something or someone finds us."

"We are hidden here and we will be vulnerable with your ribs hardly healed and your arm weak, so we will not move until you are completely well." Aleanna crossed her arms and glared at him.

"My arm is mostly healed and I do not think the ribs will affect me at all." He gave her a pleading look. He was tired of sitting around doing next to nothing.

"Then you will not mind staying here in this idyllic spot for a while longer and letting Rathe and me enjoy ourselves. You could enjoy yourself too instead of acting like a fuddy duddy."

Björn had learned when it was useless for him to say anything, and this was one of those times. He strolled away and, to have something to do, checked and rechecked the saddles and bridles, then moved out to check the horses. He kept going to see if he could find Jago.

He was gone so long that Aleanna started to worry, even though he had taken his weapons with him. When he finally returned, she chastised him, but he responded that he had barely gone out of sight.

Over the next days, Björn continued to roam, accompanied by Jago most of the time. Aleanna noted his concern for their safety by how he carried his two long swords on his back at all times and laid them down close beside him when he retired at night.

Then one day, when Jago was grazing near the other horses, he froze to attention. At the same time, Björn commanded, "Get your horses. We have trouble."

"What is it?" asked Rathe.

"Horses and riders not far away. I am afraid they may see us. Hide the horses."

Aleanna and Rathe raced to get their mounts while Jago came to Björn. There was a small knoll near their camp in the meadow, and Björn gathered them all there. They hid as best they could. Björn removed his bow and a handful of arrows from Jago's back and motioned for the other two to do the same.

Twenty or more horsemen came across the edge of their meadow. They rode for a bit and the three held their breath that they would escape unscathed. But although they were hidden, their camp was not. One of the riders suddenly shouted and whirled his horse to face the camp, followed by the rest. Then one of them got a glimpse of Björn's party on the knoll, and he yelled, pointing toward the group.

The other men stopped and stared for a long moment and then, yelling wildly, they charged. Björn didn't wait but immediately shot one off his horse and moments later another. Rathe also dropped one out of the saddle. Aleanna hit one in the shoulder, but he stayed on his mount. Björn had time to shoot another and then dropped the bow and arrows, unsheathed his swords and charged with Jago from the knoll shouting for Rathe and Aleanna to stay where they were.

Jago dodged the flaying swords and battle axes of the barbarians, satisfying himself with tremendous kicks with his hind legs on the horses. This either knocked the horse to the ground or traumatized it, and then Jago trampled the horse or the rider.

Björn was now dodging under and around their weapons, slicing and stabbing bodies with his swords. To an observer, it might appear that Björn and Jago were fighting independently but, in fact, they acted as a team; they guarded each other's backs. When a rider prepared to slash at Jago, he found himself on the business end of one of Björn's swords, and when a horseman tried to attack Björn, Jago blasted the horse or rider with his hind feet.

Aleanna found the two amazing to watch. For a bit, Rathe was content to stay on the knoll firing arrows at the attackers, but he was getting impatient to join Björn. Mounting his horse, he sped into the fray brandishing his great sword. The battle swung in the favor of the three, but while Rathe was dispatching an attacker on his left, another of the enemy to his right struck the stallion with a spiked ball on the top of the head. Stunned, the great horse dropped to his knees and rolled onto its side. Though unhurt, Rathe was caught by the weight of the great horse. As he tried to disengage himself, he was oblivious to a barbarian racing toward him swinging a spiked ball on the end of a short chain.

Aleanna gave a great scream, but before either Rathe or Björn could react, the ball crunched into Rathe's head.

As the man readied the ball to strike again, Björn attacked and lopped off the attacker's head.

Racing to Rathe, Aleanna held his crushed head in her hands but then, like the warrior she was, she leapt to her feet wielding her deadly sword while standing astride her brother's body.

Björn and Jago continued their attack until the four remaining horsemen galloped away. Not content with the escape attempt, Björn pitched his sword after the last one, piercing him in the center of the back. Taking his remaining sword, he then went about the battlefield dispatching any of the enemy still alive. After the clean-up was complete, he went to retrieve his second sword.

He stayed there for some time to give Aleanna, who was shrieking and sobbing, time to complete her immediate mourning. When her cries died down, he came to her and placed his hand on her shoulder. She covered his hand with hers, and they stayed like that for quite some time.

Finally, she rose to her feet. "I will get some wraps and prepare him for burial."

She went to the camp and got the unused wraps, and when she returned, they wrapped Rathe's body. Björn took wraps and bound Rathe's head as Aleanna averted her eyes. When they finished, Björn asked what she wanted to do with the body. She remarked that since they had no digging tools that perhaps they could gather stones to cover it.

Björn didn't tell her that it would be much easier to give him a Northland funeral by leaving him either in a tree or on a high rock. Getting a sturdy ground cloth from the camp, he and Jago went off in search of rocks. It took them three trips to pile enough of them onto the cloth and drag them to the spot Aleanna had selected as a grave site.

Björn gave Aleanna time to say goodbye to her brother even though he was concerned that the ones who had attacked them might be part of a larger group. He expected at any moment to see Jago, who was guarding them from some distance away, give a signal of approaching danger.

Her goodbye completed, Aleanna got her mare ready then mounted and rode up beside Björn. Despite her apparent composure, he couldn't help noticing the tears streaming down her cheeks. After he checked to make sure all was well with Aleanna's mare, he and Jago moved slightly ahead of her, moving away without a backward glance, leaving a noble prince and his glorious stallion dead and alone in the glen.

CHAPTER FOUR
TRAVELING

They rode for a long while, Björn tactfully avoided addressing Aleanna's grief. The terrain they traveled was rolling hills with meadows, large fields and deep forests. Björn trotted beside Jago with Aleanna on her mare right behind them.

As far as Aleanna could tell, Björn had completely recovered. Despite her deep grief, she marveled at the man's recuperative power. They made no attempt to travel hard or fast, as time was not a great factor now, and Björn said they could travel with relative ease because there was only one serious obstacle between them and Carigo.

At noon, they stopped for lunch instead of eating on the run, and they stopped several hours before dark to make camp. After the camp was set up, Björn went out to hunt, leaving Jago on guard.

Aleanna used this private time to grieve. She began by sobbing, wailing and then back to sobbing again. By the time Björn returned with a small deer, she had gathered wood and built a cooking fire. Showing no signs of her grief other than her red eyes, she made up her mind she would not grieve again. When he said he could easily have gotten a larger deer except that it would only be a waste of meat, sorrow wrenched at her heart, but she steeled herself against it. They dressed the deer together and hung it high on a nearby tree after cutting some steaks from it.

"It might be a bit tough now, but it will be much better after it ages," Björn told her. "We will butcher it in the morning and load it on the pack horse."

Aleanna cooked the steaks and boiled some greens she had picked while Björn was hunting. Despite the pall cast by Rathe's death, the meal was pleasant.

After they ate their meal, possibly as much to keep her mind off her brother as anything else, she ordered Björn to sit on a comfortable stack of blankets she had prepared, then she sat beside him.

"Now," she said, "You promised to tell me more about the Northland and your life there. I would like to know as much as you care to tell me."

Björn was silent for some time. Aleanna was sure he was trying to decide what to tell her and what to omit. She knew what a private person he was, so she told him she was perfectly willing for him not to share anything he didn't care to.

"The Northland is a land of steep, snow-covered mountains," he began. "There is only limited land where anything can be grown, and the short growing season affects the kind of crops that can be grown." He paused for a moment. "I think I mentioned before that it is a hard and unforgiving land. One mistake is all it takes to end a life.

"Most people live in cabins or caves in the lower mountains. Now do not think that Northlanders are barbarians because they live in caves. You would not believe these caves; they are spacious and provide abundant room for the people living there, and to make the caves more their own, the inhabitants cover the walls and ceilings with their own personal art work. Much of it is quite beautiful."

He looked over at her and smiled. "I was born in a cave and later considered myself fortunate to have lived my early life there rather than in a cabin.

"The land barely supports the population that is there at any particular time, and the excess population must leave when they are capable of taking care of themselves. I was one of those; I was taken from my family when I was around four by a man called a trainer who would be the only parent I would know from then on. He would not let me associate with other children and I was not allowed any kind of play. He said I had to keep my mind focused on what he was teaching me.

"First he taught me to concentrate," he told her. "We sat side by side with our legs crossed, blindfolded, and he taught me to concentrate so that I saw only a bright white curtain. I had to close out everything else and see only the curtain, and then he started doing things to distract me, like talking to me and making noises. We kept on doing this until I could concentrate on the curtain despite any distraction.

"Then he taught me to use my ears. I kept my eyes closed and concentrated while he made noises from different places, and I was to identify what the sound was and where it was. I did not think I would ever learn, but he was very patient." He gave a self-deprecating laugh. "Finally, I was able to learn a little and then it came to me with a rush. I got to where I could identify his hand when he moved it rapidly through the air, and I could tell him exactly where he was. He told me this was one of the most important parts of my training, and I finally developed enough skill that I could tell where he was simply by his breathing or the sound of his body if he held his breath.

"Then one day he put the blindfold over my ears as well

as my eyes and tested me. By using only my ears, I had developed my other senses as well. Somehow I was able to sense what and where objects were and whether or not they were moving."

He glanced over at Aleanna to find her completely engrossed in his story.

"So that is how you performed so well for my father," she said, laughing as she remembered how baffled her father was by Björn's fighting style.

He nodded, then continued, "Yes, that is how I was able to perform those tricks on your father. Next my trainer had me traverse mountain paths in the dark with my eyes and ears covered. Then we went deep into caves where there was no light and I had to find my way out. The first time I was somewhat apprehensive, but with practice it became easy."

He shifted his weight to rest his arm more comfortably. "I kept learning to sense objects at greater and greater distances. I got so I could sense something as small as a butterfly flying, and that is how I was able to know when and where those monsters were before we saw them. During this time, my trainer also taught me to use the sword and bow and arrow. At first I used a small sword but gradually, as I grew and was able to handle them, I graduated to bigger swords. I did the same with the bow. Finally, I had to use the long narrow sword I use today. It is incredibly difficult to handle, and I remember being so proud when I mastered one and then he gave me the second." Björn's face lit with pride. "I did not think I would ever satisfy him. I could slash with one and then the other, but that was not good enough. He set up two dummies and swung both of them, and I was to slash simultaneously and strike each dummy with a different stroke while they were moving. This seemed to be an impossible task, but I did it. When I finally mastered this skill, he put the cloth over my eyes and ears and I had to demonstrate the same skill handicapped. Interestingly enough, I learned to do that more quickly than I had with my eyes and ears open."

He shot her an inquisitive look, but she smiled gently and urged him to go on. "This is a very interesting tale, and do not think you can stop until you tell me everything you want to share."

"Well, then," he said, "I practiced with the dummies continuously, then he started practicing with me. First he moved his sword slowly and told me to strike, which was really not that difficult in slow motion, but then he started moving it quickly. His sword went faster until it simulated a real sword fight. It took a long time, but I was finally able to protect myself no matter what he did. Of course, I had a great advantage because I was using the long sword while he was using a standard sword like your father's."

"Your sword blades are so thin. How do they keep from breaking?"

"There is an exceptional ore in the mountains that is converted into an extremely hard metal. The metal is so hard that it takes considerable work to shape it into a sword, and the sword becomes so hard and sharp that it will cut through steel as it did your father's sword. We have skillful sword smiths who work for months to make a single sword each."

"That is incredible," she said.

Björn nodded and continued his story. "We followed the same practice with the bow as with the swords. He swung the dummies and I hit them one after the other, and he kept moving further and further away and swinging them faster and faster until he finally reached the distance limit of the bow. All this time I had my eyes and ears covered, but I was eventually able to do nearly anything a bow was capable of in the hands of a skilled bowman.

"Almost from the time he took me as a trainee, I had to run. No matter how far I ran, he was never satisfied, but as I grew I kept getting better, and in the end, I was able to run for days. Then he had me run without water. We kept working at it until I was able to run as long as three days without water."

He paused, then asked, "Are you bored yet? It is a pretty dull story in many ways."

She shook her head, and he went on with his tale. "We also worked on my strength, and I had to do all kinds of exercises, like lifting large rocks and logs and throwing them. I also had to do different exercises with my hands, arms, legs and body. One exercise I particularly liked was throwing a heavy hammer. This was to strengthen my hands and arms and to give me another weapon. We eventually changed the hammer to a hatchet. Perhaps you noticed the one I carry packed on Jago."

"Yes, I did, and it is a fearsome weapon. Please, go on."

"I had to learn to tolerate pain." He raised his arms to show her rows of scars on both arms. "At first he cut me and I had to learn not to cry out, cry or even flinch or move, and then I started cutting myself. He taught me that if I concentrated fully I would learn to feel no pain. You can see by the number of scars that this exercise took quite a while. I will not bother to show you the scars on my legs. Thankfully I succeeded while I still had some skin left." He laughed, and she joined in.

"How did you meet Jago?"

"Herds of horses run wild in the Northland. They are compact, well muscled and incredibly nimble. They have to be strong and agile to survive in the Northland. They cannot be tamed, so they are hunted for their hides and meat. Jago got caught in a landslide and was almost dead when I found him buried up to his chest in rock and dirt. I started digging and removing rocks, and all the while he kept biting and snapping at me, so I had to be careful. Finally, I extricated him to the point where he weakly pulled himself loose and stood on wobbly legs. He stood for a moment looking at me warily and then hobbled off.

"Three days later, when I was practicing with the hatchet, I saw him watching me from far off. This went on for days until one day I noticed he was closer. As the days wore on, he came closer and closer until he was almost close enough for me to touch, but I did not try. When I moved away, he followed me. This went on for some time until one day I stuck out my hand for him to smell. After taking a good whiff, he let me touch him and thus began our relationship that has become stronger through the years.

"One day, the trainer announced that I was ready to leave." Björn's face got a little sad for a moment as he remembered that day. "Of course, I wanted to stay but I knew I could not. It had been explained to me early on how some Northlanders had to leave each year, and now it was my turn.

"The trainer explained the opportunities that awaited me. One was the path I chose, the mercenary. Others were variations of that such as a bodyguard or soldier. It was emphasized since early in my training that I was not to be an outlaw because that would be easy with my skills, but it was against the tradition of the Northlanders. We were always to act ethically and morally; that was drilled into me. My trainer explained that my skill was far beyond that of men outside the Northland and that fights with them would be easy for me, even fights against numerous opponents at the same time. He continuously emphasized that, no matter what path I chose, I should behave in a way that was ethically and morally right."

"That explains a lot about you, Björn," Aleanna said.

"I suppose so," Björn said. "My trainer told me I was the best student he had ever had, and perhaps the most skilled Northlander of all. He told me he was considered to be one of the best, but my skills had dwarfed his years ago. He also said that he considered sending me out some years before, but my skills kept increasing so he thought he had a responsibility to me to keep me in training.

"It was difficult leaving the Northland. It was not only my home but it was also the only life I knew."

"What did you do to get started as a mercenary?" Aleanna asked. "I think it would be very hard unless you went out and started fights to prove your skills. And according to what you said, that would be neither ethical nor moral."

"You would be surprised what you can learn in taverns if you sit and listen," Björn said. "That is what I did, and it was not long before I learned of a possible client. When I went to meet him, I performed the tricks I played on your father. My reputation spread and I had people from everywhere seeking me out. I finally made arrangements with a tavern owner for people to leave messages for me. It is a busy place located on two main roads, and word spread that I could be contacted through the tavern. That is how your father reached me."

"Why made you decide to be a mercenary?"

"I tried other occupations for a bit and found them boring, plus it was difficult to maintain the ethical values in which I had been trained. I tried being a mercenary and found it was exciting and suited my independent nature."

"Yes," she said, "I can see that it would. But what do you do when you are not working as a mercenary? You said earlier there were times that were not exciting."

"Believe it or not, those times are rare now. Word has gotten around and, the same as your father did, people leave messages for me. Usually I have a number to choose from when I return from a task. I had quite a number to select from when I got the request from your father."

"So why did you pick this one?"

"It is not a very compelling reason. I really could not feel right about getting involved in a foolish local war, and I did not feel good about helping a young girl marry an old man." He shot her an impish grin. "I took it because I had never met a princess before and was curious, but I really had no expectation of taking the job. I thought the king would turn my proposal down and, if he did not, I would slip away."

"What changed your mind?" she asked innocently.

"You did. I came to respect and admire you a great deal. While I did not agree with your decision to marry an old man, if you were determined to do it, I felt a responsibility to help you." He smiled at her again. "On first meeting you, I observed that you were poised and self-confident, and I became even more impressed on our trip through the kingdom. What you did to start and develop the legal system really convinced me. I could not believe that a young woman like you could even see the need for such a program, let alone initiate and manage it. You have no idea how rare such a system is. I was also amazed at your relationships with the villagers. You were not the least bit pretentious with them; instead, you acted like one of them when you danced with them."

"Do not forget that you also danced," she teased. "I could not believe such a stiff man could actually have fun. That is when I decided I liked you."

Looking at her genuine smile, he saw some of the sorrow over her brother's death fade somewhat.

"I find it hard to admit, Aleanna, but I did enjoy it," he said. "I do not normally enjoy things like that. It was a new emotional experience for me, and I have been trained not to allow myself to feel emotions. My feelings were always under total control, and I have no idea why I crossed that line then. It must have been that I was relaxed traveling with you and not having any responsibilities."

"It was fun," she said. "I love to dance and I certainly enjoyed dancing with you, but I was amazed at how well you danced. You are an expert dancer. You said you had never danced, so how did you learn so quickly?"

"Watching you and the old man, I noted that dancing is not so different from fighting. Milder, of course, but it requires similar physical ability. Remember that I was trained to be an athlete."

"Well, I was certainly impressed, and so were the villagers. I received numerous comments about my 'boyfriend' and his dancing."

He chuckled. "So you thought that was better than telling them I was your bodyguard?"

"I did not want to irritate or embarrass you, but if I had told them you were my bodyguard, I would have had to go into long explanations that I did not want to go into."

They lapsed into silence. Björn went for more firewood while Aleanna tried to digest what she had learned about this man. She was glad to see that her initial impression of him as a good man was correct. While she had to admire the man he was now and she realized what an important role he played, she felt sorry for the boy who was deprived of play and having fun. He had not had a childhood. She found it hard to believe that a child had been raised without ever having the opportunity to play. How devastating it must have been to be deprived of the interaction with other children. It was no wonder that as a man he appeared to be cold, aloof, unconcerned and mechanical. She thought it was amazing that he had turned out to be as well adjusted as he appeared to be. There had to be something about the Northlanders living in that harsh environment and having to adapt to it. She thought it must have been terrible knowing that death was always so close.

When Björn returned with the wood, Aleanna was already in her bedroll. As always, she was astonished to see that if he slept at all it would be standing upright or stretched out directly on the ground. As was his usual practice, he noted where Jago was on guard and then took up his post in the opposite direction.

Aleanna lay awake for quite some time thinking about this strange man. She felt secure when she was in his presence, but she wondered at the life he led and what kind of man he was deep inside that incredible self-control. She wondered if he got satisfaction out of helping people and filed that away as one of the things to ask him. With those thoughts, she fell asleep.

The next morning was like so many in the past and so many in their future. After washing herself, Aleanna packed her bedding and saddled her mare while Björn put their cooking and eating utensils on the packhorse, along with the venison he had butchered earlier in the morning before Aleanna awoke.

Aleanna mounted her horse and, as always, Jago and

Björn trotted ahead. They moved this way until mid-day when Björn called a halt. He asked her to start a fire while he slipped into the meadow to search for bulbs, tubers and fruits.

They cooked the bulbs and tubers over the fire and ate the fruit raw. Aleanna found the vegetables amazingly good and the fruit especially tasty. After their meal, Björn gave Aleanna and her mare a short time to rest and then they were back on the road.

That evening, Björn called a halt and they made camp in a grove of trees. Aleanna took care of her mare, arranged the camp and made the fire while Björn unpacked some venison from the pack horse. When the fire was ready, he arranged it on a spit over the fire, and Aleanna brought out the fruit and vegetables and warmed the vegetables over the fire.

Over dinner, Aleanna asked the questions she was curious about. "When you were young, did you miss your home?"

"At first I did, but as time went on the memory of my home faded as my trainer began to teach me how to control my feelings and my thinking. So after a while I really did not miss it."

"Did that make you feel lonely?"

He smiled. "One of the feelings I was trained to suppress was loneliness. So, on the contrary, I enjoy my solitude."

"Does that mean you would rather be by yourself than with me?" Afraid of his answer, she hurried on. "I want to know about your feelings. You learned not to feel pain and were never allowed to play; all you did was train your mind and body. You learned iron control. What about your feelings, and what feelings do you have toward other people?"

He could tell she genuinely wanted to know the answer to her questions, but he was a little confused. "I am not sure I understand what you mean."

"I will give you some examples," she said. "I love my father and loved Rathe. You saw what it meant to me when he was killed. Is there anyone you like?"

"I will always retain the memory of my mother. It is a memory I want to keep. According to my recollection, she was very beautiful and sweet to me. She is the one soft and loving memory I have."

"What about your trainer?"

"He taught me not to regard people with care, even him. He told me it would interfere with whatever I did in the outside world. If I cared, I would not be able to kill when necessary."

"Did you at least say goodbye to your trainer?" She sounded appalled.

"No, I turned and walked away. Remember that our relationship was all business; there was no room for feelings."

"What about other people?"

"I have never thought about that. Perhaps you mean do I enjoy being in other people's company? There is Gibbons, the owner of the tavern where messages come for me. I enjoy his company, even though our relationship is business."

Aleanna was silent for quite some time, trying to work up her nerve to ask the obvious question. Finally she decided she would never have the nerve because she was afraid of the answer, so she blurted it out. "What about me?"

Björn was silent for what seemed like ages to Aleanna. She went cold at this silence, afraid of what it meant.

Finally she got her answer. "I am glad you asked because I had not thought about it," Björn said softly. "I enjoy your company and when our trip is completed, I will miss you and wonder how your life is. I enjoyed our trip through your kingdom and the talks we had. You must remember that I really do not have feelings toward other people. I was too highly trained to have them, but I developed feelings toward you during our trip. Now I must suppress them again because it is my responsibility to keep you safe until our trip is completed. I cannot allow any feelings that might interfere with that objective."

"Does that mean you erased those good memories of me?" she asked sadly.

Another long pause, then, "No, but you understand that I have to bury them because my responsibility comes first. Perhaps when the trip is completed, I can let them come to the surface again. But in answer to your original question, yes, I would rather be making this trip with you than by myself."

Satisfied with that answer, she crawled into her bedding and lay thinking about what he had said. It explained a great deal about him his coldness, aloofness and control. She thought she felt sorry for him but she wasn't sure. In a way, it must be wonderful to be such a warrior and have the opportunity to do much good in the world. Any other person would take great pride in his abilities, but Björn took them for granted. She had never met a person who was less impressed with himself than he was. With these thoughts, she drifted off to sleep.

The next day was a repeat of the previous day. The terrain remained the same quite beautiful and they traveled the same way. As always, Björn did not initiate any conversation and Aleanna was too deep in her thoughts to want to talk.

Her thoughts drifted off to Rathe, how much she missed him and what a horrible death he had suffered. She thought about when they were children, playing together and growing up together. She remembered Rathe always tried to take care of her, whether or not she wanted him to; he thought she was always too bold when she insisted on doing the things he did.

At times, she and Rathe camped far away from the castle, and the only way she could go along was to run after him with her backpack over her shoulders. She could outrun him, even though Rathe was four years older.

She remembered the time they played that they were cooking and he made mud pies and convinced her to eat one. At that time, she so believed in her big brother that she ate the entire thing, even though she had to spit out each bite. Finally, his practical jokes made her more cautious.

At first they played only with each other, but when they were old enough to explore beyond the castle grounds, they encountered children from the village. Initially the children were afraid of them, even those who were bigger than they were, and when they first tried to get them to play with them, their mothers would call them home. She and Rathe couldn't understand why the village children wouldn't play with them.

They asked one of the servants they felt close to, and she told them that they were different from those children because they were royalty while the other children were commoners. Commoners were not equal to the royal family but were expected to be subservient to them, do their bidding and work for them as she did. Neither Aleanna nor

Rathe could understand this, so she sat them down and explained it to them.

"Centuries ago," she explained, "a strong man led a large army and defeated all who opposed him, and he formed the kingdom and became the first king. When he died, his first-born son became king. It continued this way through the ages until at the present time, your father is king. When he passes away, Rathe will become king."

"What would happen if Father had no children?" Rathe asked.

"In that case, the king would take another queen and would have children until he had a male child."

"What would happen if the king died before his son became twenty-one?"

The maid, who was the soul of patience, said, "Then the first-born male child would become king and his mother would reign as the Queen Mother until her son was twenty-one years old."

Not ready to stop the interrogation, Rathe asked, "What would happen if the king never had a child?"

The maid answered that it had never happened and all hoped it would never happen, as it would cause a serious problem. No one knew what would happen.

As far as playing with the village children, the maid told them, "Simply act as though you are no different from them and keep trying to get them to play." She silently thought she would pass the word to the women of the village that the king was unhappy that his children had only themselves to play with and that he wished the village children could play. That worked, as the mothers now encouraged their children to play.

Rathe and Aleanna didn't realize that they had a great model in their father. Even though he was the king, he acted naturally and did not think he was better than others. Aleanna dozed off into a deep sleep, comforted by her memories.

The following morning, she and Björn continued their trip. Toward mid-day, they saw low mountains in the distance. Aleanna asked about them.

"These mountains are fairly easy to cross, except for one spot where the trail is narrow and dangerous," Björn told her, then he suggested they stop for lunch.

Aleanna was ready for a break, so they stopped and feasted on some delightful fruits and vegetables that Björn discovered near their camp. Her favorite was a bulb he included in the vegetable stew he made. She told him how much she liked it, and he told her it would be a beautiful red flower when it matured.

"When I passed through this area, it was later in the year, and there were fields and fields of red." He spread his arms expansively.

"It is just as beautiful now with the trees with their green leaves, the green shrubbery and the verdant long grass," Aleanna said.

Björn agreed, but said he wished she could see it when the flowers were blooming.

After eating, they traveled on and then stopped in early evening before dark. Björn again foraged while Aleanna started the fire and cut some steaks from the deer. By the time she finished, Björn returned with his bounty. She was delighted with the variety of edibles, and she cooked them so they could enjoy their meal. Instead of making the vegetables into a stew, Björn showed her how to cook them in a bit of water.

After tasting the edibles with his new method, she exclaimed that this was even better than the stew. They again had fruit for dessert.

Aleanna thought she was fit when they started the journey; now she realized how much the journey had strengthened her muscles. She noticed that she was sleeping less than she had at the beginning and, even though it was now dark, she was not the least bit sleepy, so she asked Björn if he would stay and talk with her. He hesitated, and she said firmly, lips pursed, that Jago would protect them.

Björn, leaning back against a convenient tree asked, as all men do when confronted with this situation, "What do you wish to talk about?"

She furrowed her brows and asked somewhat heatedly, "No, what do you wish to talk about?"

He thought for a moment and said, "I would like to talk about you."

"Me? Why? What do you want to know?"

"I know you are going on this dangerous trek out of a sense of duty to marry an old man you have never met. What would you do if you were not doing this?"

She was quiet and thoughtful for a long moment then, with a beautiful smile, she said, "I would marry and have lots of children. I would spoil them as babies and when I grew older, I would have lots of grandchildren."

"That will require a husband. Where will you find one?" he teased.

With an impish grin she said, "I would pick you!"

He laughed. "I cannot imagine worse husband material than me. I would not be around enough to father all those babies you want."

"Then we would have to make the best of the time we had," she retorted.

He laughed again. "You simply will not quit! But if you

were not going to marry the old king, your father would never have contacted me and we would not have met."

She pondered that for a moment and then said seriously, "It would not be all that easy anyway. I am already past the age at which most women marry. It seems that all of my friends have babies, and I have yet to see a man of royal blood who interests me so it would most likely have to be a commoner." She sighed. "I guess I would have to pick one, but it is difficult for a princess to court a man, because most common men are afraid of me." She brightened. "Of course, that could work to my advantage because a commoner would most likely be afraid to say no to me."

He thought about her answer for a moment. "Is it appropriate for a princess to marry someone who is not of royal blood?"

"I thought you knew me," she laughed. "When do you think I have been concerned about what is appropriate? Did you see any women besides me wearing trousers and boots? Or being armed like a warrior?"

Björn gave a huge guffaw at that. "Yes, I am afraid you have me there, but with all of those babies, who would run your legal system?" he asked.

"I would," she said. "Can you imagine me trusting it to someone else after all the work I have done? I could travel while I was pregnant, and then I would take the babies with me after they were born. That is one good thing about having as many servants as you want."

She stopped, and her eyes filled with tears, a few running down her cheeks. With a catch in her voice, she said, "Yes, that is what I would do."

There was silence for a long time. Finally dabbing at her eyes she said, "That would be a good life."

"And why," he asked, "would you want to marry any

man who was afraid to say no to you?"

She was astonished that he remembered she had said that. "Well, I suppose it would be boring, getting my way all the time." She smiled up at him. "You, of course, would no doubt tell me no all the time."

This time, Björn rocked with suppressed laughter, and she joined in after a couple of seconds. "I think we are both strong-willed. Such a marriage would no doubt be impossible."

After another long interval, she stretched and sighed, "Now I am tired and sleepy. I had better get to bed so I do not hold you up tomorrow."

She climbed into her blankets and, even though she was tired and sleepy, she did not fall asleep immediately. Instead she lay thinking. Tears rolled down her cheeks until sleep finally did come. Björn stayed by the campfire a while longer and then rose and faded into the darkness.

The next morning they were again on their way, giving no indication of the emotional talk the previous night.

They came ever closer to the mountains. Aleanna could see they were not very tall compared to the Ice Mountains. She thought they would be easy to cross, but as they approached them, she saw they were more rugged than she first thought and that it would be a challenge to cross them. When she mentioned this to Björn, he replied that she was correct. "There is a pass where we can traverse the mountains, and there is only one spot on the trail that is dangerous. It is quite narrow and the ground and rocks are unstable so we will have to be careful, but we should be able to make it safely. When I last came across on it, I saw that it could be treacherous, but by taking it slow and carefully I made it easily. We should have no trouble."

They went on silently as was their custom now. First

was Jago, then Aleanna, then Björn and finally the mare and the pack horse.

Late that evening, Björn called a halt. "Tomorrow we will start on the mountains so we can rest for the remainder of the day. Relax and get some rest. Jago will stay with you."

"And where will you be?" she asked pertly.

"I will be around checking things," was his cryptic response.

She thought he would be ahead of them checking out the land and ascertaining if there were dangers that might be hidden from them while they traveled or that might not have been present on his first trip. But with Jago for company, she knew she had nothing to fear.

As she had sometimes done before when the two of them were alone, she walked away from the camp and away from Jago. She was sure of what he would do so she kept a sharp eye behind her. Sure enough, she shortly caught a glimpse of him so she turned and retraced her steps to where the horse was standing.

She moved close but not too close to him. She had learned the distance he would let her approach. She took an apple from her pocket, squatted and held it out. Talking in soft, cooing words, she tried to coax him to take it, but he did not. She held the apple less than six inches from his nose and continued her soft words. Gradually she moved the apple closer, but Jago snorted, swung his head and strolled away. But he did not go far; he moved only a short distance, stopped, then turned to look at her. She felt a sense of triumph. This was the closest she had ever been able to get to him.

Jago swung his head at something, and then Björn said, "That was impressive. It looked as though the two of you were enjoying each other."

"That is the closest I was ever able to get to him, and it seems like I have spent hours trying to get him to let me touch him. The spacing will be different, but each time he lets me think that this will be the time. Do you think he is shy or merely playing with me?"

"Well, I do not think Jago is shy and I doubt he is very playful. I think that is simply the way he grew up in the mountains, to be wary of people, like me."

"Do you think he will ever warm up to me?" she asked.

"I could not say," Björn said. "I would not say that he and I have a warm relationship; it is more of a partnership, but you have spent more time with him than any human except me so I think you perhaps have a chance. Do not give up. Look at how far he has come in only a few months, and you are having to overcome thousands of year of breeding and behavior."

"That is true," she said.

Aleanna searched for wood for their fire while Björn looked for vegetables and fruit. By the time she had the fire going, he had venison and vegetables in water in their kettle, ready to cook.

This was a time of day that Aleanna especially liked because it was restful and peaceful. It was evening, so the birds were quiet and the night hunters had not roused themselves from their daytime slumber. The only real sounds were the calls of small frogs and the occasional bellow of a bullfrog.

Even Björn seemed relaxed, and this made her more comfortable. He sat on the ground across the fire from her. She began to take down the bun she always rolled her tresses of hair into when she began each day. Once she had it down, she began to comb out the tangles and occasionally to toss her head, partially to help get it into place and partially to get Björn's attention.

She couldn't tell if he noticed until he said, "You have beautiful hair."

"I did not think you ever noticed anything about me."

"Of course I do, and I have always thought you had beautiful hair."

"You never told me. Why not?"

"I do not know," he replied. "I never seem to think of it at the right time to tell you."

"Well, thank you anyway."

"I think the food should be ready." He went over to the fire and began to spoon their meal out of the pot into their dishes.

The next morning they began their ascent of the mountain. The going was not difficult, as they followed an animal trail that had the grass beaten down and many different tracks indicating that all sorts of animals used it. When she commented on the tracks, he answered that it was because of the pass ahead.

"It is the only pass for many miles, and it forces all the animals into this one path."

There were some steep places, but they got through them with little difficulty. After the Ice Mountains, it was like playing as children. She commented on this to Björn.

"Look ahead at the tall mountain," he said, pointing upward. "That is where the pass is narrow and dangerous. It will not seem like play to go through the pass unless you used to play extremely dangerous games."

"Are you trying to frighten me?" she asked.

"No, I would never do that, and I would never question your bravery, not after what we have been through together," he said. "I only want you to be prepared that we will have to take that part of the trail with great care. After all the dangers we have come through, I do not want us to come to grief from a lesser danger."

"If you are trying to warn me to do exactly as you tell me, I promise you I will."

They journeyed on in the same fashion as always Björn in front, then Aleanna, then the pack horse and the mare followed by Jago. There was not much game about so they had a lunch of dried venison and dried fruit without stopping. They traveled until late in the afternoon, when Björn finally stopped. He took his bow from Jago's back and went out to hunt for dinner while Aleanna made camp and gathered firewood.

When she had completed her tasks, she began to stroll around the pleasant little valley where they had stopped. She still marveled at all the different animal tracks she saw, but because of the savannah-type terrain, she could see why the animals did not stop but simply used this land as a corridor to what must be better land ahead.

Returning to camp in time to meet Björn returning from his hunt, she was surprised when he indicated with his empty hands that the hunt had been unsuccessful. "There is simply nothing about. I found a land turtle that I could have brought back, but since I would not care for that meat I was sure of what your reaction would be, so we have to eat out of our stores again. But this time, we can take some of our dried vegetables and dried venison and make a lesser stew out of it. I know that is not much but, believe me, it is far better than land turtle."

Despite what he said, Aleanna knew the real reason he had cut his hunt short. She had heard animal growls and knew he had returned to protect her.

"Should we save the water?" she objected. "I don't want

to run out."

"Do not worry. By tomorrow we will find a small lake where we can fill all of our water bags again."

He prepared the meal while Aleanna set the fire. Soon they were eating the stew, which Aleanna maintained was not bad.

"Yes, it is," retorted Björn. "I know you have to be getting tired of so much stew. To me, food is only fuel, so it does not really matter what I eat, but I know you prefer a great deal more variety."

"You are right, but from what we have been through, I am truly happy to have this. I know we could be going to bed hungry."

That night the loud roaring of beasts woke Aleanna. She sat up and saw Björn and Jago standing still, looking into the darkness.

She got up and walked to them. "What is that?" she asked.

"Tigers. I built up the fire so I do not think they will bother us. They are afraid of fire."

"What about that giant cat that attacked us before we got to the Ice Mountains?"

"Remember that he was afraid of the fire, but I think that because he was such a beast he had less fear than others and he certainly wanted our horses that night. But the animals you hear are not such beasts as he was, so I feel we are safe tonight."

"Then why are you and Jago on guard?"

"We are always on guard, little one. Go back to sleep."

"I cannot sleep with this going on," she said. "Do you mind if I stay with you?"

"Of course I do not mind, but I cannot believe you are afraid," he said, glancing at the sword in her hand.

"If we had trouble, I was not going to let you and Jago face it alone," she said defiantly.

"That is what I thought, but do not worry; if there is any real danger, I will call you."

"I would rather stay with you. I could not sleep anyway." She took his arm and moved closer to him. "How long have you been away from your home in the Northland?"

"It has been so long that I do not consider it home any more. I guess the closest thing I have to a home is the tavern where I get my messages. I stay there occasionally and after an adventure, I stop there for messages."

"Do you miss not having a home?" she asked.

"Since I have never really had one, I guess I do not know what to miss. What about you when we get to the castle of this old king? Will that become your home?"

She looked at him sharply. "I guess it will be, but I can see what you mean. It will never really be home."

The sky in the east started to lighten.

"It is almost dawn," Björn commented, "and the hunters seem to have stopped their hunting. At least they are not roaring about it. We should pack up and be on our way."

"I agree," she said, hopping up to go pack everything so he could load the pack horse.

They started up a mountain taller than the rest.

"Is this the mountain with the dangerous pass?"

"You sure ask a lot of questions, Princess. Yes, it is, so we will camp outside the pass and traverse it tomorrow, as I want us to be rested and have full daylight when we challenge it. It will not take us long to cross, but we need enough time and light to see our way clearly."

They traveled all that day, stopping only for a brief lunch and a rest for the horses and Aleanna, although she remarked that she didn't need the rest. Björn responded that he realized that she might not need the rest but the horses did.

That evening, as usual, Aleanna made camp while Björn went off in search of fresh meat. He soon returned with a pigeon and a rabbit along with some fruit. Combining all the ingredients, they put together a delicious dinner.

After dinner, Aleanna sat on her on her bedroll. "What will you do after you have delivered me to the old king?"

Without hesitation, he replied, "I will return to the tavern and see if there are any interesting requests for my services."

"But this has been such an adventure that you should take a little time off to rest."

He laughed softly. "What you call an adventure is only the usual for me. That is why I am in such great demand. People often seek the impossible from me, and I take those jobs that appear to be most interesting. That is why I am here with you."

"I would think you would take the jobs that offer the most money."

"I guess I am a strange mercenary," he said. "Money is not why I do this. I have spread the rumor that, if I do not get paid, heads will roll, but that is simply to keep things on an even keel. If I gave my services away, as I sometimes do, people would not value them. This work has made me a rich man but that is not why I do it."

"If not for money, why do you do it?" she asked.

"For the opportunity to meet beautiful princesses like you."

"And how many have you met?"

"Only one so far, but surely there are more like you. I will have the word spread that taking care of beautiful princesses is my number one interest and those are the jobs I will take."

"You are usually so serious but sometimes, like now, you are absolutely absurd."

He chuckled. "You are right. No, I will continue to take those jobs that interest me. Anyway, I am sure there are no more princesses out there like you."

Aleanna blushed. "Now stop teasing me and tell me why it is that you do what you do if it is not for the money?"

"As you have no doubt noticed, I am good at it." He paused for a moment, as if considering her question more thoughtfully. "When I say I look for opportunities to take on tasks that interest me, I also mean those that right some wrong people have suffered. You would be surprised at how much injustice there is in the world. I do what little I can to make a few things right.

"I do not do this because I have to. My needs are small and I am a very rich man. I will never be able to spend the wealth I have accumulated. I even have the man at the tavern give some of my money away for worthy causes when he finds one. He has become known far and wide as a benefactor of the poor and complains that he is pestered too much, but he is a good man and I know he enjoys doing it."

Silence reigned for a long time, then Aleanna said with tears in her eyes, "I knew you were a good man but you are even better than I thought. Why is it that there are so few men like you?"

"There are many like me, Aleanna, and many are better. Rathe and your father are two good examples. Think of all the good they have accomplished. They cannot do the things that I do because they do not have the skills, but your father does the best he can and Rathe did as well. And doing good is not limited to men; think of what you have accomplished with the legal system you established. That is an incredible accomplishment."

She smiled. "I understand what you are saying. People should strive to do the best they can and, if they can accomplish that, they are heroes."

"That is what I believe, Aleanna. People cannot do more than they are capable of doing, and we cannot expect more from people than they can give. I think you are giving me far too much credit because I am simply doing what I can, the same as both you and your father do, and as Rathe did."

It grew quiet again as Aleanna thought about his statement. "I would not have expected a warrior to also be a philosopher."

"Just because I can fight does not mean I am dull-witted. As I travel a great deal, I have plenty of time to think."

With that subtle rebuke, Aleanna apologized, said good night and stretched out on her bed. She thought about what he said. She had come to admire him for his courage and fighting ability, his gentleness toward her and because she discovered he was a good and decent man. Now she found him even more unique and appealing.

Bright and early the next morning they were looking at a long narrow pass. Aleanna shuddered just looking at it. "How are we to cross this?"

"We will stay in the same formation, except I will change places with the pack horse. I do not think he will be as careful as I can and I want to be close to you."

"Still looking out for me?" she quipped.

"That is what I am being paid to do."

At a signal from Björn, Jago started to navigate the pass. He kept as close to the mountain as possible and walked with extreme care. On the other side, the pass dropped off abruptly into a deep ravine. Without a word, Aleanna followed on her mare and close behind her came Björn, followed by the pack horse.

The pass was narrow for quite some distance, then it broadened out again. Slightly more than halfway across, it became even more narrow. Aleanna hugged the side of the mountain, as did Jago and Björn.

Suddenly, the pack horse panicked and began to whinny and rear and kick. Gravel and small rocks began to fall, followed by larger stones, and then it seemed as though the whole pass gave way. Björn grabbed Aleanna around the waist and pitched her ahead. She landed where the ground was groaning but was still stable, and on all fours she scrambled as fast as she could to solid ground. Jago moved rapidly ahead of her. The ground trembled under her but she kept going. None too soon, the ground stabilized and the noise of the rocks stopped.

Jago stopped ahead of her and looked back. Sitting on the ground, she turned and did the same, and was shocked to see that the trail behind her was gone, along with Björn, the pack horse, and her mare. She inched back to where she thought the ground was firm and looked down.

Far below in the ravine, Björn lay among the rocks, almost covered with them. One boulder looked like it was covering him from the hips down. He lay there unmoving, and she started screaming at him but got no response. His head was clear of the rocks, and he was on his back with one side of his face showing. She could not tell if he was breathing; he appeared to be dead.

Suddenly Jago appeared in her line of sight, making his way to Björn where he began nuzzling Björn's face. Aleanna's heart leapt as she decided Jago would not try to awaken him unless he was alive. Her next thought was, how did Jago get down there? If Jago could get down there, so could she. She climbed to her feet and, still walking with care, started moving down the pass away from the shattered path. The pass became wider and the bank into the ravine became less steep and she finally she came to a spot where she could tell from marks in the dirt and dislodged rocks that this was where Jago must have descended. It looked treacherous, but she was pretty certain that if the horse could climb down it, so could she. She left the trail and began to descend. She started by lowering herself inches at a time, thinking back to times when she and Rathe played at climbing cliffs, and she decided this was no worse than some of those.

That memory gave her confidence she needed, and she moved more rapidly but still with care, wondering if she would ever reach the ground. Finally, after a few scary moments, she made it.

The ravine was full of fallen rock that made it rough going. She ran where she could, walked where she could not, and clambered where she had to. She thought she was making terribly slow progress, but she was actually moving quite rapidly for the terrain. Finally she saw Jago up ahead. When she reached him and started to go to Björn, the horse moved between them.

Each time she attempted to reach him, Jago blocked her. She yelled at him in frustration, but that did not move him. Peering around the horse, she saw Björn, still lying lifeless, his face ashen.

As she stared at him, a joyous thrill went through as she saw his chest move as he breathed. She turned back to Jago more determined than ever. Crouching, she softly called his name, and to hear the soothing sound of her own voice, told Jago how important it was for her to reach Björn. She continued talking with cooing words, and somehow managed to edge past the protective horse.

Reaching Björn, she felt his throat for a pulse, and rejoiced when she found it. "Thank God you are alive," she said, not knowing whether to laugh or cry. One thing she did know was that she had to get the rocks off his body. As she began this task, there were so many stones that she was sure his body was shattered. She was able to remove all of them, even some quite large ones and then, only the large boulder covering him from his hips to almost his feet remained.

Going to the boulder and standing astride Björn, she attempted to move it, but it did not budge. In desperation she shoved it with all her strength and was able to rock it a bit. Realizing that this only made it worse on Björn, she went to him and put her hand on his forehead. He felt cold to her touch, but she could see he still breathed.

"Oh, how am I going to get you free from that rock?" she moaned. "Jago, can you help?" An idea began to form in her mind. "Of course you can." She turned to the horse. "I hope I can arrange things."

She stepped over Björn and began looking for the pack horse. She found it some fifty yards away, lying amid the rocks. His neck was broken, but it wasn't the horse she was after. She took the rope and unfastened it from the dead horse.

Returning to Björn, she made a harness to go around the rock and tied the other end off in two sections to make a makeshift harness. Placing the harness around her body, she pulled. She called to Jago, making sure he was watching her as she strained on the rope. Stopping to rest, she noticed he was watching her curiously. Straining again, she called, "Jago, please come help me." She did not strain on the rope as she knew it was hopeless. but she put on a good act by pulling the rope tight and groaning.

Periodically she stopped to talk to the horse. In the cooing voice she had used earlier, she begged, "Come on, Jago, together we can do it. How can I convince you to help me?"

Pausing, she held the rope out toward the horse and kept moving the rope toward him as she continued talking softly and calmly to him. He watched her with interest, but she could not tell if he did not get the idea, was reluctant to come close to her or simply didn't want to be put in the harness. She kept cooing at him and holding the rope toward him, but he did not move.

She put the rope back on and again pretended to pull, keeping her eye on Jago, who still watched. Finally, to her great surprise, the horse came to stand beside her. Still talking, she took the rope and placed it around his chest. He began to strain against the rope, and she raced over to Björn, got behind the stone and cried to Jago, who began to pull. The rock gave a little under her hands, and then it moved faster and rolled off Björn.

She rushed to him and cradled his head in her lap. To her immense surprise, his eyes were open. He gave her a faint smile and said weakly, "I really scared you that time."

"How badly are you hurt?" she asked.

"For the ride I took, I do not think I am hurt too much. I am afraid my left leg is busted up but I will not know about the rest of me until you get me up. If I am to live, I must get up. We cannot stay here." He peered down his body toward his leg. "Is my leg broken?"

The leg bent at an odd angle. "I am afraid it is, Björn," she said.

"Fortunately for me, that big rock did not land on me," he said. "It landed right beside me and then rolled onto me. What about you? How did you manage?"

"When you tossed me ahead, I kept crawling and reached solid ground. Then I saw Jago down here with you and kept going until I found where he had climbed down. Really, I thought you were dead."

"I think I blacked out for a while because I felt Jago nuzzling me and then I do not remember anything until I felt the rock move. How is Jago?"

"He is right here," she said, calling to the horse. "You will not believe what the two of us did. I got the rope and tied it around the rock, then I tied the other end into two sections to make a harness. There was no way I could move the rock by myself so I had to get Jago to work with me. I showed him what to do and kept coaxing him, and then he came and let me put the rope on him. With him pulling and me pushing, we got the rock off." She sat back on her heels, looking inordinately pleased with herself.

"He let you put the rope on him?" Björn exclaimed.

"It took awhile but finally he did. I think he needed time to understand what it was he had to do and once he understood, he acted quite willingly."

"That is absolutely amazing," Björn said. "I would not have believed it possible. I know Jago is smart enough to learn something like that, but the fact that he let you do it shows he trusts you completely. I did not think he could come to trust anyone that much other than me." He smiled up at her through his pain. "All that work you did coaxing him finally paid off."

"And for you," she retorted.

"Most certainly for me." He grimaced. "We had better figure out how to get out of this hole. It would not be easy at best, but with me crippled, it will be a while before I am ready."

"But what will we eat? I have not seen any sign of game and it will take some time for you to heal and get out of here."

"You are right on both counts," he said, "but we do have food. There is vegetation and we have an entire horse to eat." Again, a smile creased his face. "That will certainly be enough for us."

"A horse!" Aleanna shrunk back at that thought.

"Yes, a horse. When you get hungry enough, you will be glad we have it. You would be surprised at what people will eat that they normally would never even consider to keep from starving. I will not tell you some of the things I have eaten."

"Like what?" she asked.

"Well," he said, "I once got so hungry that I ate my moccasins, although I soaked them thoroughly first. There was not much taste but at least it was something in my stomach. Remember that I once told you that food is just fuel for my body, so I will eat nearly anything that provides nourishment. Believe me, that horse will look delicious before we get out of here."

"I am sure you are right, but I guarantee I will not develop a taste for it." Aleanna shuddered. "I do not think it is possible for me to get that hungry."

"All I ask is that you eat it," he coaxed. "You do not have to like it. I do not want you getting so weak that I have to carry you out of here. Now, could you find something to splint my leg with?"

Aleanna set out, keeping an alert eye out for her missing mare. She would hope the mare was safe and concentrate her efforts on helping Björn. She searched for something to make a splint, but all that was available in the ravine were small scrub trees scavenging for a foothold in the rocks, and those that had made it to a size adequate for a splint were badly deformed and crooked. Finally she found one she thought would work and cut it with the hatchet she had taken from the dead pack horse. Trimming it, she set it in a place she could find when she returned and went in search of another. It took several hours to find another one she thought was satisfactory, and she cut and trimmed it, then returned to pick up the first one.

She had been gone so long that she was concerned about Björn. She had not seen tracks of wildlife in the ravine, but she was worried because he would be helpless if something did find him. When she returned, though, she found him safe and sound asleep. She checked to see if he were sleeping or had passed out again, but from his even breathing concluded that he was merely asleep. Checking the length of the splints against his leg, she concluded they would be adequate.

Realizing that, deep in the ravine as they were, darkness would come early, she decided to make use of the daylight left, Collecting a knife and the hatchet, she went back to the pack horse. She assumed she could dress it the same as a large deer or elk, so first she gutted and skinned it. She had time to quarter it, but by then it was dark.

She returned to Björn and touched him. He was still sleeping, but he was shivering. Tucking his blanket tightly around him, she lay down next to him as close as she could and put her arm around him. Soon he stopped shivering and rested peacefully, and it wasn't long before she fell asleep as well.

She was awakened several times by Björn moving in his sleep, but each time was able to get back to sleep. It was still dark in the ravine when she awoke and got up, although she could see light glowing above them on the mountain.

"So you are awake," he said.

Aleanna started. "How long have you been awake?" she asked.

"Not very long. I appreciate you keeping me warm during the night. I remember being very cold when I went to sleep."

"It worked both ways, as you kept me warm as well, but I wonder how either of us got any sleep here in these rocks."

He started to say that she could have found a more comfortable spot but then caught himself and instead said, "I wonder if you could get some supplies off the pack horse for a rough breakfast."

"I already have," she said. "I took everything off the horse before I field-dressed him. I was not able to hang him because there are no trees tall enough, but I do not think there is anything here to bother him. I also got you two limbs for splints."

"Did you remember to get them long enough for me to walk?"

"Yes, I remembered from when you broke your arm from your fight with that snow monster. I checked and these are long enough. I will have to set the bone now."

She took the bone in each hand and, as gently as possible but with considerable pressure, put the bone back in place. Surprisingly, Jago stood motionless as she removed the powder Björn had used earlier from the pack. She took the powder and rubbed it gently on the area of the break, then mixed some with water and had him drink it. Next she took the bindings she had gotten from the pack horse and, placing a limb on each side of his leg, bound them securely.

"How is that?" she asked.

"I think it is fine," he said. "Help me up to see if I can walk."

She bent down and, taking her arm, he struggled to his feet. Once he was up, he tested the splint that reached the ground just below his foot so the splint and not the foot touched the ground.

"While I am up, we can try to find a good place to camp."

She frowned. "I do not know if there are any good places, but I found a spot while I was searching for your splint that I think will provide a decent camp, at least better than this."

With his arm over her shoulder they walked in tandem, carefully avoiding rocks that might trip him. When they reached the butchered horse, Björn admired her work, telling her she had done a great job. After resting for a few moments, they resumed their slow journey. They had to stop at frequent intervals and Aleanna helped Björn lower himself to the ground to rest. Each time, after a short rest, he raised his arm seeking her assistance so they could continue their painful trip. At last, they reached the spot she had selected.

She helped Björn to the ground so he could stretch out to take weight off his leg, then she backtracked to where the pack horse had fallen and retrieved their bedding, along with the pack that held their stores. Returning to camp, she stretched out a bedroll and helped him crawl onto it.

"I know you prefer to sleep right on the ground, but you are going to sleep on Rathe's bedroll. You will be more comfortable on the bedding than on the ground, and you no longer have to prove anything to me, so lie there in as much comfort as you can get."

"I do not have much choice, do I?"

She ignored him. "How are we going to get out of this ravine?" she asked.

"As soon as my leg is sufficiently healed, we will search for a way out. How about that place where you and Jago descended?"

"I do not think that way will work, especially with your bad leg." She looked around. "I am concerned because there are no animals here because if there were places to get here, there would be some sign of animals. I hope we are seeing no sign because there is no food here." She checked on him again before continuing. "That would explain the lack of animal evidence, but do not think about now. The first job we have is to get you well."

Collecting some of the dried venison, and dried fruit and vegetables from the pack, she brought the food to his bedroll and sat beside him. He surprised her by sitting up by himself as she extended her arm help him. She thought about reprimanding him but then wondered what good would it do? She had learned long ago that he was the most stubborn man she had ever met, but it showed her he was determined to take care of himself as much as possible.

After they ate, washing the meal down with water, Aleanna pulled Björn's blankets over him, then laid her bedroll next to his and crawled into it.

"Are you warm enough?" she asked.

"Yes, I am fine," he said. "Thank you for taking such good care of me. I hate to be a burden on you because I know how difficult my injuries are to you."

"Difficult!" She sat up. "You saved my life and now you are complaining that I take care of you. I do not know if you are ungrateful or simply stupid. You and I are traveling as partners, and although you may be the senior partner, we are still partners. You saved my life and now it is my job to help you mend."

"I know, but it is extremely difficult for me to be helpless and to have someone to take care of me," he said. "That has happened to me only once before, and now this is already the second time while with you. But you are correct; we are partners and I am most glad to have you as one. In my present condition, I would probably die here without you."

"If it were not for saving me, you would not be lying here helpless; you would have saved yourself. But thank you for agreeing that we are partners."

She lay back in her bedding but she did not sleep. The pride of this strange man! she thought. But she understood; he had been trained to be independent. His life was that of a lonely mercenary, and he made no personal attachments and was close to no one. Each job he took was merely that—a job. She was sure he derived personal satisfaction out of helping people, but that didn't mean he formed relationships with them.

She remembered their talk about her being a job, and she didn't understand it. She was concerned for his welfare, she enjoyed his company and realized that she cared a great deal for him; she had to be more to him than a job. She would miss him a great deal when he had delivered her to the king, but at least she had the privilege of knowing him and having his company for such a long time. She thought that he was the most uniquely marvelous man in the world. The only bad part would come when his job was completed and he left her in Carigo. She lay thinking like this for a long time before finally going to sleep.

They stayed there for some time while Björn healed. In addition to his broken leg, he had deep bruises all over his body but, being Björn, he healed rapidly. They ate the horse meat, along with the dried fruits and vegetables. She thought about how Björn had insisted they take the time to dry the food, thinking he was being prepared for something like this. He knew their trip would be dangerous and didn't want to be stranded without food.

Björn was soon up and walking with his crutch. Aleanna found another small tree he could use as a cane. With that, he was able to move about with her, and they began to search for a way out. Their searches were limited because they had to return to camp by nightfall each day, but one day Björn took off the splints and walked without them. He limped and walked slowly, but they were able to make much better progress than before.

The time came when Björn took some of the horse meat they had dried, along with the other dried food, and they abandoned their camp to search until they found a way out. When they came to the spot where she and Jago had descended it was, as Aleanna had said, impassable as a way out, so they kept going. They found a few places where Björn thought it was possible, but each time Aleanna ruled it out as being too difficult and he realized she based her decision on his crippled leg.

After several hours, they found a place that Aleanna agreed they should try. Laying down their packs and putting a cord on each one, they started their climb. At a motion from Björn, Jago went first, scrambling up the cliff, knocking rocks in his wake. He hit several spots where he had to struggle, but he eventually made it to the top.

Björn wanted Aleanna to go next, but she insisted that he go. He started up the steep slope, carefully placing his feet and using his hands to balance and pull himself up, but he struggled, and Aleanna hurt just watching him.

He took rest breaks regularly, at last reaching the top and scrambling over the edge.

"And you did not think I could do it. When will you ever stop doubting me?" he shouted.

"From now on, whenever you say you can do something, I will always trust you," she laughed, mostly to cover her relief. "I was concerned that you might fall and hurt yourself all over again, fearful at the thought of trying to catch you or break your fall if you did fall. Now I will come up." She positioned herself to make the climb, grabbing the cords attached to the packs and tying them to her back. As she climbed, these gave her a little trouble, but except for a few places, she made it with comparative ease. Impressed, Björn told her what a great job she had done when she came over the edge and sat beside him.

"This trip has really toughened me up," she said. "I do not think I could have done it before we left home. I thought I was in good condition, but I was not prepared for this. From the way my clothes fit now, I think I have become very lean."

They got up and pulled the cords with their supplies the rest of the way. Since it was mid-afternoon and the pass had widened considerably, Aleanna suggested they make their camp there and get an early start in the morning. Björn agreed.

To Aleanna's relief, her mare had made her way above them on the pass while they progressed through the ravine and up the cliff face. She was waiting for them, delighted to see her mistress safe and sound.

CHAPTER FIVE
CARIGO

Björn wanted to travel as soon as they awoke the next morning, but Aleanna insisted they travel only far enough to find a really good camp. Björn thought she was doing it for his sake and objected strongly.

"Are you trying to get rid of me as quickly as you can? I thought you said you enjoyed my company." she asked.

"No, that is not it. I guess I am simply accustomed to being in a hurry when I am working."

"Well, you do not have to work all of the time. We will stay long enough for the leg and the bruises to heal, so look for a good spot where we can be comfortable for a time."

They gathered their supplies and started on the trail again in search of a better camp site. Jago was leading, Björn astride the mare whom Aleanna had convinced him to ride and she brought up the rear. Björn had not wanted to ride, and convincing him had not been easy for Aleanna. It was only after she threatened to make the site they found permanent that he allowed her to help him onto the horse. Secretly, he was impressed with how naturally she took charge when he was incapacitated.

They had to travel much further than Aleanna expected, but finally they found a spot beside the trail that she pronounced satisfactory. She helped him down from her mare by giving him her shoulder to hold to and putting her arm around him so she could ease him to the ground. After making him as comfortable as possible, she unloaded their things and, although it was late in the day, she took her bow and quiver of arrows and started off to hunt.

"We are still near the trail so perhaps you should take your sword as well," Björn said. "There could be large animals passing through that might decide you would make a good meal."

"I guarantee you that I would be a prickly meal," Aleanna said, but she got her sword before she left.

She slipped into the woods, moving stealthily, passing up a small herd of deer because she didn't want a whole deer to carry and she didn't believe in wasting meat. Traveling on until almost dusk, she spotted a squirrel as it ran up a tree. Sitting with her back against a tree, she got an arrow ready. She watched silently, waiting for the squirrel to stick his head out, then put an arrow through it. She notched another arrow and waited, and before long, she saw another head and put an arrow through it as well. Gathering up the two small carcasses, she retrieved her arrows and returned to camp.

Björn was asleep on Rathe's bedroll, so Aleanna quietly cleaned the two squirrels and got them ready for dinner. At the smell of the squirrels cooking in gravy, Björn awoke. "I see your hunt was successful."

"And I see that your stomach is not injured."

She told him of her plan to move their camp site and he agreed that would be wise. When the meal was ready they ate hungrily. As they were both tired, they fell into their beds and Aleanna was soon asleep.

Björn raised himself to a sitting position. He was able to stretch out and reach his bow and quiver of arrows. He remained in a sitting position, holding his bow with an arrow notched through the remainder of the night.

When Aleanna awoke, she stretched and then saw Björn on guard. "Have you been up all night?"

"Oh, I have to admit I was not much of a guard," Björn said. "I dozed off occasionally, and I am not sure how effective a guard I would be with my injuries. We relied on Jago last night, but I felt I had to do my part."

"Sometimes I get so angry with you."

"I know, but this is the way I am. I am afraid I cannot change, so please try to bear with me."

They broke camp, Aleanna demanding that she do all of the work of packing. When everything was ready, they began to travel parallel to the trail but far enough away that Björn thought they would be safe from any marauding beasts. After traveling almost half the day, Aleanna found a good spot, and they unpacked and set up camp. It was a pleasant open spot surrounded by trees that gave it a secluded look, and Aleanna found it cozy.

They stayed at the site for eleven days. The first ten Björn spent exercising while walking on his crutch, then he got rid of the crutch and walked without it.

Watching him, Aleanna said, "I have never seen a man recover as you do."

"Give the credit to my ancestors," Björn grunted. "Remember that in the Northland one has to get over injuries quickly. In that unforgiving land, you either recover or die. I think that only the strongest who recovered most quickly survived and brought us to where we are today. So I deserve no credit; I was fortunate enough to be descended from a long line of strong, healthy people."

"That sounds reasonable," she said. "But whatever the reason, you appear to be completely recovered. Do you want to move out in the morning?" She dreaded his answer because she wanted to stay in this idyllic spot as long as possible.

"I think it is time," he said. "I am healed and we have had time to dry some jerky, vegetables and fruits to sustain us as we travel. Once we clear this mountain, there is a level plain all the way to Carigo; we should make good time."

"I will be sorry for the trip to end."

"I am surprised to admit that I will be, too. I have never enjoyed a trip or a client so much." He gave her an appraising look. "Perhaps when the old king dies, you will contact me to take you home again."

As alert as he always was, he did not see the tear in her eyes as she responded. "Who knows what will happen in the future? We cannot predict it, only plan for it."

"Well, plan to contact me if you ever want to make the return journey."

They rode on. The days passed uneventfully, and barely over three weeks later, they made their last camp in sight of the Carigo castle. Björn said they should have a feast to celebrate their safe journey. Aleanna didn't reply but only walked a short distance away; the time she had dreaded was here. She had let her imagination run away with her and let her think the journey would never end, but here it was. She composed herself and walked back to find the camp empty, so she assumed Björn had gone out hunting.

She sat on her bedroll, dividing her life into three parts. There was the first part of growing up and living in Kallthom, then there was this journey. The third was coming next, and she anticipated that she would spend the rest of her life in Carigo. She was certain that no matter how pleasant her life in Carigo was, it would never match the first two segments of her life. Those two were simply too important and meant too much to her. She would never forget them.

Aleanna sat with her arms wrapped around herself and thought about what her life would be like in Carigo. What would be expected of the queen? She assumed she would assist the king in conducting formal affairs. As the king was so old, she presumed she would have a great deal of time to herself, but she knew herself well enough to know that she could not sit idle.

She wondered what she could conjure up that would be useful to the people. Perhaps her legal system would be needed but, if not that, she was sure she could find something. She also wondered how much resistance she might encounter, but knew the strength of her own personality and how cleverly she could operate when she wanted to. She had to admit that if it were not for the sorrow of leaving home and taking leave of Björn, she would be looking forward to her life in Carigo.

By the time Björn returned with a partridge, she was combing out her long black hair.

"I see you are getting beautiful in preparation for meeting the king," he teased. "But you do not have to do much. Even smudged as you so often were on our trip, you would still be the envy of the women of the castle,"

Aleanna blushed in spite of herself.

Quickly changing the subject, Björn reported, "We are so close to the village surrounding the castle that this area is evidently hunted a great deal. I had to work hard for this bird, but I got a look at the village. In my experience, the size of the village at the castle is determined by the size of the kingdom and the activities within the castle. Since this is a large village, I assume the kingdom is large and there is a great deal of activity inside the castle."

"What did you see?"

"Not much, only the usual hustle and bustle of a typical village and, of course, a great wall surrounding the castle. Off to one side is what appears to be a mine. There is a lot of mining machinery and piles of what looks like coal, but it could be just about anything. When things come directly from the earth, most of them look like coal or lumps of dark dirt. Are you aware of any mining that goes on in Carigo?"

"There is nothing that I know of, but that does not necessarily mean anything since Carigo is so far from Kallthom. I am sure we will find out soon enough." She kept brushing her hair vigorously. "I should not be so vain, but I want to look as good as I possibly can for the king and his court." She put the brush down and came to eat.

"Umm, this is quite good," she said after taking a bite.

"It should be quite tender, Because you were working so hard on your hair, I had time to cook it slowly."

"Time passes quickly when I brush my hair," she said. "It gives me time to think."

"And what were you thinking about, Princess?"

"About what my life will be like in Carigo, and what my responsibilities will be. I hope they do not expect only a figurehead because unless I am busy doing something I consider important, I will go crazy. I have a feeling that I am going to run into opposition trying to get things done."

"I am sure it will not be anything you cannot handle. I cannot imagine anyone keeping you from doing something you want for long."

She smiled over at him. "Well, I hope there will not be any difficulty, but I can be diplomatic and clever. I would hate to be labeled a troublemaker immediately, so I will be patient and take my time. I want things to go smoothly in Carigo. After giving up so much, leaving Kallthom, losing

Rathe and making this almost impossible trek, it would be terrible if I had a miserable life here."

"You are making trouble for yourself before we have even gotten through the gate," he admonished gently. "It is generally true that the bad things we expect never come true. Remember what I expected to find in a princess? More or less a spoiled child whom I would never agree to serve as bodyguard. Instead I found this beautiful wonderful woman whom it has been a pleasure to accompany."

She blushed again. "I hope you really mean that."

"You know I always mean what I say."

"Of course I do. It is simply that it is so important to me. I respect you so much that what you think of me means a great deal to me."

"I did not know that," he said.

"As well as we have gotten to know each other, you should have known it."

He moved off to stand guard as she went back to brushing her hair and thinking. What a strange, wonderful man! He had perilously risked his own life to toss her out of danger at the rock slide, and there were other times when he had stood between her and death. She knew he would find it ridiculous, but she was sure that as fierce a fighter as he was, he would willingly have given his own life for hers.

She thought he liked her in his own way, but she had no idea he considered her wonderful and beautiful. Now she was afraid she would blush every time he looked at her. To prevent him from seeing her now, she stopped brushing her hair and curled up in her blankets and stopped breathing when she felt his presence in the camp. She didn't know how she was aware of him because she hadn't heard him, but she knew he was there. Feigning sleep as well as she could, she knew it would never fool him. Feeling he was watching her, she shivered.

As she thought about him and their relationship, she let her mind wander. She had never thought about it because it was impossible for more than one reason, but she realized she wanted to spend more time with him, to even share intimate time with him. She fantasized that tomorrow she would tell him she had changed her mind and wanted to go on with him, knowing that she really wouldn't, but it was a wonderful fantasy. She drifted off to sleep.

The next morning she awoke much later than usual. She wondered if it was because she stayed awake longer than usual the night before, but it was more likely her restless sleep caused by wisps of dreams she could barely recall.

She combed and then brushed her tangled hair. When she was satisfied with it, she got out the packet containing her dress. Even though she opened it repeatedly during the trip to shake out the wrinkles and refold it in a manner to randomly spread the creases and keep any from getting too deep, she gave it a dejected look as she examined it. Hanging it on a tree branch, she got the two pots they had and, filling them with water, she placed them over the fire.

When they were boiling, she started to take the pots but Björn beat her to it. She directed him to place the pots directly under the dress. After several repetitions of this, she shook out the dress, which still looked mussed. Frowning, she decided it was the best she could do.

"Please turn your back while I dress," she said as she prepared to change.

Once she had the dress on, she asked him to turn around and help her with the buttons on the back of the dress. Then she smoothed out the dress and asked," How do I look?"

"I am not a good person to ask because I think you

always look wonderful. But if you are asking how you look after completing our journey, I think the king and his court will be most pleasantly surprised. You can be sure you will not disappoint them."

"Well, this is as good as I am going to look. We might as well go and meet this old king."

Björn took the few possessions he wanted for his continued trip and, abandoning the rest, Björn helped Aleanna mount her mare and leaving Jago to fend for himself, they started for the village.

The village was like many others, built in a random order as it had grown through the years. The houses were of logs with thatched roofs, different sizes, some quite large, most of them medium-sized and some simple cabins. There were people working and children playing. The most interesting thing they saw was the opening to a mine. There was a great deal of machinery, and Björn commented it was used to send miners up and down and to bring the ore up. He saw that it was set up with a large sluice to separate gold ore from the dirt and rock.

"What is it?" asked Aleanna.

"A gold mine, evidently a prosperous one from the amount of dirt they have strained away from the ore. That is why the village is so large. It takes a great deal of manpower to operate a mine. Carigo must be quite prosperous, but if it is typical of other villages, the wealth primarily goes to the wealthy and only a little to the rest of the kingdom. From the difference between the village and the castle, Carigo is typical."

Aleanna thought the castle huge. It was one-half again the size of the Kallthom castle, and it looked absolutely impregnable with tall thick walls, turrets high on the walls, and a massive gate.

"Is there any way this castle could be successfully attacked?" she asked.

"It would take a great many men but it could be done," Björn replied. "I would approach it the same way we discussed the weakness at Kallthom. It appears that the protection is primarily at the front and sides, so there is probably much less at the back. I do not know if you can tell from here, but the keep is located at the rear of the castle. It is always placed where it should be most secure. I think this shows they are not expecting any trouble from the rear, if trouble comes at all. Yes, I would attack the same way, feinting an assault at the front and bringing my main force in from the rear as quietly and quickly as possible."

"But surely a large troop movement would be noticed," she objected.

"I am sure it would be, but most likely not in time. I am sure the peasants would send alarms to the castle, but they would most likely be ignored because those in the castle would consider it to be preposterous. It could be done but, as I said, it would take many men."

They entered the great wall and drifted toward the castle on what seemed to be the main street. There was a great deal of activity, and Aleanna guessed that it must be market day. All around them men and women were hawking their wares.

"Freeesh vegetables, right here."

"Young tom turkeys, the best tasting you could ever have."

"Honeeeey, the lightest you have ever seen. You have to see this."

And there was much more of the same.

Aleanna bought a fresh apple for a Kallthom gold piece.

"I have been wanting one of these for months."

The crowd rippled and rushed around them and, for the most part, they were ignored. If they received any attention at all, it centered on Aleanna's dress. Noticing repeated stares, she commented that she seemed to be the only female dressed for a ball.

"That dress does make us sort of stand out," was Björn's rejoinder.

Aleanna had never seen anything like this and was fascinated. There were stands selling trinkets, jewelry, shoes, clothing of every manner, fruits and vegetables of all types, and almost everything else imaginable. Aleanna stopped every ten paces or so to check out first one thing and then another. Björn followed her slow pace and wasn't the least bit perturbed.

"You are the most patient man I know. Any other man would be shouting at me to move on."

"After what you have been through, it is good to see you enjoying yourself."

She gave him a dazzling smile and went on with her shopping. She combed through the items in the stalls, exclaiming occasionally when something caught her eye. When she found a pendant and tried to buy it, she didn't have Carigo currency and this vendor refused to accept a Kallthom coin.

Björn came to her side and handed her a small gold nugget. The saleswoman looked at them strangely and said she couldn't take it because she didn't know its value. Björn said it was worth at least four Carigo gold pieces, and he would be satisfied with one in change. She examined the nugget with great care and agreed. Aleanna again gave him her bright smile and thanked him.

"It was worth it to see your smile," he laughed. "I hope

you can find other items you want, perhaps these pickled pigs feet? Would you like to gnaw on one of these while we walk?"

Aleanna grimaced with disgust. "I cannot think of many things I would like less, but perhaps we can find something else." She moved on through the crowded aisles.

Björn thought they should be heading toward the castle, but he was enjoying the time with Aleanna. He was as close to being thrilled as it was possible for him to be. Her hair was combed and lustrous and she looked alluring in her gown; he thought she had never been so beautiful. But then he realized how long it had been since he had seen her all dressed up and groomed. If the people of the palace are not thoroughly thrilled with her as well, there was something drastically wrong with them.

As dusk approached, people began to take down their merchandise from the stalls. Aleanna saw a last fruit stand that an elderly man and woman were dismantling and asked Björn if she could have one final apple. Björn gave his small grin and purchased one for her.

"I have not forgotten that we have not eaten since breakfast," he said.

"I have been enjoying myself so much I had forgotten that. No wonder those apples tasted so good."

They moved on toward the castle. The great doors were open and people were streaming in and out. They entered with a group of people.

As Aleanna looked around the interior of the castle, she realized it was enormous; the Kallthom castle would fit inside with room to spare. She had never seen anything so imposing. "And I am to be queen of all this," she said, not realizing she had spoken aloud.

Taking Björn's arm, she whispered, "Where should we

go?"

"I think the royal quarters would be located behind that large arch." He pointed to a large, heavily decorated arch with three uniformed soldiers on each side. The squads faced each other, and they carried long spears.

Björn guided her toward them. As they approached, the first two soldiers crossed their spears to block their way.

One of the soldiers said harshly, "State your business." He glared at them with hostile eyes.

"This is Aleanna, Princess of Kallthom," said Björn. "We are here to meet with your king."

The soldier frowned at them for at least a full minute before he growled, "Wait here." He disappeared into the interior of the castle for what seemed ages to Aleanna before he returned with a small man in a long white robe.

"I am Rohla, the prime minister," he said, smiling broadly. "And you are Aleanna. I must say we were not expecting such a beautiful young woman," he said, extending his hand.

Taking his hand, she said, "This is my bodyguard, Björn."

Rohla also shook Björn's hand. "Come, I will take you to the king," he said pleasantly.

He nodded to one of the soldiers to take the mare.

"You have traveled a great distance," Rohla said. "How did you evade our watchers out on the plain? We have been watching for months. In fact, we had almost given up hope of your arrival." The prime minister spoke in a solicitous, friendly manner.

"We did not come across the plain," Aleanna told him. "We crossed the Ice Mountains."

"But I thought was impossible," Rohla said incredulously in a startled voice. "We have never heard of anyone taking that route. According to rumors, it is filled with monsters and barbarians. How in the world did you make such a trip safely with only one bodyguard?" He peered at her, perplexed.

"Björn is not just any bodyguard, and my brother started with us but was killed along the way."

"Well, then, come with me, and I will take you to the king," he said, taking Aleanna's arm and leading the pair down a magnificent vaulted hallway with murals and frescos on the walls and ceilings. It was the most beautiful thing Aleanna had ever seen, but then they entered a huge chamber that took her breath away. It was also vaulted with inlaid gold and covered with frescos and murals as well as gorgeous tapestries. Aleanna thought how rich this kingdom must be and wondered how she would be treated.

Rohla led them to a magnificent golden throne. On the throne, or rather in it, sat a little wizened, wrinkled old man. Aleanna was startled. How could they have wanted her to come all this way to wed an old man who looked as though he wouldn't last another day?

Rohla started to lead them to the king down a line with soldiers with spears. Björn reached and drew Aleanna back, pushing her behind him as the soldiers moved toward them with spears pointed at them. Björn drew his swords in a flash of motion and half-turned toward the entryway they had entered as more soldiers scurried there.

"We know who and what you are, Northlander," said Rohla. "You can possibly kill these soldiers, but are you sure you can keep them from killing the princess while you do?"

Björn remained still, but he held his swords ready.

"Why are you doing this?" Björn asked.

"Surely you have noticed that the king is a senile old

man. What need would he have of a beautiful young wife?" Rohla's voice dripped venom. "But that is not the reason I brought you here. We have formed an alliance with Delph, and we will inform your father that we have you captive and the only way he can get you back is to surrender to us."

"My father will never agree to such a thing," Aleanna said calmly.

"Possibly not. I know I would not if I had a daughter." Rohla continued staring at them malevolently. "But perhaps he is more sentimental than me. We shall see. If he does not surrender, it will take longer and lives will be lost because Delph and Carigo's armies will unite and we will march on Kallthom. One way or another it will happen. Now put down your swords, Northlander, before the princess gets hurt."

Björn glowered at the prime minister, and Aleanna could see his black eyes boring into the man. Aleanna thought they had better kill Björn now or they would live to pay for their ignorance and arrogance. Finally Björn tossed his swords to the floor with a loud clatter and, taking the knife from his belt, he tossed it on the swords.

"I am sure you understand, Northlander, that we have to put restraints on you." Rohla nodded at two of his men, who brought wrist and leg chains that they fastened around Björn's ankles and wrists. The leg bracelets were unique in that the middle link was large and round instead of being oval. One of the men hooked a short chain to this middle link and gave a jerk but Björn didn't budge.

Rohla shrugged. "If you will follow my men," he said with mock politeness, "they will see to your needs."

Forty men lined up on each side of Björn, and one holding the chain jerked it again. This time Björn did not resist but went along quietly, wondering why they thought it necessary to have so many men guarding him.

They led him to a cage that Björn could tell was at the top of the mine, and he noticed that it operated on a combination of chains and gears. The group entered the cage, leaving only two men at the top. Björn saw an eight-team rig of horses attached to a long chain, which in turn was fastened to a large gear over the cage. Björn thought this was the way they brought the cage back up from the mine.

One man threw a lever and the cage slowly rattled to the bottom, where a man opened the door and Björn was forced out of the cage. Proceeding along a tunnel with torches spaced regularly to illuminate the floor and sides, they traveled for some distance before they turned to enter another tunnel that branched off to the left and sloped downward. There were no torches here, but several of the soldiers lit torches they carried. After they walked down this tunnel for some minutes, Björn felt the presence of a large group of men ahead of them and then heard voices. When they reached the source of the voices, he saw two rows of men chained to each wall, and he estimated that there must be at least two hundred on each side.

"This man is very dangerous, so put him in the middle of the chain where it will be more difficult for him to escape, if he can at all. He is supposed to be a Northlander, whatever that is," said the soldier in charge. "He looks kind of scrawny to me."

"I have heard of them," another soldier said. "They are a strong barbaric race from the mountains northwest of us, but I agree with you. He does not look dangerous or barbaric."

The end of the chain was fastened to a large pin that was inserted through a large block. One soldier took a large hammer and began to pound on a key that was through the pin at the bottom. When he had it loose, he pulled the pin free from its base and out of the chain. The soldiers spread out to keep guard over the men as this action released the prisoners from their ankle chains. When they reached the approximate center, they brought Björn over and ran the chain through the center link of his chain, then re-threaded the long, heavy chain back through the leg irons of the men. An officer ordered a soldier to remove Björn's wrist chains then, looking at Björn smugly, he turned to leave, ordering his men to follow. They marched out of the area in two lines.

There were no lighted torches on these walls, so the prisoners sat chained on the cold floor in total darkness. Björn could see, but he knew the others were unable to see anything, not even the difference between light and dark.

The prisoners started to talk around him and, at first, the sounds came to him in a jumble. Then he heard them ask, "Who is this new man?" and a man on one side of Björn poked him and asked him who he was.

Björn responded, "An enemy of the prime minister."

"We all are," the man said, then he asked, "What crime did you commit?"

"None that I know of, except the prime minister considers me a threat of some kind."

"Many of us are here because of the prime minister. He has become a dictator since he took over from the old king. Most of us are here for minor crimes if we have committed any crimes at all. I think his real motive is to get free labor instead of having to pay for it. That way he keeps more of the gold from the mine."

The man fell silent and there was only silence in the darkness except for the clang of a chain when someone moved.

With Björn's heightened senses, he could hear a multitude of sounds. He heard the sound of breathing and sighing, and occasionally the sound of someone crying.

As always, his mind started to work on how he might escape, and he thought about how he was restrained. A long chain ran through the center link of each man's chain and was fastened at each end by a pin inserted through a metal slab, which had a key through it at the bottom to keep it secure. The officer told the soldiers not to leave him at the end of the line and, if they had, he would have already unfastened the pin and be free. But now what could he do?

He drew up his right boot and examined the clasp around his ankle. The clasp was two half-round pieces of thick metal with pins holding each end. Retrieving the small knife he kept in his boot for emergencies, he began to saw silently back and forth on the pins. Even though the knife was made from the metal of the Northlands, and thus much harder than the pin, Björn realized it would take considerable time to cut through it. Then he would have to cut through the pin that held the ring around his other ankle. Still, in order to finish, he had to get started. He was extremely patient by nature, but was concerned about Aleanna. What was she doing and what was happening to her?

Aleanna's heart sank as she saw Björn being led from the chamber. Her first concern was that they were going to kill him, but she knew that even unarmed he might be a match for the soldiers surrounding him. She knew he had not fought them for fear she might be injured or held hostage for his good behavior. Then she thought of her own predicament, realizing she was helpless for the first time in her life. It definitely was not a good feeling.

Rohla sidled close to her. "Well, my dear, I am sure you want to get the traveling dust off and you must be hungry." He nodded to a nearby soldier, who left the room and returned with four middle-aged women. "Go with them," the prime minister ordered. "They will bathe you and dress you for dinner."

One woman took each of Aleanna's arms and they marched her out of the room and down a long hallway. They moved her through a set of rooms and halls, finally arriving at a luxurious bath set inside a spacious, ornate room. The bath was already filled with steaming water, and after the women undressed her, she walked into the bath and gingerly sat in the hot water. In spite of her sense that she was a prisoner, it felt wonderful. One woman bathed her back and two others each leg while the fourth washed and dried her hair and started to arrange it. When they finished, she got out and walked to the front of a large mirror. She liked what they had done to her hair. Her body smelled of the fragrances of the bath water.

The women led her into the next room where a beautiful dress hung on a padded hanger. They helped Aleanna into it, and she found another mirror in this room, placed so she could take stock of her appearance. She decided it had been a long time since she had looked and felt this pretty. It was apparent that the trek she and Björn had completed had been good for her appearance, for her body was toned and firm. She smiled inwardly at the thought that only a man like Björn would find her hard body attractive. Other men, as she had learned primarily from her brother Rathe, preferred softer, rounder women, and she thought she might have an advantage, as she certainly did not want to appear attractive to the prime minister.

The women slipped delicate shoes on her feet and placed a beautiful comb in her hair, completing their task by hanging a gorgeous diamond pendant around her neck. As she started to thank them, she realized that if their work did not satisfy the prime minister, he would surely have them beaten.

She was led by another route to a huge dining hall filled with people. A hush fell over the crowd as she entered, and Rohla rose. Moving to her side, he extended his arm, and she took it, allowing him to lead her to her place at the head of the table.

"This is Princess Aleanna of Kallthom, who has graciously agreed to join us." He started applause that was picked up immediately by the crowd.

Aleanna noted that all the men and women were dressed impeccably, also noting that a pair of uniformed soldiers guarded each exit.

Rohla held her chair so she could sit, then a servant seated him. "You look lovely, my dear," he purred. "We are honored by your presence."

"Well, I am not honored at being tricked into coming here," she said, matching his tone of voice.

"In good time I will explain all to you. Now, let us have a leisurely meal and tonight you can rest. Tomorrow I will take you on a tour of your castle and your kingdom."

"I do not see any sign of my bridegroom."

"That will also be explained in good time. Now let us enjoy this feast." The prime minister turned to his food and began to eat fastidiously.

The table was loaded with meats, seafood, vegetables, fruits and delicacies. Rohla passed her a dish she failed to recognize, a slimy small object served in butter with its shell. She hated to ask what it was, but she did anyway.

She was not going to eat something she couldn't identify.

"It is escargot, or snails," Rohla told her.

Aleanna's stomach turned, but when she saw him and others eating them, she tried one and found it to be far better than it looked. Someone passed her a dish of eyes. She didn't know what they came from, but she tried one of these as well. Contrary to the escargot, these tasted worse than they looked. Everything else she recognized as not being out of the ordinary, and all in all she thought it a delicious meal.

The meal ended with a dessert of a sweet cake topped with honey, followed by wine—more types of wine than she thought possible. Taking a glass of white wine, she found it much too sweet for her taste, so she sipped at it. Rohla noticed and asked if she would like to try a glass of a different wine. He asked what type of wine she preferred.

"This is too sweet for my taste, prime minister, but I am not very experienced with wine."

"We will try to get you exactly what you like." He selected a red wine and said, "This wine is dryer, but not so dry that you will find it bitter."

She took a sip. "Yes, this is much better," she said.

As the diners finished their wine, the prime minister rose and a servant edged back Aleanna's chair. She arose, but noted that everyone else stayed seated. Rohla offered his arm and, with a servant following, led her from the dining room. They walked down a hallway until they came to a door. The servant opened the door to what looked to Aleanna like a very small room, and she was surprised when the servant stepped into the room behind them.

Seeing her baffled look, Rohla explained, "This is an elevator. It is powered by a strong man in the basement of the castle pulling on a long rope attached to a gear which, in turn, is attached to the top of the elevator. He hauls the elevator up by pulling on the rope and lowers it by slowly releasing the rope. Because of the way it is designed, one man can operate it easily. Its purpose is to keep us from having to walk between floors. As you perhaps noticed when you approached the castle, the floors are quite high and walking from the first to the top floor can be quite arduous."

Rohla nodded to the servant, who rang a bell, and the cage began to move upward. It creaked and clanged but rose steadily. When it stopped, the servant opened the door and Rohla and Aleanna stepped out. They walked down another hallway and Rohla stopped at a door guarded by soldiers on each side of the door. The prime minister held the door open for Aleanna to pass through. She almost gasped at the luxury of the bedroom, but caught herself to avoid giving him the satisfaction of knowing he surprised her. At the center of the room was a huge canopied bed, and the other furniture in the room was equally impressive. A maid stood by the bed on which was laid a white lace nightgown, both feminine and beautiful, for Aleanna.

"I will leave you for tonight," said Rohla. "The maid will help you with your ablutions and nightgown, and will turn back the bedcovers."

"You are talking to a woman who traveled over a thousand treacherous miles to get here and you think I need help getting into bed?"

"I apologize if I offended you. I was only trying to be a good host."

"I thank you for it, but it really is unnecessary," she said, her shoulders stiff.

"I will leave the two soldiers outside your room for protection," he told her. "I would not want anything to happen to you on your first night with us."

"And just what could happen to me?"

"One never knows." He gave her an oily smile. "It is only a precaution. I do not want you to think you are in any danger; I am only thinking of your safety. If there is nothing else I can do for you, I bid you good night."

Motioning to the maid, he followed her out of the room.

Aleanna sat on the edge of the bed, wondering where Björn was and how he was. Was he still alive? She thought of him as indestructible, but during the course of their travels, she realized he wasn't. At the same time, she was confident that, if they were so ignorant of Northlanders that they let him live, he would eventually escape and wreak havoc on their captors.

She still didn't understand why she had been brought here. It was obvious that marriage to the old king was merely a ruse, but for what purpose? The only reason she could think of was for them to hold her to blackmail her father. She smiled; obviously they didn't know her father. He would never hand over his kingdom, even to save the life of his daughter. She brushed her hair and readied herself for bed. Even though she was so preoccupied she thought she would never sleep, she gradually drifted off.

The next morning she awoke late. The sun already hung in the sky above the horizon. Here she was, her trip over by only one day, and she was already getting lazy. As she stretched, the events of the previous day came back to her in a rush. A crushing feeling shivered through her as she thought of Björn, and she wondered what had happened to him. He was alive; that much she knew because she was absolutely confident she would know if he were dead, but where was he and what was he doing?

Finding another exquisite gown hanging in her

chamber, she prepared for the day, somewhat surprised that she actually felt comfortable after all those months of wearing trousers. Walking to the door, she opened it, startling the two guards.

One of them said, "Princess, you should have rung the bell and we would have had maids come to assist you."

"Thank you, but as you can see I managed quite well. How do I contact the prime minister? He promised me a tour of the kingdom today."

"I will get him immediately." One of the soldiers hurried away down the hall.

Aleanna spent the time he was gone by staring at the remaining soldier, making him squirm in discomfort. Shortly, the other soldier returned with the prime minister.

"Princess, you should have called for us," said Rohla, out of breath from hurrying. "Princess Aleanna, you must start acting like a queen. Your people expect it." He held out his arm and said, "Let me escort you to breakfast, then, if you approve, I will give you a tour of your castle and kingdom."

"That will be fine, but why do you keep calling it my kingdom? The king and I are not yet married."

"That is simply a formality. We will have that taken care of shortly."

They arrived at the elevator and he escorted her in. A soldier rang the bell and the cage descended, swaying a bit. At the ground floor, they walked to the most ornate room Aleanna had ever seen. The walls were gold and the ceiling was trimmed in gold. She gasped.

"It is quite a beautiful room, yes?" Rohla said. "I had our breakfast set here because I think it is the most impressive room in the castle."

"It is beautiful," she said. "But where do you get all the

gold?"

"We have our own mine that is quite productive. It has been active for many years, and we have incorporated much of it into the castle. But you will see all of that when we have our tour. I think you will be quite impressed."

He held her chair for her and then sat beside her. He nodded, and servants began to bring food. The breakfast was almost as expansive as the banquet the night before, with eggs, bacon, ham, sausage, hot cakes, biscuits, gravy and more than a dozen different kinds of jams and jellies, honey and syrup. Aleanna thought she would become plump in no time by eating here.

Rohla kept up his patter during breakfast, telling her about the great things they would see. She would see the greatest castle in the world and the most peaceful population, the hardest workers and the most bountiful farms.

"Can I also see the gold mine?"

"The gold mine is no place for a woman," he said. "It is a dirty, dangerous place and goes far below ground. They say that years ago, the gold was picked up on the surface but, as time passed, we had to go deeper and deeper. Now parts of the mine are at least a mile deep." He shook his head. "Not only that, but there are occasional cave-ins and at other times, the miners hit pockets of deadly odorous gas. Those are a few of the things that make the mine so dangerous."

"If it is so dangerous, how do you get men to work there?"

"Most of the workers are convicts. It is much easier to keep them restrained deep under ground and much more economical."

"Are they released when their sentences are over?"

Aleanna asked.

He laughed. "They are all sentenced for life, not even getting out when they die. We simply dump their bodies into one of the unused blind alley tunnels."

No doubt that is where Björn is, she thought without showing her alarm. She would have to think of some way to get him out.

At the conclusion of the meal, Rohla held his hand and led Aleanna from the room. He showed her around the castle, starting with the first floor, pointing out all the things he thought were points of interest. He was especially proud of the great hall where they had dined the evening before. Aleanna had no choice but to follow him as he gave a tour of the three floors of the castle. Even though the rooms were beautiful, Rohla told her about each one in a boring monologue.

They took a break in the tour to eat a light lunch and, afterward, Rohla asked if she would like to rest. She said she was fine, so he escorted her into the courtyard where the market had been held the day before, but today it was empty of market stalls. When she inquired where they were, he told her they had been removed for the day in preparation for her tour. "We cannot have the queen in the company of common people," he said.

He called for a carriage and helped her into it. "Now we will see the countryside."

Carigo Castle was set on a large plain. Mountains reached for the sky in the faraway distance but, for miles around the castle, the land was flat except where there were enormous piles of dirt mixed with rock.

"Is that the gold mine?" she asked.

"Yes, Princess, that is the gold mine." Disinterested, Rohla turned the conversation toward other features of the castle.

At the end of the day, they returned to the castle. Taking Aleanna to her room, Rohla ordered four maids to assist her in removing the dirt from the day and to prepare for dinner. Aleanna insisted she did not need assistance, but this time he would not take no for an answer. She resigned herself to the unnecessary and unwanted assistance.

When she was prepared for dinner, Rohla led her to the same room where they had eaten breakfast rather than the great hall of the night before. Instead of dining alone, they were joined by a small number of dignitaries. Rohla led a lively discussion in which he included Aleanna and, at the end of dinner, he rose and pulled her chair back. Again, she was escorted to her suite and again he insisted the four maids wait on her.

When the servants had helped her bathe and dress in her nightgown, one of them brushed her hair until it shone in the candlelight. After she dismissed the maids, she got into bed and lay there thinking. She had asked questions about the gold mine, but all she had learned might be useful was that a huge elevator built on the same principle as the one in the castle was used to take men up and down and the ore up. She was not sure how this information could help her, but now she knew that was the only way to reach Björn.

A door at the corner of her room that had been locked when she tried it opened and Rohla entered dressed in a bed robe.

"What are you doing?" she asked, startled.

"I have come to bid you good night and help you get to sleep."

"What do you mean, help me get to sleep?"

He didn't answer but simply slid out of his robe and

crawled into bed beside her. She was so taken aback that she was too slow to stop him from placing a hand on her breast.

"No," she shouted. Doubling up her knees and kicking out, she sent him sprawling out of bed onto the floor.

He picked himself up and said peevishly, "So, you are going to be difficult." He pulled a cord near the head of the bed and she heard a bell ring faintly in the hall. Four soldiers entered the room, and one man subdued her while the other two grabbed an ankle each and the other one her wrists. Then the one who held her released his hold and took one of her wrists. As the men held her stretched across the bed, Rohla said with a leer on his face, "You are going to wish you had been cooperative, my dear."

CHAPTER SIX
ESCAPE

Using his boot knife, Björn continued cutting on the left ankle bracelet. He knew it would be long tedious work, possibly taking weeks. He cut as quickly as he could, putting as much pressure as possible on the knife, working through the night. Occasionally he stopped to examine his work and was disappointed at the lack of progress. He had no idea of what had happened to Aleanna and, for perhaps the only time in his life, he felt a sense of panic. She was in danger and he was helpless to protect her. His only consolation was that eventually he would cut through the chains and be free to find and rescue her, and the prime minister and his cohorts would pay dearly.

He heard the elevator descending and then men talking. When the elevator stopped, he heard the sound of many men marching toward them, along with the clanking of armor. When the men arrived at the cell, an officer yelled, "Get up!"

Slipping the knife back into his boot, he pulled himself erect with the rest of the men. One soldier worked on the chain fastener, pulling the holder from the hole in the bottom of the pin holding the chain. The pin was withdrawn, and he heard the clank and rattle of the chain hitting the floor, then felt the long chain being drawn through the large links attached to their legs. When the prisoners were free, the officer gave the order to march.

Björn turned with the man in front of him and followed him down the passageway. Most of the men were evidently so used to the chains that they had adjusted their walking to accommodate them. There was still no illumination on the walls; the only light came from the torches held by the soldiers.

With the guards in front and in back, the prisoners shuffled down the corridor, then turned into another corridor when ordered and proceeded further to an area with more illumination. Finally, of their own accord, they halted, picked up shovels and picks, and began to work. Björn selected a pick at the order of one of the guards.

The prisoners with picks pounded them into the rock to chip pieces from it, and the men with shovels picked up the pieces and tossed them into a cart. When the cart was full, a team of two donkeys pulled it away. Another cart was pulled into place and the process continued.

After being chained all night, Björn actually enjoyed the labor. He held back to only minimal strength, not for concern of tiring himself but to keep his captors from learning his true strength.

The mining continued until what Björn judged to be mid-day. The guards called a halt to the work and the men slumped to the ground, exhausted. The soldiers passed among them distributing pieces of bread and tins of stew. They were fed well, Björn thought, but he was sure this was to keep up their strength rather than out of kindness. After they finished their lunch, they were allowed to rest for a bit and then were called back to work.

The air was so dirty the men could barely see, and coughing was constant. Even Björn felt the effect of the deadly toxic air. Occasionally a man fell and was pulled from his job while the work continued unabated. The longer the day went on, the more men fell until, at last, the guards halted the work.

The rest of the miners were ordered to pick up the fallen men and were herded back to their sleeping area, where the chain was refastened. The guards departed, and the men slumped, too tired to even talk. The only sign of life was the coughing.

Björn slipped the small knife from his boot and continued to work on the chain. A short time later, a half dozen guards returned with their meal, which was the same as they had been served for their noon meal. The guards left them to finish eating in the darkness and when he finished, Björn got back to work on the chain and continued to work through another night.

Each day was like the first. Their tins were filled with gruel in the morning, they went to work, they worked until mid-day when they were fed the same fare as the day before and after a brief rest were ordered back to work. Then they were led back to their sleeping area where they were chained at the end of the day, fed and left in darkness.

Björn went back to work on the chain. Again he worked through the night. When the guards returned in the morning, he slipped the knife back into his boot, checking the depth of the cut. Not much, he thought, but he had time. He only hoped that Aleanna did.

The days continued in a seemingly endless progression and, for the rest of the men, it appeared to be so, but Björn would not accept that. He kept cutting at the chain until one night he felt the knife go all the way through it. He was exhilarated, but he also had a sense of dread because it had taken so long and he still had three more cuts to make.

How was Aleanna faring? They would have to keep

her alive, as there would be no point in killing her. Her life did not trouble him, but her treatment did. From his impression of the prime minister, he would put nothing past him, but that kind of thinking would not cut the chain so he went back to work.

The next day, the cut in the chain did not hamper Björn's walk as it was still fastened and would be until he could make another cut and move the large chain through the incision he made. The next day began and ended, but now Björn felt a genuine sense of progress.

That night after they were fed, he went back to work on the chain, taking care to cut through a spot far enough apart to allow the large chain to slip through when he was ready. Time continued unchanged until Björn felt the cut over three quarters of the way through the chain link. He stopped cutting at that point. He was sure the link would hold, but he didn't want to tempt fate. Next he began cutting the link around his right ankle. The work on the chain continued, as did the work of the mine. Time seemed endless, timeless and hopeless for all but Björn. He knew that in the near future he would extricate himself from the chains and escape.

Then one night, the knife cut through the last remaining steel. Immediately Björn went to work on the parallel cut and eventually, it too was cut almost through. Slipping the knife back into his boot, he rested the remainder of the night. He had rested only a few hours since entering the mine, but felt guilty even for that, although the short rests helped him maintain his strength. Each night he rested again to ensure that he was alert and at his full strength when it was time.

Through the following several nights he worked through the chain on his left wrist, then the right, systematically repeating the process. He had to make four cuts each, but they did not have to be as far apart, as the chain connecting his wrists was smaller than the large chain snaking through the links at his feet. It seemed to take forever, even for a man as patient at Björn, but his progress continued until he fully expected to have the chains cut through during the following night.

Björn could hardly wait for the day to end. He had been imprisoned a long time, and now his hopes were achieved. The cuts were finished, each link was pulled through the chain, and he was free.

He had formulated plans through the long days and nights. The plan called for him to start releasing the rest of the men at night when he thought the castle and village were asleep.

Björn moved so silently that not one man in the chain awoke. Without a sound, he moved down the corridor until he came to the elevator shaft. Just as he thought, there were chains hanging down from above as part of the elevator mechanism. Grabbing the chains, he climbed up the shaft.

At the top, he paused, peering around to get his bearings. He needed to figure out his location from the castle and the village. He looked for the soldiers' quarters, even though they were most likely within the castle grounds. After orienting himself to his surroundings, he began to move. He watched for people or lights indicating anyone was still awake, but all was quiet. As he approached the castle gate, he saw no guards on the outside, but he suspected there were several on top of the wall.

Traveling down the wall away from the gate and away from where he suspected the guards would most likely be, at some distance from the gate he began to climb the wall.

It would have been impossible for anyone else, but Björn found hand and foot holds in the blocks of the wall. Taking his time, he ascended silently then, pulling himself to the top of the wall and with only his head projecting above the wall, he surveyed the area carefully. Nobody and nothing moved so, pulling himself onto the wall, he began to make his way back stealthily back to the gate.

He reached the gate without any sign of another human. Satisfying himself that there was no one on the other side of the gate, he walked across the top of the gate and reconnoitered the entire wall and the turrets on the walls. Then he returned to the gate. Evidently they felt so secure inside their great wall that they saw no need to post guards.

During his walk along the wall, he examined the castle and the castle grounds. There was one long building that appeared to be a barracks. Björn lowered himself into the courtyard and, after a quick search, he found the door that allowed people to exit and enter without having to open the gate. This door was locked with a heavy bolt on the inside. Sliding the bolt back, he slowly opened the door. Although it was not noiseless, Björn was convinced that when he and the men from the mine entered, there would be only minimal noise. He left the door closed but unlocked.

Next he examined the barracks. He prowled silently around the entire building, finding only two doors, one at each end. The doors were fastened from the inside. Gratified with his progress, he slipped away to the outside door and, leaving it closed behind him, made his way back to the top of the elevator shaft. The elevator was in place. Scouting farther, he found the stables holding horses but, more importantly, he discovered the mules that pulled the elevator. Harnessing a pair of them, he led them to the elevator and hitched them to it in preparation for when he was ready to bring the men to the surface.

Releasing the elevator brake, he allowed it to descend slowly into the shaft. When the elevator stopped, he climbed down the chain and, returning to the men, released the pin from the chain and woke the first man. The man couldn't believe Björn was free and thought it was some kind of trick.

While Björn was attempting to explain it, several other prisoners awoke, and they were as astonished as the first one had been. Even though the pitch blackness made it difficult to communicate, Björn was finally able to get them relatively quiet while he pulled the large chain through the links of the first several men. Somehow he was able to get them to hold still long enough for him to take the axe he had found and brought down with him to break the chain.

The pounding woke all of the men, and they began to shout. Those who had pulled the chain through their links began to stagger about the corridor, tripping over their chains and falling over each other. Björn was thankful their sounds would not carry to the surface. With a great deal of effort and more patience, he was able to break all the men free of the chains. Gradually, he was able to get the men to link hands, with the first man holding his.

He led them down the corridor to the main tunnel and then to the elevator shaft. At the shaft, he got the men's attention enough to listen to him.

"I am going to climb to the surface, and then I will send the elevator down," he whispered hoarsely. "The elevator will not hold all of you at one time." Björn explained that, if they were smart, they would wait until all the prisoners had ascended and then enter the castle grounds armed with tools they could find.

"We have to defeat the soldiers if we are to have a chance to escape," he said.

When all were ready, Björn climbed to the top of the shaft. Grasping the lines, he got the mules to pull the elevator to the surface. The men were packed inside the elevator and hanging on the top. They got off the elevator and began to run away, as Björn had expected them to. He let them go and lowered the elevator, and kept running the elevator until all the men were above ground. He was disappointed but not surprised that all of them had run away.

Making his way back to the castle gate, he entered through the door he had left open. He heard the other escapees noisily gathering tools and implements to serve as weapons, followed by their cries as they raced away. Most were on foot, but some had the foresight to get mounts from the stables and were making good time as they escaped. He had no doubt that most of them would be captured and put back into the mine.

Running toward the castle, he heard the sound of soldiers waking up. He got there as the barracks doors were flung open and the soldiers poured out. They ran to the gate, but were held up momentarily as they struggled with the bolt in the door. Björn had closed it so the soldiers would be unaware there was anyone loose on the grounds, then he bent the bolt holding the small door so the soldiers would have to take the time to open the large gates, which he hoped would give the men he had freed from the mine as much chance as possible.

The soldiers finally had to climb the stairs up the wall to open the gate. Björn watched to be sure they were fully engaged before surveying the castle. The soldiers and others in the castle had heard the commotion outside and were coming out the front door. Björn slipped to the back and began to climb.

Aleanna had also been forming a plan of escape. She was sure if she could slip through the gate she could outrun any pursuers. There were always two soldiers at the gate, but these guards did not seem very alert and she did not think it their job to guard her.

She had complete freedom of the castle yard, and she took daily strolls accompanied by one of her servants. Making sure she visited every part of the yard, she was particularly careful to walk closely inside the castle wall all the way from near the back of the castle, then back past the gate and beyond. When she first did this, the guards appeared nervous, but they seemed to become inured to her visits as they became routine.

Aleanna thought she had a good chance of breaking past them. The biggest problem was her dress; she knew that no matter how thin a dress she wore, it would still restrict her movements. She solved the problem by deciding to wearing her old trousers under the dress, wearing a dress she had expanded into an extra-large waist size. Thinking she could shed the dress once she was away from the accompanying servant, she would be able to move around unencumbered. With no hope of finding her mare, but knowing Jago had not been captured, she would find Jago and the two of them would find Björn after she escaped.

But she had to wait for the right moment; she knew she would only get one chance. If they caught her on her first attempt, it was sure to be her only one. She didn't know how they would restrain her, but she thought it would definitely be the end of her yard privileges.

She waited until one of the weekly fairs was in the courtyard. As usual, she feigned interest in most of the booths and exhibits, but this day, she took more time than usual. Waiting until late in the day when people were starting to exit the grounds, she blended in with a group, lowering her head and moving quickly away until she was sure she had evaded the servant. Then she slipped between two booths, removed the dress and donned the hat she had hidden under the dress. Pushing her hair up under the hat, she was certain she looked enough like a young man to escape all but the most discriminating examination.

The moment came. She mingled with some vendors leaving the grounds, moving past the gate and the soldiers that guarded it. Keeping her eyes on the guards, she sauntered through, hugging the side of the fence opposite the guards. With her attention distracted, however, she ran into a donkey a man was leading into the grounds. Startled, the donkey jumped, knocking Aleanna off balance. She fell to the ground, and the jar of hitting the ground knocked off her hat, causing her long hair to cascade over her face. As she got to her feet, the arms of a suddenly alert guard pinned her from behind.

The guard held her and another gave a cry of alarm as he sprinted to the aid of his partner. Between the two of them, they subdued her, then led her back to the castle, each guarding taking an arm. They were met by the chief captain, who sent for the prime minister. When the minister appeared, both soldiers tried to explain at the same time what had happened.

Rohla looked at the disheveled Aleanna. "I guess we will have to keep a closer eye on you," he said, directing the captain and his men to return her to her third floor room. Arriving at her room, the captain opened the door for her, motioned for the two soldiers to guard the door, then gave her a long look before he departed.

Aleanna threw herself onto the bed and sobbed. She rarely cried, but she felt completely hopeless. How could she rescue Björn? She didn't mind so much about herself, but she spent a good deal of time worrying about him. All she could do was assume he was in the gold mine with the slaves, and so far had not been able to extricate himself and come to her aid. Still, she had complete faith in him because she knew how difficult it was to kill him; she was also convinced that, if he were still alive, he would eventually come for her. And she knew in her heart that he was still alive.

Her only major problem now was putting up with the prime minister. Aleanna was grateful that in addition to his small stature, he was small all over. While that might ease the pain of their mating, it did nothing for the humiliation and embarrassment she suffered. His visits had dwindled to only once per week, and that was still too many, but at least it was not as frequent as it had been at first. The whole thing had now become routine; Rohla always asked if this time he could be gentle, and her reply was always the same obscenity. He pulled the cord to signal the guards, they forced her into submission, and the prime minister had his way with her.

She had decided early on that it was not sexual urge that drove the prime minister; rather it was his way of showing power and control over her. The rest of the time he ignored her, for which she was grateful.

That evening, Aleanna heard loud shouting outside on the grounds and then inside. She heard the soldiers running away from her door and waited for the sound of the elevator before carefully opening the door. The dark hallway was empty so she hurried down the hallway toward the elevator. Just before getting there, she ran into someone in the dark. She struggled, but her captor held her tightly.

"Aleanna, Aleanna." she heard in a hushed whisper.

Pulling back to look at him, she stifled a sob when she recognized him. "Björn, it is you!" She pulled him to her, hanging on for dear life. "I knew you would come for me." She leaned back to get a better look at him. "You do not look any the worse for wear. Where did they keep you?"

"I was chained in the mine, so I had to cut through the chains to free myself. I managed to accomplish that only last night."

"I heard a lot of shouting a few moments ago. What has happened?"

"There must have been at least two hundred slaves chained with me," he said. "I freed them as well, and they made a great deal of noise escaping. That drew the soldiers out against them, which gave me the opportunity to search for you."

She hugged him again as tightly as she could. "But how did you find me so easily?"

"It was simply blind luck. I picked the third floor because it seemed the darkest, entered a window and was starting to search when I literally ran into you."

"What were you going to do if we had not run into each other? Search the entire castle?"

He laughed softly. "If I had to, but I thought with all the distraction of the slaves trying to escape, I could do it fairly easily. I was going to start here on this top floor and search every room." He looked down at her seriously. "I was going to keep on searching until I found you."

"We need to get out of here," she said.

"Do you know where my weapons are?" He looked around, checking everything.

"No," she said, "I have not seen them because I am sure no one here could use them, certainly not the swords and not even the bow. But, if I had to guess, I bet they are in the armory on the first floor. That is where we should begin our search."

Instead of the noisy elevator, they took the stairs. They stealthily made their way from landing to landing. At the first floor, Björn surveyed it carefully, but saw no one.

Since the floor appeared deserted, they slipped silently along the walls and sped across several open spots, making their way to what Aleanna thought was the armory. As they slipped inside, it was obvious that she was right, for they found themselves surrounded by all manner of weapons. Armor, swords of all sizes and kinds, battle axes, maces, spears and bows with arrows were stacked and shelved all along the walls.

There was no sign of Björn's swords or bow, and they were disappointed until Aleanna noticed a door at the end of the room. Moving warily toward it, they cracked the door and found a collection of obviously valuable weapons inside, including intricately designed swords, adorned battle axes, and bows with ornate designs. The room resembled a museum rather than a weapons depository. Björn's weapons were displayed on one of the shelves, the swords in their sheaths and the arrows in their quiver beside the bow. Slipping the sword harness onto his shoulders and handing the bow and quiver to Aleanna, he asked which was the safest way out.

"A door at the back," Aleanna said quickly, "but I need a sword." She selected a fine-looking weapon, saying, "I want to be of some use if we meet anyone."

They moved out of the armory into the great room, and there was still no one in sight. "Follow me," Aleanna whispered, leading the way to a door at the rear of the room. The door was locked from the inside, but that was no problem except for the noise of the bolt opening. Opening the door, they stepped outside. There were two soldiers there but they were too far apart for Björn to attack at once. He charged one and, with a violent slash, took the man's head from his shoulders. Meanwhile, Aleanna engaged the other one. She was more than holding her own when Björn arrived and thrust a sword into the man's center.

"We are lucky they did not sound an alarm," said Aleanna. "What do we do now?"

"Find Jago."

"How will we do that? We have no idea where he is."

"We will let him find us," Björn said. "With all the noise, he will know something is amiss and start looking for us. There is too much commotion for me to sense him."

"How will we get out of the castle grounds?" she asked. "You can scale the wall but I cannot."

"There is only one way and that is through the gate," he answered. "It will be risky, but we have no other choice. Even if we move quietly, I am sure we will be detected. If and when we are, leave the fighting to me unless someone gets past me and you are in danger. I do not want to hurt you by accident. Come on."

They hugged the castle wall, moving silently to the front gate. A crowd of women were grouped inside the gate looking outward and Björn, with Aleanna close behind, walked quietly toward them. One turned and saw them, telling the other women, who turned to look at them curiously.

"I hope they keep their mouths shut," Björn grunted. "I

hate to kill women."

But the women said nothing, apparently not recognizing either of them. In the darkness, Björn was only a man, and Aleanna looked like a man with her hair up under her hat and dressed in trousers instead of a dress. When they got close, however, the women became wary and called to the soldiers on the outside.

Moving quickly, Björn and Aleanna passed through the women, who parted to let them through, probably because the pair had their swords drawn. Outside the gate, three soldiers rushed toward them, two leading. Björn skewered one through the heart, and with his other sword slashed the second man from his breastbone to his waist. Without pausing, he drove a sword through the third man. All three fell without a sound.

They moved away from the castle in the direction where it seemed most quiet. Several soldiers came around the corner of a house some distance away leading three captured slaves. The soldiers and their captives paid no attention to the pair no doubt taking them for villagers as they moved off to place the slaves in security. Herding the slaves in front of them, the soldiers marched through the castle gate. Björn and Aleanna walked on until they reached the village.

"We will try to lose ourselves among the houses," Björn whispered against her ear. "Watch out for people milling about so they do not spot us."

Moving around one of the houses, they saw a small crowd of people at the end of the short lane between the houses. The villagers were looking in the opposite direction, but before Björn and Aleanna could back into the shadows, one turned, saw them and raised an alarm. Björn began to run, Aleanna hard on his heels. The villagers ran after them, calling for soldiers.

Björn thought of going back to silence them, but decided it would cost too much time and effort. At a juncture of two lanes, a group of people appeared in front of them, approximately a dozen armed men, some with swords and lances, the rest holding farm implements such as hoes, scythes, rakes and shovels. They moved menacingly toward Björn and Aleanna.

Björn knew they were no danger, thinking they were trying to defend their womenfolk. Not wanting to kill the innocent fools, he darted between houses with Aleanna following. They heard the shouts of villagers, who were joining forces with the first group. Aleanna and Björn kept running, and were almost clear of the village when they encountered a group of eight soldiers.

Without hesitation, Björn attacked. He drove his first sword through one of them while driving his other sword through the heart of a second. Not pausing, he took the head off a third, driving his second sword through the midsection of another. He did the damage quickly, ending the stroke by slashing the midsection of the fifth soldier. As they saw the carnage created by the madman in their midst, the other three soldiers stood transfixed with fear.

With his swords raised, Björn shouted, "Run!"

Needing no further invitation, they turned and fled, and he let them go.

"I am glad you let them go alive rather than killing them," she said, "but we may live to regret it."

"We may, but I do not like to end any life needlessly, even that of an enemy. We should move on."

They had gone only a short distance outside the village, and encountered no one else on their silent trek. They came to an area of clean and open fields, with only a few trees for cover. Knowing they must keep going, they stayed as close to the stone fences as possible for what little cover they might provide.

They had traversed a short distance when they heard shouts behind them. Turning, they saw a group of almost twenty soldiers in pursuit. They broke into as fast a run as they could, not stopping at fences but simply vaulting over them. Looking back over her shoulder, Aleanna saw them dropping further behind them. She and Björn continued running until they reached the woods and disappeared into it, far away from the soldiers who were now out of sight.

They stopped, Aleanna gasping for breath. Between gasps, she asked, "What will we do now?"

"We will move slowly through these woods," he said. "Somewhere we should find Jago."

"Do you really think Jago will have waited this long for us?"

"I am certain he is still here because he would never leave me as long as he thought I was alive." He sounded completely sure of himself.

They continued walking quietly through the woods parallel to open fields.

"Do you think there is any chance of running into the slaves or soldiers?"

"Possibly soldiers who have given up the chase and others who have captured slaves and are returning with them. But there is little to fear. I will hear them before they are even aware of us." He gave her an encouraging smile. "We should keep moving, stay out of their way and keep looking for Jago."

They occasionally heard soldiers but, as Björn predicted, they had no trouble avoiding contact. They continued their trek, finally coming to a large open plain with many soldiers in the open.

"We will have to stay here until they leave or until darkness hides us," Björn said.

They settled down to wait in the cover of the trees. As the sun began to fall over the horizon and light began to fade, some of the soldiers started back toward the castle. Others stayed on the plain, and soon Aleanna and Björn saw bonfires flame up.

"Can we move now?" she asked.

"Not yet," Björn said. "We will wait until it is darker and there is no danger of being seen."

"Remember, Björn," she said quietly, "that I cannot see as well as you in the dark."

"That will not be a problem," he told her. "I will take your hand and lead you, warning you when we come to something you might trip over."

When it was completely dark, they moved out. Keeping well away from the bonfires, they traveled across the plain, eventually arriving at the other side where they encountered more woods. Björn continued to hold Aleanna's hand and lead her carefully, and they had gone only a short distance when they heard noise ahead of them, including the whinny of a horse.

"Is that Jago?" gasped Aleanna.

A few moments later, Björn was talking softly to Jago. Although she could not see them in the darkness, she doubted that Björn was stroking Jago and the horse was nuzzling him like she and her mare would have in the same circumstance. Rather she thought they would be standing close enough to each other, just happy to be together.

Björn came back to her, followed by Jago. Instinctively, Aleanna reached up to stroke Jago's neck and, to her surprise, he let her for a few seconds before backing away.

"Amazing," Björn said, evidently pleased that Jago and Aleanna could communicate. "We should go. We have passed the bonfires so we can return to the plain and move more quickly. We have nothing to fear until daylight."

They moved back to the open plain, but Björn continued to hold her hand. The sun was beginning to peek over the horizon when he called a halt. "We should step back into the woods and find a secure campsite," he announced.

When they found a spot that he found satisfactory, he said, "We will stop here and rest. I will hunt down some food while you nap. When you wake up, we will move out again."

Aleanna made herself as comfortable as she could on the ground and, tired as she was, she fell asleep almost immediately. Björn left Jago to guard her and went to hunt.

Aleanna awoke to Björn squatting next to her, gazing at her. "What is it?" she asked.

"Nothing. I was watching you while you slept. You looked so peaceful, and I doubt that you have slept well since we were captured, even though you had a soft bed to sleep in."

"I have not." A beautiful smile crossed her face. "I also think this is the first time I have smiled. What have you found us to eat?"

He held out his hands to her, and she saw he had quite a harvest. They ate the bulbs he had gathered along with some apples and pears.

Then Björn said he had to leave, which startled Aleanna. "I have a job to do," he told her.

"What is it?" she asked.

"I will tell you when I get back."

"Do you really have to go?"

"Yes, it is something I must do, and I cannot leave here without doing it. Please wait for me. I should be back in no more than three days, though I expect to be back much sooner." He indicated a large bag lying close by. "I have gathered enough food to last you, and you know how to gather more and even trap a small animal for meat if you wish." Seeing her crestfallen face, he said gently, "Do not worry; I will be back."

"I still do not know why you have to go when we are free."

"You will have to trust me," He picked up his swords, leaving the bow and arrows. Without a word, he disappeared into the woods.

Björn moved out of the woods, trotting at a fast pace, the same pace that he used to run for days without stopping. He didn't stop until he got back to the village. When he encountered workers in their fields and others with their livestock, he faded into the woods, and no one saw him. He reached the village when the sun was starting to set, and he settled down to wait until dark.

When darkness came, he arose and began to steal silently through the village, avoiding homes with lights still on. Coming to the palace wall, he scaled it at a point far away from the guards. He surveyed the grounds; there was no movement, and he waited patiently, knowing he had most of the night if need be. Long before then, however, he rose and descended the wall. Moving to the front of the gate, he climbed the stairs. Moving like a shadow, he approached the guard. There was a snap as he broke the guard's neck, then he lowered the body to the ground. Descending to the ground, he repeated the action on the other side of the wall.

Moving across the vacant grounds to the front of the castle, he came to a door on the side. It was unguarded but locked. Björn pushed on the door at the lock, gradually increasing his exertion. Eventually the door splintered and swung open, and Björn darted inside and sped up the stairwell. The breaking of the door had made considerable noise, and he was sure guards were on their way. Sure enough, they came pouring out of two rooms on either side of the great room like hornets responding to a threat to their nest.

By then, Björn was gone. He raced to the top floor and found the trap door to the attic that he had noticed earlier. Moving a chair under the door so he could reach and open the door, he hung onto the ledge and kicked the chair away. Pulling himself into the attic, he closed the trap door and went to the far end of the single long room to hide in the event they thought to look in the attic.

The soldiers sounded like they were milling about without purpose. Then someone, probably an officer, arrived and took charge. Björn heard him order some of the men to search the main floor, others to search the second and still others the third. He ordered a squad of men outside to check the grounds in case the break-in of the door had only been a feint, leaving one man to guard the door.

Björn settled down to wait. He could hear what sounded like a thorough search of the castle. After a while, someone opened the trap door, and a soldier stuck his head in as he held a torch aloft. He gave the room a cursory look and disappeared.

Björn continued to wait. Eventually silence returned, and Björn left his hiding place, opened the trap door and poked his head down for a look. It was empty except for two soldiers guarding a door at the end of the long hall.

Björn knew he had no choice; he couldn't stay there forever. When he thought they weren't looking, he dropped to the floor. His landing was noiseless, but one of the soldiers saw him. Björn sprinted the length of the floor and pressed one sword completely through one man and placed the point of the other sword against the throat of the second. Björn said, "Stand still if you wish to live." The man got very still.

"Where is the prime minister?" Björn asked. When the soldier responded that he didn't know, Björn thrust the sword through his neck, killing him instantly.

Assuming this was the minister's room being guarded, he knocked on the door and said loudly, "We have caught one of them."

"Where did you catch him? How many more are there, and what were they doing?"

Björn said nothing. He heard Rohla come to the door and unlatch it. Björn immediately slammed his body against the door as hard as he could. The door struck Rohla so hard that it propelled him across the room to land against a large chest, unconscious.

Taking a sheet from the bed, Björn cut strips and bound and gagged Rohla securely. Picking the official up, he threw him over his shoulder and fled from the room down the hallway to the stairwell. He made his way softly to the first floor with his burden.

Carefully checking the great room, he saw a group of soldiers gathered round the broken door. They had called a carpenter from the village to come repair the door, and he was working on it diligently under the watchful eyes of the soldiers.

Björn waited patiently for them to leave. He felt Rohla start to stir and, without guilt, he laid the man on the step and struck him on the skull with the hilt of his sword. Rohla lapsed back into unconsciousness, and Björn continued to wait. Before the soldiers left, the prime minister began to stir again, and Björn again rapped him on the head.

Finally, the door was repaired to the satisfaction of the soldiers, so the carpenter left and the soldiers retired. Björn picked up the still unconscious Rohla and placed him over his solder. Warily, he took a good look around the room and saw that it was empty.

Cautiously, he made his way to the mended door. He saw that the carpenter had done an excellent job and the door was probably stronger than before. Silently sliding the bolt, he pulled the door open and slipped through it. Laying Rohla on the ground near the gate, Björn went some distance away and climbed the wall. He moved silently down the wall to the turret on the right side of the gate. The soldier inside appeared fairly alert as he kept watch on the ground beyond the castle. Suddenly, a shadowy figure rose from the floor, there was a snap, and the man slipped lifeless to the floor.

On his stomach, Björn slid his body across the top of the gate, knowing that in the darkness, he would be unseen. At the turret on the left side of the gate, the guard was sitting on a bench sound asleep with his body propped against the wall of the turret. Another snap, and the gate was unguarded.

Descending, Björn found the prime minister awake and trying to work the gag out of his mouth. He forced it back into Rohla's mouth and made sure the binding was still tight. Opening the door in the gate, he yanked Rohla up and tossed him across his back, then moved through the gate and into the village. He broke into a run when he heard dogs beginning to bark, pulling one sword out and holding it ready in case he ran into any villagers. He really did not wish to kill one, but he did not want to be slowed down either.

He heard the villagers getting up, but he was through the village and onto the plain before any could find out what was wrong. The dogs were still barking and some ran a short distance onto the plain before they stopped and returned to the town. The villagers gave up quickly and returned to their homes.

Björn continued to run, Rohla bouncing against his shoulder. A good distance from the castle, Björn turned and headed deep into the woods. Putting the prime minister on the ground, he went to look for the right tree. When his search was successful, he returned, picking Rohla up and throwing him over his shoulder again.

When he got to the tree he had selected, Björn threw Rohla to the ground and used his knife to cut the ropes binding the man's ankles, taking a great deal of skin and flesh. Rohla's eyes went wide with pain and he tried to scream through the gag.

Björn had thrown a rope over a high limb and tied it off on another limb. A noose dangled a short man's height above a small limb directly below the high one. Björn carried the prime minister up the tree and out onto the small limb. Standing him on the limb and holding onto him, he slipped the noose over Rohla's head and tightened it around his neck. He then pulled the gag from Rohla's mouth, and the man immediately began to scream. Björn let him scream until he was hoarse and breathless.

When he finally stopped screaming, Björn told him he was being merciful. Instead of killing him outright, he was

The Northlander

giving him a chance. It was possible he could escape from his bonds or, if he continued to scream, some woodsman might hear him and rescue him.

"Why are you doing this to me?" Rohla asked. "Is it because I had you imprisoned?"

"No, that was nothing. It is because of what you did to Aleanna."

"But why does that concern you?" Rohla whined. "Any prominent man has the right to take any woman he wants, be she married or single."

Björn shook his head in disgust. "That may be true here in Carigo for any other woman, but not for Aleanna. All the time you had her, she was under my guardianship. Whether I was free or not, she was my responsibility. If you knew anything about Northlanders, you should have known I would escape and come for her, and then come for you." He grinned at the frightened Rohla, an evil grin designed to scare the wits out of him. "But I will not kill you, no matter how much you deserve it. As long as you balance yourself, or if someone hears your screams and comes to help, you will live. The choice is yours."

Björn stepped off the limb and dropped lightly to the ground. At first, the screams were for him to come back but, when he was out of sight, they changed to cries of help.

Starting into his usual fast trot, Björn sped away, the screams following. Before the cries were out of his earshot, they changed to choking and gasping.

"He had better balance than I expected," muttered Björn with sarcasm.

Trotting toward the camp where he had left Aleanna, he moved at the same pace that enabled him to travel for days without stopping and without water. When he got to the camp, morning had broken and light had brightened the landscape.

Aleanna was tidying up the camp when he arrived. As soon as she saw him, she beamed with a beautiful smile, then ran to him and hugged him with relief.

"You had me so worried," she said. "After getting you back, I would have been heartbroken to lose you again. Why did you do that to me?" She held him away and looked him in the eye.

"I told you it was something I had to do."

"What was it?" she demanded.

Björn was silent for several seconds. "I suppose you should know," he said. "I went to take care of the prime minister. I could not leave his actions toward you unpunished."

"Why did you do that? Was it for me or for you or both of us?" She searched his face, then said, "It was for you. But why? I was safe and secure and I knew you would eventually come to get me."

"If he had only kidnapped you and enslaved me, I would simply have killed him. But for what he did to you, killing was too easy. I know you are going to ask what I did and that you are not going to give me any peace until I give you details." He took a deep breath. "I took him deep into the woods, put him on a small limb with his hands tied behind him and his neck in a noose tied to an upper limb. And yes, I heard him gurgling before I was out of hearing." He watched emotions flood across her face.

Then she smiled at him. "I guess I am more of a barbarian than you thought. My only regret is that I was not there to push him off the limb. You are sure he died?" she asked.

"I did not go back to check, but I am sure he did. The sounds were unmistakable."

She buried her face against his shoulder. "How did you know what he did to me?"

He held her tenderly. "From knowing men like that. Small men like that are often driven to control when they achieve power," he told her. "I knew you would not be safe from him, but there was nothing I could do. I thought of fighting them when they first trapped us but, while I might have gotten out, I did not think I could get you out safely. I was afraid that if I tried you might be hurt or killed."

He disengaged himself. "Now we need to break camp and move out. We have to go quickly in case Rohla's men mount a pursuit."

They moved quickly for the next three days, stopping only to allow Aleanna to rest. Finally, Björn decided they were out of danger and could rest and take their time.

CHAPTER SEVEN
RETURNING HOME

They rested that night, and even though Björn said they could rest the next day as well, Aleanna insisted she was ready to travel. So they were back on the road again, but with a difference now Björn walked instead of running, and Aleanna walked beside him.

She knew Björn was taciturn by nature, but she asked him to share details of his escape. To give him a break from talking, she told him of almost all her adventures, assuming correctly that he did not want her to tell him everything.

"I spent most of my days roaming the castle grounds, trying to think of a way to escape," she said. "I examined the walls and the castle to see if I thought your plan of attacking the castle would work."

"And what conclusion did you come to?" he asked.

"I thought it could be done but, like you said, it would require many men."

"Well," he said, "I am glad we agree." He grinned down at her. "What else did you think about?"

"Escape," she answered. "All the time, I was determined to escape. During market day each week, I made sure to spend all day at the booths and displays. It was like a fair, with shows of all kinds—flamethrowers, singers, a strong man, and pet animals, including a monkey on a chain in a small man's jacket. Strange animals from afar are especially fascinating," she said. "but I made sure I visited every booth, exhibit and act, and spent the entire day lunching on snacks from the various booths when I was hungry. I always stayed until most of the merchants and players had gone."

She paused, thinking about her failed escape attempt. "Finally I was ready. I put on my old slacks and fastened my hat under my dress. Two booths near the gate were handy, so I slipped between them and changed. I tried to slip out with a crowd, but I did not watch where I was going and I bumped into a damned donkey. The encounter startled him and he knocked me down."

Björn started to laugh, but a look at her face told him that would be an inappropriate response. "So what happened next?" he asked.

"They had me before I could get back on my feet and run. I was so disappointed I threw myself on the bed and cried when they put me back in my room."

"What were you going to do if you had escaped?"

"I did have a plan," she said a bit defensively, "or at least part of one. I was going to find Jago and have him help me find you. I suspected you were in the mine because Rohla said that was where they kept prisoners, but I had no idea how we were going to rescue you, or even get down into the mine. I thought that between the two of us, we would have a chance. It was better than doing nothing."

"You were certainly very brave," he told her.

"Not really. What could they do to me but take away my yard privileges and lock me in my room? Even when they did that, I was sure I could talk them into releasing me in the company of a soldier." She smiled up at him, rather pleased with herself.

She stopped and, leaning against him, took off one of her shoes and shook out some dirt. Then she put it back on and started walking again. "I was a fool to have had this crazy girlish idea of saving my kingdom. I wasted all of your time and got Rathe killed, and now I realize how unrealistic it was."

"You cannot blame Rathe's death on yourself," Björn said. "He insisted on coming, and it was his bravery that got him killed. I do not consider my time wasted because otherwise I would never have met you."

"Am I really worth that much to you?"

"Of course you are."

They traveled in silence for a long time. Then Aleanna asked, "What will you do after you deliver me to my home?"

"I had not given it any thought," he said. "I rarely plan very far ahead unless I am planning one of my contracts. Then I make sure I have planned carefully, but I mostly let things happen."

"Surely you had a definite plan of what you were going to do after you escaped from the mine."

"Actually, I had a plan even before I left the mine. I told the other prisoners that, to have the best chance of escaping, they should arm themselves and attack the soldiers in their barracks. I knew they would not listen, but at least I told them." He shook his head as he remembered the escape. "They were afraid of the soldiers and so anxious to get away that they could not wait. I am afraid most of them went back to their homes and were easy to recapture. No matter what they did, it would give us cover for our escape."

"Did you also plan what you were going to do with the prime minister?" she asked.

"Yes, I did. I knew the plan would only work if I could get him out of the castle and grounds alive. If I ran into serious trouble, I was ready to kill him and escape. But I managed to make it happen exactly the way I planned," he said, sounding a bit proud of himself. "And, before you ask, because I know you will, I thought about you a great deal of the time. I wondered how you were coping with your captivity and how they were treating you. I wasted some time being frustrated that I had to wait so long before I could escape to rescue you. But I knew it was inevitable that I would rescue you."

They made camp at nightfall. As Aleanna lay in her bedroll, she looked at the heavens, which were covered with stars from horizon to horizon, and she took that as a good omen. She thought that now, for the first time in their journey, they were not committed on their destination. They had to return to Kallthom to see her father but, beyond that, she wasn't sure what would happen. She knew that with Rathe gone, she should stay and take care of her father, and she should also marry and have children so there would be an heir to the throne. She wondered briefly if Björn would marry her and settle down and raise a family, but she knew she had to get that idea out of her head. There would be no tying Björn down and, even if she could, she was positive he would eventually be unhappy.

A shooting star streaked through the sky and she thought it might be a good luck sign that her dream with Björn could somehow be possible. It would take several months of steady travel to make it back to Kallthom, and she was sure she could get Björn to slow down. She doubted that the remainder of his fee was important to him and that he could be easily persuaded not to race back. This could be another part of her life she had not planned for, and it would perhaps be the happiest time of her life.

She rolled over in her bedroll, relieved that she did not have to sacrifice herself for her kingdom and live among strangers for the rest of her life. Since Björn freed her, she no longer had to worry about being a captive. And she was spending time with Björn, the man she loved. That thought startled her, and then she realized she had been thinking of it for some time. Only the thought that their love was impossible kept her from thinking of it consciously that and the fact that she doubted if he returned her feelings.

She wondered what he was thinking. Would he be pleased when she told him that she did not wish to hurry back? She knew he liked her and enjoyed her company, but he might be in a hurry to take off on another adventure. As she was falling asleep, she decided she would discuss it with him in the morning.

In the morning, after eating, she did just that. "Are you in a hurry to return to Kallthom?" she asked.

"Not necessarily," he said, "but I was certain you wished to return quickly to see your father."

"We had to race so hard to get to Carigo that I would like to take our time on the way back," she responded with a bright smile. "I would like see the country and enjoy myself, sort of like a holiday. Do you have anything pressing to get back to? I mean, are there any important jobs you have to do right away?"

Björn gave her a small crooked grin. "No, there is nothing I need to race back for, and as I have never had a holiday before, it might be fun." He paused as if thinking it over. "That is a strange word for me to use—fun. I do not think I have ever had fun in my life, so it should be interesting to try."

"Then it is settled," Aleanna said with a smile and a toss

of her hair. "Be sure to pick the most scenic route for us so we can enjoy it all."

Björn took off, leaving Aleanna and Jago to follow. She caught up by running, but he moved ahead with a long, fast stride she had trouble adjusting to, as if unaware of her.

"Slow down," she protested. "I thought we were not going to be in a hurry."

He slowed his pace. "Sorry, I will have to learn to take it easy," he said with his patented grin.

They moved on at the pace Björn set for them. It was a beautiful day, and many flowers were in bloom. Aleanna exclaimed over first one and then another patch of them. "I do not think I have ever seen so much beauty," she exclaimed. "Or perhaps everything is now more beautiful since we have escaped."

At mid-day they stopped for a lunch of bulbs, tubers and fruit. Afterward, Aleanna lay back on a blanket and enjoyed the moment as birds sang, butterflies fluttered about, and the sun was warm on her skin.

"Can we stay here and relax for a while?" she asked.

"You are in charge, so we will do whatever you want," replied Björn softly.

They stayed for two days, and Aleanna remarked that it was perhaps the most peaceful place she had ever seen. Low mountains rose ahead of them and to the south, and far to the north the Ice Mountains loomed. Their spot was a rolling prairie with meadows, woods and many different colors of flowers. Aleanna was thrilled to be in the midst of all the flowers, and Björn pointed out those that had edible bulbs.

"Surely you see the beauty of the land!" she exclaimed, throwing her arms wide to encompass the landscape.

"While I was growing up, all I was concerned with was survival," he said, and she thought she detected a note of sadness in his voice. "That left no time for appreciation of something so unneeded as beauty and appearances.

"That is horrible," she said incredulously. "You are missing the most important things in life. What is life worth if you cannot take time to enjoy things?"

"I never learned to enjoy things, I suppose," he commented. "I was trained to defend myself, to live off the land, and to be honest and true to myself. Flowers were only a possible source of food, and hills and mountains were merely something to climb. I am sorry but I simply do not understand what you call beauty. Perhaps you could teach me."

"Do you think I am attractive?"

"Of course, I do."

"Attractive in what way?"

Björn paused, then said, "I think you are attractive, even beautiful, compared to other women I have seen. I never thought about it because I was never attracted to a woman, although I have observed numerous slave auctions where attractive women were sold. I guess I appreciated their beauty, but never thought to purchase one, and what would I have done with one anyway?"

"Have you never found anything attractive other than women? That is a very narrow view."

This time, his pause lasted for quite some time. "I find beauty in living things," he said finally, "like that giant tiger Jago and I killed. I found the giant white snow beast especially beautiful, and I regretted having to kill both of them." Giving her a quick glance, he went on. "Those killings were necessary for us to survive. I never kill anything needlessly, not even an insect; there is simply too much needless killing in this world. Many would call me a killer, but I do not consider myself one."

"But do you find beauty in inanimate things? Do you remember when you found me in the snow? I thought it was a winter paradise, so beautiful that I did not want to come back to camp." Then she gave him an impish look. "But I guess I have to be grateful that you find me beautiful."

"I do, but perhaps you can teach me to appreciate non-living things as well, but I have controlled my feelings for so long that I am sure that might be a tall task."

"I accept the challenge," she said, clapping her hands with happiness. "Since we are resting here, it might be a good time to start." She cupped his chin and pulled his face toward the north. "Look at the Ice Mountains. Notice how they are jagged with sharp points that reach into the clouds as though they were punching a hole through the sky, then look at the low mountains in the distance. They look gentle and inviting—do you see that?" He nodded, and she swung her arm out, as if to gather their surroundings close to them. "Here it is so peaceful and graceful, all is beautiful, and as there is nothing here to threaten us, we can relax and enjoy ourselves."

"I could never do that. Remember I was trained for years to always be on guard, no matter where I was, so I cannot relax here even though it may seem peaceful. One never knows when some danger may present itself. I am afraid that if I relax my guard, we may find ourselves in danger."

"But we have Jago to protect us," she countered. "Surely he will warn us if we are in danger."

"Yes, he will, but two guards are better than one."

With a mischievous grin, she said, "I guess I will have to work with you on relaxation."

After their break, they moved on. Björn set the pace comfortably for Aleanna and though they moved steadily, they took so many detours to examine things she found interesting that they progressed slowly.

Suddenly, they came upon a small lake that Aleanna thought was beautiful. "Number one," she said, "in our lesson on beauty. Open your eyes wide and see how the water moves with the breeze, along with the willows swaying along the bank. Do you see what I mean?"

He did as she told him, taking everything in with his hunter's eyes. He saw other things, like the reflection of wispy clouds in the lake, and ripples that went through the water with living things beneath the surface.

Even though it was still only mid-day, she insisted they stop and take another break.

"I have not had a complete bath since we left Carigo," she declared, "and I want one now. This lake looks clear and inviting, so it will serve my purpose well."

"Well, then," Björn said, collecting his sword and bow and tossing the quiver of arrows across his shoulder, "I will be off to hunt. I will leave Jago close by to guard you."

He turned, disappearing from sight into a nearby stand of trees. Aleanna took off her clothes, folded them, and laid them neatly on the bank. Testing the water with one foot, she found it to be the perfect temperature, and she slid into the water, letting it soak into her. An excellent swimmer, she spent the next several hours swimming, then she sat on a large rock near the other shore and soaked up the sun. She couldn't remember when she had last rested in the sun.

She became drowsy and dozed off for a time. When she awoke, she looked toward where they had stopped, expecting to see Björn. He was nowhere to be seen, but she could see that he had made camp across the lake, so she dove off the rock and swam to their camp.

When she reached the shore, she stood up to her ankles in the water and called for Björn. She had to call several times before he answered.

"Come here," she called, not knowing if he would or not.

When he appeared, he averted his eyes from her.

"Are you bashful?" she asked. "Are you afraid to look at me?"

He still wouldn't look at her. In fact, he turned as if he was going to leave.

"Stay here," commanded Aleanna in a strong voice.

Björn halted, his back to her. She stepped out of the water naked and walked up to him. Taking him by the front of his shirt, she demanded, "Do you ever bathe?"

"Of course I do," he said. "I was waiting for you to come out and then I would go to the far side and bathe."

"What is wrong with this side?" she asked softly.

Reaching down, she tried to pull his shirt over his head. He resisted by keeping his arms at his sides, and she noticed he still would not look at her. She almost stopped, realizing how desperate she would be if he rejected her, then she continued to tug at his shirt. Finally, she took one of his hands and raised his arm so she could get his top over it, and did the same to the other arm so she could pull it over his head.

His beauty stunned her; even with his scars, his body was ruggedly attractive. Instead of large muscles like Rathe's, his muscles were sloping rather than large and bunched. She much preferred his.

Finally he looked at her, but quickly looked away.

"What are you trying to do?" he asked in a quiet voice.

"You have said before that you thought I was beautiful and that you liked to look at me. Why are you afraid to look at me now?"

He was silent, looking further away from her. "That was when you had clothes on," he said. "I am sorry, but seeing you unclothed embarrasses me."

"Surely you have seen naked women before."

"Yes, but those were slave girls."

"Surely you looked at them."

Again silence, then he replied, "Yes, I did, but that was different."

"And how was it so different looking at them and looking at me?"

"I did not care about them," he told her, "and I feel close to you. It is a feeling I have never had before. It frightens me, and I have never been frightened of anything."

"You mean you have finally met something you are afraid of, not a gigantic snow beast but a mere girl." She smiled a bit. "That is all the more reason for you to look at me. Come, let us go for that swim."

She tugged at his pants and, getting them loose, lowered them to his ankles. She slipped off his moccasins and then his pants.

She stepped back to admire his body, amazed to see only a few scars.

"Magnificent," she murmured. Taking his hand, she led him into the water and waded out to where it was chest deep.

Still worried he would reject her, she worked up her nerve to give him a complete bath. When she was finished, her fears increased because he stood without moving and still refused to look at her. Taking his hand again, she led him back up to the beach and somehow got him to lie on his back.

Moving slowly so as not to startle him, she slid on top of him, pleased to notice his organ was extended and certainly far larger than the prime minister's. Working up all of her courage, she raised herself on her knees and inserted him into her. She rocked up and down gently, building up to orgasm for both of them. As she climaxed, she felt him explode inside of her.

She let out a loud cry of joy, and Björn immediately opened his closed eyes. Grasping her arms and moving out of her, he blurted, "Did I hurt you? If I did…"

"No!" she cried. "That was the sound of happiness, not pain. It was wonderful!" Encircling his body with her arms and legs, she held him close. "Why were you so afraid to look at me and to do this?"

"I have never done 'this' before and, as I told you, I care so much about you." He glanced away. "I know I can never give you what you need, a reliable husband and children."

"Forget about that," she whispered. "How did that make you feel?"

"That was the most wonderful feeling I have ever had in my life. I do not know how to explain it. It is something I have never experienced and know nothing about." He stared into her eyes. "It frightens me a little; it is the only time in my life that I felt totally out of control."

"Well, now that you know how wonderful it is, perhaps you will not be so shy and reluctant the next time."

"I do not know if I dare another time," he laughed. "If there is to be one, you will have to help me like you did this time."

"Do not worry," she said, "you can count on that."

She curled up against him and drifted off to sleep.

Björn lay awake thinking. What was that experience?

Would he want to do it again? He was wondering if the pleasure warranted the loss of control, because losing control was the most frightening thing Björn could imagine. Then his thoughts turned back to the wonderful experience, and he too went to sleep.

They stayed at the lake for six days. At first, Aleanna had to coach and lead, but then they made love repeatedly. One day after making love Aleanna slid next to him and said hesitantly, "I am in love with you, Björn. Is there a chance that you love me?"

There was such a long silence that Aleanna was sorry she had asked the question.

Finally, he spoke. "I do not know. I have heard other people speak of love, but I have never experienced it, so I do not know what it is. I suppose I loved my mother, but I was young and that was so long ago."

There was another long silence while Aleanna's tension grew even greater.

"Let me try to explain," he said. "For the first time in my life I am aware that I have feelings. In the past, I felt outrage at injustice, which was why I set out to change what I could, but this is the first time in my life that I have had feelings for another person. I know that I care about you a great deal, and after I got to know you on the trip, I enjoyed your company. When we were captured and I was taken away, I worried about you constantly. When we got away, I had no choice but to go back and avenge you for what the prime minister did to you. Now I cannot even think of being without you."

Aleanna smiled a gorgeous smile and embraced him. "I think you are innocent and wonderful at the same time. These things you describe tell me that you are in love with me and do not even know it. Now that you know it, we should start discussing what to do when we return to Kallthom."

Raising himself on an elbow, he asked, "What do you mean?"

"I must tell you that I intend to stay with you. Now that I have found the man I love I am not going to lose you, so we can either stay together at the castle, or I can leave and travel with you."

Björn was quiet for a long time as he digested her statement. Finally, he said, "Even though I like your kingdom, I am not sure how long I would be happy there because I have never stayed in one place for any length of time. And I would be apprehensive about you traveling with me. Do you remember all the problems we encountered on our trip? You could have been injured or killed numerous times. I would not dare risk your life."

"Would you have to continue to be a mercenary? We could travel and see the world. Surely between the two of us, we have sufficient wealth to last us. Would it be worth it for us to be together?"

"I am afraid I would always be worried about you."

"Now you are being silly," she laughed. "You know I can take care of myself, and we can defeat any dangers together. Let us consider it settled." She ran her fingertips across his chest, feeling little goose bumps on his skin. "We will spend some time at the castle visiting with my father and then we will start our journey. If it is agreeable to you, we can return from time to time to visit and then be on our way again."

"I do not know..." Björn began.

But Aleanna interrupted, "I told you it is settled so we do not need to discuss it further." She held him close, laying her head on his chest and soon, listening to the regular beating of his heart, she fell sleep.

They spent their remaining three days at the lake, enjoying their surroundings and making love almost constantly. On the third day, Björn announced that they should be moving on because they were becoming far too comfortable.

They set out with Björn still setting the pace.

"Have you had time to think about me and how you feel about me by now, Sir Björn?" she asked.

Again, there was one of the long periods of silence that left her breathless with apprehension.

"I have thought a great deal about what you said about us staying together. I do not think I will fit in at the castle; I am too different from the people there. As far as traveling together, I do not know." Again, he paused, as if thinking what to say next. "I could stop being a mercenary and thus not expose you to unnecessary danger; I am not opposed to that. We could travel and see the world, and although I do not think that would be overly dangerous, I am sure we will encounter challenges. That is the way the world is. You got a taste of it on our journey."

"So it is settled," she said. "We will travel together and experience the world. But how do you feel about me now? Have you had the opportunity to sort out your feelings?"

He was quiet again, then he said, "I must be in love with you because I want to stay with you always, no matter where you go. I would even like to raise a family with you, but that would be difficult while traveling."

"Nonsense," she laughed. "Gypsies have families, and surely we are as competent as they. We will get a wagon and even hire a driver if we wish. We can take care of the babies and travel as a family."

"You think of everything, do you not?"

"I feel I must try to think how we can build our future together and stay happy. I have never been so happy in my life and I do not want to lose the way I feel right now. Does that make sense to you?"

"Yes," he said simply.

They traveled on in silence and finally stopped at midday for lunch.

"Tell me more about this world we are going to see," Aleanna said.

"As I said, it can be a dangerous place. There are large cities with many, many people. In most of these cities, there is crime such as murder, thievery, and corruption and, in many places, there is limited freedom for the people because a dictator rules it, as was the case in Carigo." He paused to take a bite of fruit, then continued, "We have to avoid such cities because slavery is a way of life, and men would try to capture you and sell you as a slave. Because of your beauty, you would bring a high price. Even outside the big cities, there are bands of brigands who would want to kidnap you, so I am afraid there is constant danger."

"I will disguise myself like I did when I tried to escape from Carigo. It will not take much because I prefer trousers when I am riding, and I could wear a man's shirt, tie up my hair and wear a floppy hat. I think I could fool most people except under close scrutiny. Anyway, that is what I will do. It is the way I would want to travel even if we were not trying to disguise me. Tell me more about the world."

"You are full of questions," he said, but he went on. "There are vast areas where there are few people, maybe only hunters and trappers and families trying to survive on their own in the wilderness. These people prefer solitude to living among others, and I have almost always found them friendly when I visit them. Of course, I rarely visit because you know how being alone is so important to me." He pulled her close to him, planting a quick kiss on the tip of her nose. "Up until now, that is, but even now I would like it to be only you and me. Then there are villages and hamlets of many different sizes and types, some self-sufficient and filled with people who do not like big cities, but do not wish to live alone. Other villages are on major roadways or crossroads, and they serve the needs of travelers. In some areas, there is much trade; I have seen caravans as long as several miles loaded with all kinds of merchandise.

"Then there are small kingdoms like Kallthom and Carigo surrounded by small villages. Some of the people in these kingdoms are free, such as your father's; others are more like Carigo. All in all, you will find much diversity and discover that the world is a most interesting place."

That evening when they stopped, Björn went hunting while Aleanna made their camp. Björn returned with two partridges and a variety of bulbs and fruit, and they enjoyed a fine dinner. Afterward, Aleanna laid both bedrolls side by side.

"From now on, it will be up to Jago to do most of the guarding," she announced. "You will have to guard from beside me."

Björn's response was his signature grin as he lay down next to her. Aleanna did not really expect him to stay there all through the night but, when she awoke several times before daylight, and although he was always awake, he stayed next to her.

"Do you ever sleep? Are you still keeping guard while lying here instead of standing watch?"

He smiled. "You know I rarely sleep; it is another trait of my ancestors. I must admit that I enjoy lying here next to you more than I like standing watch, but I must also admit that most of the time I am still alert and able to detect danger."

"What do you mean by most of the time?" she asked.

"When I am absorbed in thought our future together, I leave guarding to Jago. During these times, I have thought of many questions to ask you."

"And what are those questions?"

"How long you wish to stay at Kallthom this time and what you will say to your father? I cannot imagine he will be thrilled with the news, either about your relationship with me or leaving with me. How often you will you wish to visit your father, because that will influence how far from Kallthom we can go and how long we can stay."

She pondered these questions, then wrinkling her brow, she answered, "I would like to see my father for at least several weeks if you could bear an extended visit. I would like to return to Kallthom once or twice a year and stay a week or two," she said thoughtfully. "The primary things for us to consider are to be happy and content. I trust you to show me wonderful places, so I will leave our travels and pace up to you."

They had breakfast and moved on, and Aleanna said, "Now that this is decided, there is no reason for us to dawdle on the trail. We will make straight for Kallthom."

One morning, Björn was concerned when Aleanna awoke in the morning throwing up. It was unpleasant, but washing up afterward, she found could eat and then travel. Björn wanted to know what the problem was. He thought it must have been caused by something they ate, but she replied that it was most likely stress from the thought of returning to see her father and Kallthom.

When it happened again the following morning and

most mornings thereafter, Björn was beside himself. She always appeared to be fine a bit later in the day and showed no additional signs of being ill. Aleanna tried to reassure him that it was merely a woman thing. Though somewhat mollified, he was still very concerned. Finally the sickness ended, and Björn was much relieved.

Björn selected the easiest route in their travel, but it still took another month to reach Kallthom. They made their final stop at a tavern in a small village at the outskirts of the kingdom. Taking a seat at one of the tables Aleanna ordered ale while Björn was satisfied with water.

"You drink an incredible amount of water," Aleanna commented after Björn requested a pitcher of water be brought to their table.

"I am much like a camel," he responded. "I can go long periods without water, so when I have the opportunity to drink, I fill myself."

When the barmaid returned with another ale, Aleanna asked her to stay for a moment and provide them with news of the kingdom. "How is the king?" she asked.

"We do not have a king," the woman said. "The old king died about six months ago. He seemed to have a heart attack and keeled over, and the doctors said he died immediately. The king's five advisors are running the kingdom, waiting for the return of Rathe, his son, who will then become king." Dumbfounded, she helped herself to some water from the pitcher on their table, pouring it into a her cup.

"Prince Rathe and Princess Aleanna have been gone for almost a year, and people are wondering if Rathe will ever return. If he does not, they will have to figure out some way to select a king or find some other way to rule in the absence of a king." The woman moved on to serve other customers.

Aleanna had a stricken look on her face. She asked no further questions and neglected her ale. Putting her head in her hands, she was silent for a long time. Finally, looking up, she said solemnly, "You will have to leave me."

Björn was bewildered. "Why am I to leave?"

"I cannot explain. you must leave now," she responded sadly. As she turned to leave she said, "Please do not follow me, you must leave the kingdom immediately."

She rose and walked out of the tavern with her head held high. Björn followed her outside the tavern, watching as she walked away toward the castle. She did not look back. He stared after her long after she had disappeared.

He knew the news of the king's death had been the reason she made the decision to leave him. She had frozen up at the news of the death of her father. The only possible reason he could think she would betray her feelings for him was so that she could marry someone of royal blood, and raise a son to be king. She was devoted to her kingdom and her people, but he couldn't imagine them allowing her to act as king based upon her explanation of royal succession.

Then he thought about himself. She had told him firmly to leave, so no matter what his feelings were, he had no choice. He walked down the lane and out of the village.

Giving no thought to where he might go, he realized he was heading in the direction of Gibbons' tavern. That was only natural, he thought, because it was the closest thing he had to a home. Even after some serious thought as he walked, he had no idea what he would do. All he could think about was how alone he felt, and he couldn't imagine going on without Aleanna. During his life, he had controlled his feelings to the point of not having any. Now she had broken through his barriers and he was helpless.

He needed time to think about why Aleanna had sent

him away. She told him she loved him and he believed her, and she said she would always love him and would be heartbroken if she ever lost him. He believed that as well.

Why hadn't she told him the real reason instead of telling him to go away? But she had walked away without further words, leaving him standing there alone. She was the most honest person he had ever met, and he couldn't understand why she had broken off their relationship so suddenly.

He had never felt this badly. All the hurt from the numerous times he was injured did not compare to this; his physical body could recover, but he wasn't sure his heart ever would. Remembering how he had always controlled pain, he knew that was what he had to do now. He had to put her and his feelings for her out of his mind. He tried, but little remembrances of her kept sneaking back into his consciousness. He pushed them away, but he kept seeing things that reminded him of her flowers, birds, and the scenery all had their effect on him. No matter where he turned, something was there to remind him of her.

Finally, using all the mental discipline drilled into him years ago, he was able to put her out of his mind.

Aleanna marched out of the village and across the countryside that was so familiar to her. Even though she recognized many of the people as she walked through the villages, she kept her floppy worn hat on and her hair tied under it.

When she reached the castle, she didn't wish to reveal her identity, but she was forced to before she could enter the castle. She took off the cap and shook out her hair so the guards recognized her, and they waved her in. Going to her quarters, she sent for several of her maids and asked them to help her get the trail dust off her and make her presentable to meet the council of the kingdom.

She soaked for over an hour in a hot bath while the women combed and brushed her hair. Stepping out of the water, she allowed the women to dry her, then finished combing her hair into the style she preferred, which was straight down with a swirl at the top. After applying perfume to her body, she asked for the dress she considered her most attractive. They brought her the dress, along with matching shoes, and helped her into it. Looking in the mirror, she was satisfied with her appearance.

She told two of the servants to get the advisors and have them come to the throne room. When the advisors arrived, they found her sitting on the throne. They were speechless.

"What are you doing?" one of them finally gasped. "You have no right to be on the throne!"

"I have every right," she responded. "I will soon be the Queen Mother and will serve until my son is old enough to serve as king. That will be when he is twenty-one."

"You are pregnant?" one of the advisers asked.

"Yes," she said simply.

"How do we know you will have a boy?"

"And how do we know who the father is? The child must be fathered by someone of royal blood."

She stood her ground, and gazed at each of them. "The father is the king of Carigo, and I can feel it is a boy. Besides, the case is moot because, even if it is a girl, I will simply marry one of our court and eventually have a son who shall become king upon reaching the proper age. Starting now," she said imperiously, "I shall rule as the Queen Mother."

CHAPTER EIGHT
CONFUSION

Björn sat in his usual spot in the tavern, a rear table where he sat with his back to the wall. Gibbons had moved a group to provide room for his friend. He asked if he wanted anything, and Björn shook his head.

Björn had arrived three days before, after being gone for many years, and every day he sat silently waiting out the business hours. He drank water when Gibbons brought it to his table, but he refused any offer of food.

Gibbons was worried. Björn had been like this for nearly thirteen years. He'd go out on a job, come back, and wait several days before he took another one. This behavior began after he returned from the job in Kallthom. While he was normally taciturn, he was now completely uncommunicative between jobs. This time, he sat in the tavern for six days, moving only to relieve himself and to take a drink of water.

Working up his courage, Gibbons nervously approached his friend. "Would you like to know how I spent your money while you were gone this time? It has been so long since we have seen you."

Björn said nothing, not acknowledging Gibbons in any way.

"I want you to look at a request that came while you were

gone," the tavern keeper said. "It is from a grandmother and more interesting than some of the jobs you have taken in past years. Her family and another have been feuding for almost a century." He looked at Björn to see if there was any reaction, and was disappointed when there was none. He went back to his story. "Most members of both families have forgotten what started the feud, and now it has degenerated into an eye for an eye. They continue the killing out of vengeance. The grandmother has sent this request; she will pay you to stop the feud."

Gibbons stood there nervously, but Björn gave no indication he heard. Then he reached out for the paper and asked, "And how am I supposed to stop it?"

"She did not say, but she has heard many great things about you and she thinks you will find a way."

"Now why should I take such a ridiculous job? Does she want me to kill all of the men on each side to stop the feud? That is the most obvious solution." Björn glared at his water cup. "No, thank you, I do not care for such an assignment."

"At least read the letter," Gibbons pleaded. "From what she has heard about you, she thinks you could come up with a peaceful solution. In any case, whatever you do, they will be no worse off than they are now. You might consider it a challenge to think of a solution and make it work."

"Gibbons, I am not in the mood for challenges."

"That is all the more reason for you to take this job." Gibbons was persistent. "It will get your mind off your troubles and, more importantly, get you out of my tavern."

For the first time, a slight smile touched Björn's lips. "I am disappointed, Gibbons. You are the only friend I have in the world, and you want to get rid of me."

Wudo looked up from cleaning tables. "I am your

friend, too, Mr. Björn."

"Yes, you are," Björn agreed. "I guess I miscounted. Gibbons, I have you, Wudo and Jago. I must not forget Jago."

"Then you will take the job?" Gibbons said, his eyes hopeful.

"I will give it some thought."

Björn read and reread the letter, contemplating quietly for several hours, then asked Gibbons to bring him some food.

With a big smile, Gibbons brought what he knew were his friend's favorite foods. Björn finished the meal, washing it down with a large pitcher of water. When Gibbons started to bring more food, Björn waved him away, asking only for more water. Drinking a large cup of the cool liquid he rose, picked up his sword harness, and fastened it around his chest and shoulders. Gathering up his bow and arrows, he stepped out of the tavern, leaving Gibbons with the big smile on his face.

"Where is Mr. Northlander going, Mr. Gibbons?"

"He is going to work again," replied Gibbons. "I think he is back with us."

Björn strode in the direction of Rugers, the city from which the letter had come and a short time later, Jago joined him.

Rugers was more than five hundred miles away, and Björn knew they could make it in five days if he kept up a brisk but not rapid pace.

The travel was easy. The land rolled without any hindrance to their path until they reached a river they had to swim across. The swift current swept them a considerable distance downstream. Reaching the other shore, they encountered nearly impenetrable stands of reeds and other vegetation in the marsh along the river. Björn let Jago beat down a trail he could follow, and when they finally reached dry land, the way became easier again. Gradually, the land changed to rocky terrain, and they had to make their way past an immense cliff that extended far to the south.

Suddenly, Björn heard the shouts of men and the clash of swords in the distance. With no intent to get involved, but curious, he headed toward the sounds. When he arrived at the scene, he saw nine men battling a woman who had slipped into a cleft in the cliff and was battling the men one and two at a time. Bodies of two men she had killed showed she was more than holding her own, but time was on the side of the men.

Björn watched the duel with interest, noting that the woman was an expert swordsman, as good as any he had ever seen. She was more than a match for two men when they entered the cleft to face her, but he saw she was tiring. It would take some time, but the men would eventually prevail.

The woman was tall, broad-shouldered and well muscled, and she had the movements of a highly trained athlete.

Approaching the battle scene from behind the men, he saw their concentration was so fixed on the woman that they did not notice him. He could tell the woman did, but could pay no attention to him.

"Why are you trying to kill her?" Björn asked when he was close enough to be heard.

"She is an assassin," said one man. "She kills only for money. She must be killed!"

Björn continued to watch the duel. His feelings were mixed. He had no use for assassins, but this was a woman against insurmountable odds. He wondered if he would feel differently if it were a man, then decided he wouldn't. He would take the side of the underdog and then sort things out.

He drew his swords and shouted, "Enough. Leave her alone."

Three of the men turned to face him with their swords ready.

"Do not be fools," he shouted. "I am a Northlander. You have no chance against me."

Either they were unaware of what a Northlander was or didn't believe him, and three broke off their attack on the woman and charged him. The first man made a slash at Björn, and he sliced the man's blade off at the hilt, driving his second sword into the man's heart. As the other two ran at him together, he slashed the second man through the midsection and then drove his other sword into the third man's throat. The man wounded in the midsection screamed, drawing the attention of the rest of the men, giving the woman the opportunity to drive her sword through the man attacking her. This left five men.

"Do you all want to die?" asked Björn. "Pick up your fallen comrades or bury them here on the spot. We will leave and you can do whatever you wish in peace. You can see you have no chance against us."

The men talked it over, then one said, "You may go. We want no further trouble with either of you." Those attacking the woman retreated, and she emerged from her place of security. Without a word, the woman and Björn walked away, Jago trailing.

"I suppose I should thank you," she said.

"Not necessarily," replied Björn. "Are you an assassin?"

"No, I am a mercenary. There is a big difference, although at times it is difficult for people to see the difference. On this last contract, I had to kill a number of men to accomplish the job. That is why they mistook me for an assassin."

He smiled. "I am glad because I will have to kill you if you are."

"Why is that?"

"I hate killers and I hate needless killing. Remember I warned those men to leave instead of trying to fight me. I am also a mercenary."

"And you are a Northlander," she said. "Is your name Björn?"

"You have heard of me."

"I have heard you are the most dangerous man alive." Her eyes bored into his, as if she hoped to get her answer there. "Is that true?"

"That is a huge statement. After all, there are many dangerous men in this world." As an afterthought, he added, "And women."

"Where are you going?" she asked.

"To Rugers. You?"

"I am also going to Rugers. I have a job there."

"I will not ask what you are going for," he said. "That is your business and none of mine."

"I appreciate that. Since we are going to the same destination, perhaps we can travel together. I would like to learn more about you."

"We can travel together but, as far as knowing me, I am afraid I am a dull subject. You know my name. Could you tell me yours and where you are from?"

"I am Gelda and I come from the interior. The nearest

city is Baldor, which is far south and a bit west of us. Do you know where that is?"

"Yes," he replied, "but I have never been there."

"From what I have heard," Gelda said, "you must be an interesting man."

"I doubt that, but I will travel with you. It should make the trip more pleasant and make time pass more quickly."

They moved off together. She was dressed in black slacks and a multi-colored man's woolen shirt with her trousers tucked into worn boots that at one time were probably black. Her close-cropped blonde hair was uncovered, and she was Björn's height and probably weighed almost as much. Her high cheekbones gave her a wild, exotic look, and Björn thought she looked quite formidable and attractive.

He continued to move in the casual stride he had been using before he met her, and he noted with interest that she had no trouble matching his pace.

"How did you got into the mercenary business?" he asked. "It is a most unusual occupation for a woman."

"As you saw, I am good with a sword, and I have never met a man I could not defeat in a fair fight. I have done a number of things—soldier, bodyguard and guardian of merchant travelers. She smiled over at him. "But I like being a mercenary best because I enjoy the variety. What about you? How did you get into the business?"

"The same as you, I am sure. How did you first get started?"

She gave him an appraising look. "I started as a soldier, then I took up body guarding and merchant caravan guarding and finally became what I am now."

"How did you get so good with a sword?" he asked.

"From hours and hours of practice." She changed

the subject smoothly. "I had heard about those long thin swords, but could not believe the stories first. I was told you use both swords at the same time, and I wondered how you could walk with two such long swords. But I see how you do it; you have a way of walking in a rhythm that keeps the swords swinging free of you. How did you learn that?"

"The same as with the sword. Practice and more practice."

They lapsed into a comfortable silence, as if they had known each other for years. Björn continued to wonder about Gelda, noting that she was as good with a sword as any man he had ever seen. Strong and graceful, she had a special way of moving that bespoke extreme confidence. With her skills, she had a right to be self-confident.

They came to a deep wide ditch that Björn thought Gelda would have to go around, but she took a run and vaulted easily over the ditch. Björn and Jago followed.

They stopped at mid-day for a break. She knelt, eating from her store of dried vegetables and jerky. "I have heard about your horse, and I must admit he is not anything like I expected. He is small to have accomplished all that I have heard he has done."

"Jago is worth his keep," Björn laughed. "Actually, more than his keep, because he is no trouble at all and takes better care of me than I do of him," he said, "and many are fooled by his small size."

"Where did you find him?" she asked.

"In the Northland," Björn said. "He was a wild horse like the rest of his kind when he and I met, and he is still extremely independent."

"You talk about him as if he were a person," Gelda said, amused at the close relationship between man and horse.

The next morning, Björn was in the camp when Gelda

awoke. After exchanging pleasantries they got underway, again lapsing into silence. They continued at a slightly faster pace as Björn noted that Gelda seemed to want to move faster. When it was almost dark, they stopped.

Gelda built a small fire and pulled out more of her food, offering some to Björn, who declined. Between bites she asked, "You never seem to be hungry. Do you ever eat?"

He sprawled out on the grass, leaning his head on his arm. "Of course I do but it does not take much to satisfy me. If it will satisfy you, I will accept some of your dried fruit and vegetables."

She handed him some of her supply, and they ate in amiable silence, then Björn faded into the darkness, and Gelda didn't even notice he was gone until suddenly he wasn't there. She thought he must have continued on, so she made herself comfortable on the ground and fell asleep. When she awoke, she was surprised to see Björn standing across the burned-out fire from her.

"Where did you go last night?" she asked. "I thought you were gone."

"Jago and I were guarding. Neither of us needs much sleep so we make ourselves useful."

"Did you think there was danger?"

"Not necessarily," he said, "but, at times in the past, there has been. I want to take every precaution."

"So you were guarding me while I slept." She chuckled, then looked up at him. "I want you to know, Björn, that I am a very light sleeper."

"Light enough to notice this in your sleep?" he asked, holding up a huge snake.

"Where did you find that?" she gasped.

"He evidently sensed you and was about fifteen feet away from you when I spotted him." He tossed the serpent into the bushes. "I am afraid if you had been by yourself, you would have been his lunch by now."

"Well," she shrugged indignantly, "It looks like it does pay for a girl to have a bodyguard, a big strong alert man around to keep her safe."

"I did not mean to make you angry," he apologized. "If I had thought it would offend you, I would not have shown it to you. I did not mean to put you down; it is only that you and I are very different. Just as I require little food or water, I also need little sleep. Usually Jago and I take turns catching short naps while we are standing."

"And I apologize for being rude," she said, satisfied that he meant no disrespect. "Men always think they need to protect poor helpless women. It always makes me angry."

"I have seen you in action, so I would never consider you needing help. This snake prowling about and stalking prey as large as a human is unusual. When I first saw it, I did not see a threat. It was only when it sensed you that I became apprehensive."

"But it did not target you." she said.

"Perhaps because I was standing and thus looked like a larger target," he said. "I really do not know."

"Are you sure you are not trying to frighten me?" She looked a little skeptical.

"Are you frightened?"

"No, not in the least."

"That is the answer I expected. Are you ready to move on?"

Smiling brightly, she said "Thank you, and yes, I am ready." Fastening her sword around her waist, she picked up her traveling bag and started out with Björn and Jago following.

They could not keep a straight course because they had

to detour around some great cliffs. Björn let Gelda set the pace, and they made good time. At mid-day they stopped again to rest, and Gelda made herself comfortable on the ground and napped for a few minutes. Björn took the time to search for food, leaving Jago with Gelda. He was fortunate and brought back some apples and plums. Gelda clapped her hands with glee.

"I suppose you think I am acting like a little girl," she said.

"No, I think you are acting like someone who likes apples and plums."

"Thank you for getting them while I rested."

"It was no problem, and you are welcome," he said. "They were easy to find, and I like them, too. We should eat what we want and then get on the trail again. We can snack on them as we walk."

They walked until almost dark and, when they stopped, Björn made a small fire from the branches of a dead tree while Gelda arranged the fruit for their dinner.

"Is it a problem for you to go without meat?" Björn asked.

"I prefer to have it, but can do without it."

"Tomorrow, we will stop earlier in the day and hunt for our dinner."

"I will certainly agree to that," she said. "As I said, I prefer to have meat."

Gelda sat on the ground while Björn sat back on his heels. After the meal, she started to get as comfortable as possible on the ground, and he got up to go stand guard.

"Do you really need to guard us?" she said softly. "If you could hear that snake from outside our camp, surely you can hear one from here. Let Jago guard us for tonight, and you come lie with me."

Björn was speechless for several seconds, then he said, "I am sorry, but I cannot."

"Do you dislike women, or is it only me you do not like?"

"If you are asking if I like men in that way, the answer is no. I like you very much and find you very attractive." He drew up his shoulders. "There is another woman I love."

"So are you married, or is that woman waiting for you?"

There was a long silence before he replied, "No, I am not married and there is no one waiting. There is someone I care for whom I am afraid does not care for me, at least not in the same way I care for her."

"Then come to me," she pleaded.

"I cannot get her out of my mind," he whispered. "I am truly sorry." He turned and walked from the camp.

The next morning, Gelda was her normal cheerful self with seemingly no hurt feelings from being rejected, and again they were on the road early.

"We should make it to Rugers today," she said.

"I agree, perhaps shortly after noontime," he calculated.

At his estimated time, they walked into the city. Just inside, they took leave of each other, and Björn never expected to see her again. Aleanna had opened the door to his feelings, and he realized he liked her now but he couldn't say why, other than that she was good company on the trail. He thought about her strange occupation, especially for a woman. He shook the thoughts from his head, and he and Jago started out to find the family home of the grandmother who had written him.

The house was a huge mansion with four floors and flying ramparts making it appear larger than it was. Björn found it both impressive and intimidating. Leaving Jago at the side of the road, he banged the knocker at the front door, and it was opened almost immediately by a maid accompanied by two soldiers.

"How can I help you?" asked the maid.

"I am here at the request of Mrs. Gordo, the elder Mrs. Gordo. I am Björn. She has sent for me," he announced.

"Please leave your swords with the soldiers and I will take you to her."

"I will keep my swords and remain here," he said firmly. "Please get her and bring her to me."

"It is difficult for her to come all of the way down here," she told him. "You should go to her."

"Please go and ask her what she wants done, for I will not give up my swords," he said, thinking of what had happened the last time he surrendered his weapons. "She will have to come to me, I will be allowed to go to her with my gear, or I will simply leave. Will you ask her?"

With a nod from the soldiers, the maid disappeared into the dark interior of the house. Returning shortly, she said Björn could keep his swords and come with her. The soldiers grudgingly motioned to Björn to follow, with one preceding him and the other following. Björn kept his mental concentration on the one behind.

They progressed through the mansion, taking one wide, winding staircase after another. Finally, they climbed a set of narrow steps, entered the top floor and walked down a hall to a sitting room filled with beautiful furniture. In a large, overstuffed chair sat an elderly woman. Björn was surprised to see that she did not seem decrepit at all. She was plump with rosy cheeks and a lap robe covering her. Her bright eyes sparkled.

"Welcome, Northlander. I apologize for the behavior of my guards. They are not to blame, of course, and were following standard procedure. I neglected to inform them that you were an exception." She pointed to another armchair in front of her. "Now, please sit and let me explain our problem."

He sat balanced on the edge of the chair.

"As I explained in my letter, our two families have been at war with each other for at least a century. The current generations do not even know why they are fighting; all that has been forgotten through the years. Now they fight to avenge an act by one family and then the other reacts, and so endlessly it goes." She smoothed out the lap robe almost nervously, then looked him straight in the eye. I have corresponded with my equal in the rival family, and she shares my feelings. We feel that someone like you might be able to stop this continuous killing. You are an outsider who is a skilled fighter, so perhaps you can talk some sense into them." Leaning forward, she said, "Perhaps you can make them listen to reason."

"What makes you think they might listen to me?" he asked.

"For one thing, you could make them listen to you. Neither my counterpart nor I have had any success, and we are desperate. We cannot see any solution to this mess. You are our last resort."

"I am not sure if I can accomplish what you want. One thing I am sure of is that, if I try, people will likely get hurt."

She shrugged. "They are getting hurt now."

"But if I try and things turn ugly, you may regret calling for me."

"We discussed that. We are depending on your good judgment to keep that from happening."

He rose. "You have to understand that, once I set things in motion, I may not be able to control them. Once I start, people could get hurt no matter what I do."

"We must trust you," she said, "and I am willing to do so."

"Then I will do my best," he said with a dubious look on his face. "Can you have the most influential members of your family meet with me as soon as possible?"

She turned toward the soldiers. "See that Brian, Folder, Euler and Simson come here at once," she ordered. Without question, they turned and left immediately.

"What are you called, Mr. Northlander?"

"My name is Björn, just Björn."

'Well, Mr. Björn, please make yourself comfortable. Can we get you some tea or coffee while we wait?"

"Tea is fine." He sat back down.

She sent the maid for tea, then continued. "Let us get acquainted. My name is Bernadine and I have had eight children, seven of them boys. Four of the young men lost their lives in this senseless war. I mourn for them, and for the young men who continue to be killed. I also mourn for the men of the Giller family who have been killed. I have tried talking to them but have gotten nowhere, and I hope you have better success. Now, please tell me about yourself."

"Tell me what you have heard about me."

"Very well," she said. "I heard that you are an incredible warrior, especially skillful with your swords, but I also heard that you are honest, which I understand is somewhat rare for people in your profession. You are very adept at solving problems, although I am not sure you have ever been presented with something like this. I am also led to believe that you are quite expensive and woe to anyone who tries to cheat you out of your fee. Is this how you would describe yourself?"

Björn gave her his small crooked smile. "I do not think

I would say all that, but if that is what people here believe, it might make my job easier."

The maid brought the tea, and he and Bernadine talked at length.

The four men she had sent for drifted in one at a time, and Bernadine introduced them as they arrived. Each reacted nervously and quizzically to Björn. The two swords that Björn had propped against his chair seemed to intimidate them, Björn noticed with some satisfaction.

Bernadine explained the purpose of Björn's visit and told the men she wanted their cooperation. They were the most influential men of the family and should set a good example.

The men looked at Björn, then Euler asked, "What do you intend to do?"

"That depends on you. Do you want the feud stopped?"

Glancing at the others, Brian said, "The Gillers will never accept a truce."

"If I can convince them, are you willing to try?"

There was a long silence. Finally, Brian said, "If you can convince them, we are willing to give it a try, but how are you going to get them to agree?"

"Are you tired of the killing and want it to end?"

"Of course we are," responded Folder, "but when they kill one of ours, we have no choice but to retaliate."

"Which family was the last to suffer a loss?" Björn asked.

"The Giller family." Folder clinched his fist. "So we are on guard against an attack."

"If the Gillers agree to a cease fire, will you also agree? The only thing you have to lose is time—the time for the Gillers to respond if they break the agreement. Are you willing to meet with representatives of their family if I can get them to agree?"

Folder said they would like to discuss it first among themselves, so they left the room and were gone for some time. When they returned, Folder said, "We will meet with the Gillers, but only if they agree to meet at a neutral place."

"Very well," Björn said. "Name some neutral places."

They were evidently expecting that question, and Folder listed four places, but Björn could see they were skeptical that the Gillers would cooperate.

"What if I agree to stay around for a while to keep an eye on things? I will slay the first man or men who break the truce," Björn suggested. "That way there will be no one to seek revenge against anyone but me."

"That will not work," Brian interjected. "They will just kill you."

Björn chuckled. "You will find me difficult to kill, but that is not your problem unless it is you who breaks the truce. Bernadine, who is your counterpart in the Giller family?"

"Her name is Mary, and I believe she will be as cooperative as I am. Although we have never met, we have corresponded at length." She paused, then nodded. "Yes, I think she will be amenable to your idea. It is the only thing that I think has a chance to work. What do you boys think? Are you willing to give it your whole-hearted support?"

They whispered among themselves, then Brian said they would.

"Bernadine, I will get back to you on the response of the Gillers," Björn said. "If they agree, I will set the time and place for your conference."

He picked up his swords, said goodbye to the grandmother and the men, and with the servant leading the way, he left the mansion, leaving Jago behind grazing.

The Northlander

Following the directions provided by the Gordos, he headed for the Gillers' home. As he arrived, he suddenly sprinted to the interior corner of a nearby building, drawing his swords and preparing to meet a group of men he sensed.

They rounded the corner and came directly toward him. There were almost twenty of them, making Björn wish Jago was with him. But in the corner with his back against the wall, only three could attack him at one time and the length of his swords gave him a definite advantage.

They charged. He skewered the first, slashed the second, then drove a sword through the third while simultaneously taking the head from the shoulders of a fourth. From his battle experience, he had learned that there was nothing more frightening to an enemy as witnessing a companion having his head severed from his body.

But these men were determined. A fifth lost his head, and the sixth and seventh had swords driven through their midsections. Seven bodies piled up gave the men pause. For one thing, they made it difficult to get at Björn.

Sensing the fight was not yet over, he leapt across the bodies and attacked. His swords swished through the still air, severing the head from one man with a downward stroke and slicing his next opponent's head from his shoulders with the same stroke. At almost the same instant, he recovered, driving one sword through a man and the second sword through another. Now, with Björn untouched and eleven bodies on the ground, the men stopped, then turned and fled.

"Well done," a familiar voice said from a short distance away. "That was most impressive, even more impressive than what you did to the men who were attacking me. You are certainly everything I heard you were, and it is too bad you have to die."

Björn turned and spotted Gelda. "What do you mean, die?"

She grinned. "I told you I was a mercenary, and I was hired by the Giller family to kill you. They do not want any interference in their affairs; even now, they are planning a major attack against the Gordo family."

"I should have let your attackers put you out of your misery," he said calmly. "You are an assassin, yet you did not try to kill me on the trail. Why not?"

"Because I had not yet received my fee." She started toward him.

"I have seen you fight and you are an outstanding swordsman, perhaps the best I have seen except for a Northlander. You have seen on two occasions what I can do. Do you really think you have a chance against me?"

"Of course I do," she laughed. "And I have already accepted my fee, so there is no turning back."

"I do not want to hurt you," Björn said. "Please back off and let me be on my way."

"As I told you, I have already taken my fee. Now, as you must know, I am honor bound to complete the contract." She drew her sword and approached. "Why is it you do not want to fight me? Do you still have the silly idea that you must be chivalrous to a woman?"

"That is not it at all. Remember, I have seen you in action." He saluted her with his bloody swords. "It is because I came to like you on the trail. In the past days, I realized that I have only four friends, and one of them is a horse. I felt you and I were close to becoming friends."

"I felt the same," she said. "Remember that I asked you to share my bed, and that is not something I do promiscuously, but this has nothing to do with that situation; this is business." She moved a little closer, her sword ready. "As you are also a professional, I thought you would feel the same way."

"I still do not want to kill you."

Gelda charged to attack. Björn slipped one sword back into the scabbard, thrusting her sword aside with the other. They fought for some time with Gelda attacking and Björn parrying each thrust. Finally, Gelda stepped back and swiftly drew a knife from her belt, throwing it at Björn, who caught it in his free hand.

"Now that is a nasty little trick," he commented.

Breathing hard, Gelda said, "But you are not fighting me; you treat me like I am a girl you do not want to hurt."

"All right; let us continue, and I will thrust my sword through your belly button."

Red-faced, she launched herself at him again. Björn sliced her sword at the hilt with a flick of his wrist.

"I am sure that is embarrassing," he said. "but it is much better than having your belly button removed."

She stood there with her chest heaving, clutching the sword hilt. "How did you do that?" she gasped. "That sword is the best steel made; the sword was made especially for me."

Björn, still wary, stood still. "That, as you can see, is the second best steel," he said. "A good sword smith can easily repair it. Do not feel bad about not completing your mission. Accept that you have given it your best and leave Rugers immediately." He took two steps toward her, sword ready. "If you stay here and try to complete your assassin's contract, I will have no choice but to kill you." Without another glance at her, Björn stepped around her, leaving her fuming in the road.

The Giller residence was similar in design to the

Gordo home but possibly a little bigger. Björn pulled the handle of a bell outside the main door. The grounds of the mansion rang with the peals of the bell. A man dressed in the uniform of a male servant opened the door. "Yes?" he asked.

"I am Björn. The elder Mrs. Giller will know who I am. Will you tell her I am here?"

"Wait here," said the man, closing the door in Björn's face. Björn thought it rude, but thought maybe that was the way things were done here. The man returned and told Björn to follow him.

Björn followed the servant to the rear of the house, through a large sitting room and into an equally large bedroom. Sitting up in a huge wooden bed was a dried-up crone of a woman, quite old, with wispy white hair and a narrow face. But when she spoke, her voice was strong and authoritative. "So you are the young man Bernadine and I sent for," she said. "Please call me Mary. I understand you have already been hard at work killing our soldiers. I suppose I should be angry with you, but they probably had it coming. Did they attack you?"

"Yes."

"Then the fools got what they deserved. I assume you have met with Bernadine. Did she tell you what she wanted?" Björn nodded, and she continued. "Then you know the problem, and that we want the feud to end. Did you come up with any good ideas? Tell me, what do you think?"

"We decided to try to get the heads of both houses to meet in a neutral place to discuss our plan," he said.

"And what is this great plan?"

"You will have to judge whether or not it is great. I will explain to the men the trap they are in. One house is transgressed against and then wreaks its revenge on the other house, and so the violence continues year after year."

He saw that she was listening intently, and continued, "What I am proposing is a cease-fire. If anyone on either side breaks the armistice, I will kill him. Consequently, there will be no one from the other side to retaliate against. If both parties agree to this, I will remain in town long enough to make sure there is no breach of contract on either side. After I am gone, if the peace is broken, you or Bernadine can send for me. What do you think?"

She smiled. "I think it has a chance to work, but you are putting your life at great risk. Are you sure you want to do this?"

"That is what you are paying me to do and, speaking of pay, can I assume Mrs. Gordo sent the first payment? If so, your house is responsible for the second half."

"That is agreed," Mary said, and then she spoke to one of the servants in the room. "Sana, take the key," she took a key from around her neck, "unlock the chest and bring me the money bag."

Sana did as instructed and brought the money bag to her mistress. Mary counted out some gold pieces and handed them to Björn. "I understand this is the amount Bernadine sent you. Is this sufficient?"

"It is sufficient, but it is not owed until the job is completed."

"Take it now," she said. "We may not know if your plan works until years have passed."

Turning to Sana, she gave her the bag to replace in the chest, and asked her to summon Roget and Jed.

When these two men arrived, she introduced them.

"Now, then, who was so foolish as to send soldiers to kill Björn, since the result of that got them slaughtered."

Both men looked sheepishly at the floor. "Just as I suspected," she glared, "it was the two of you. If you had bothered to ask first, I could have told you such an amateur attack would not work on the Northlander. Now, here is what my counterpart in the Gordo household and I have decided." She related Björn's plan to them.

"But they transgressed against us last," protested Roget. "It will always be uneven if we do not respond."

"As I recall from when I was a little girl, it was our family that committed the first crime. If that is correct, we are now even. Now, at which of these places do you prefer to meet?"

"How can we know we will be safe at any of the locations?" asked Roget.

"There are only four men coming from the Gordo house. You may also take four." She looked at Björn for approval, and he nodded. "In addition, Björn will be there to keep trouble from breaking out. Can you agree with this?"

"Has the Gordo house agreed to these terms?" asked Jed.

"They have," Björn said.

The two talked quietly for a bit, then nodded their approval of a location.

Björn told them to meet at the place they chose with their four men within the hour. He would get the Gordo people to join them for the conference. The male servant led him from the house.

As he left the Giller mansion, heading for the Gordo home, he was deep in thought. He went over his plan in his mind, deciding exactly what he would do and say. Walking slowly, his thoughts soon drifted to Gelda, and he wondered if she had taken his advice and left town.

Then, as so often happened, his thoughts returned

The Northlander

to Aleanna, and he recalled the things they had shared. Remembering all the things she had taught him, especially acknowledging his emotions, made him miserable.

Suddenly, a figure leapt out from the shadows. A hand held a knife aimed at his chest, but having already sensed the presence, was prepared. He grabbed the knife hand and turned it back into the chest of his attacker. It was Gelda, who died immediately in his arms. He lowered her to the ground and, standing over her body, he regretted that she had not left when she had the chance, but felt some small satisfaction for removing an assassin.

He continued his trek to the Gordo home. When he got there, he told the men where to meet. He told them to bring only the four diplomats, as there would be only four Gillers. Reminding them that he would be there to settle any trouble, he left and proceeded to the designated meeting place.

The Gordos arrived first, followed shortly by the Gillers. Björn had one family sit on one side of a long table and the rival family on the other side. He introduced them, and repeated the plan before asking if there were any questions. After a long silence, Brian Gordo asked the Gillers if they would forego avenging the last of their family killed.

"Our grandmother told us she remembers it was one of our family who did the first killing," Paul Giller said finally. "Now we are even and can stop. We are willing if you are."

Brian responded that his family would honor the agreement. "I am certain Björn can and will do what he said if either side breaks the truce, and I respect that. Is there an agreement we should sign?"

Björn reached into his shirt and produced decorated documents that spelled out in detail the verbal agreement. The four Gillers signed two of their documents and gave one to the Gordos, while the Gordos did the same.

Björn thanked the men for agreeing to peace, and told them he would check in on them again in a few years. Then he and Jago headed back toward Gibbons' tavern to see what other tasks awaited them.

Seven years later, Björn returned to Rugers with Jago. He called at the Gordo home and asked to see Bernadine. Without hesitation, they led him to the same room where he found Bernadine sitting in the same chair with what looked like the same blanket across her lap. Greeting him warmly, she asked a servant to get them some tea.

"Now," she said, "how have you been, Björn?"

"Fine, thank you for asking."

"Have you received the annual messages I sent to the tavern to inform you the truce was still holding?"

"I received your messages and thank you for them," he said, "but as I was passing by, I wanted to stop to see for myself. Has there been any trouble since your last message?"

"None," she said, "The truce is holding well, thanks to your brilliant plan."

Björn set his tea cup on a table next to him. "During the peace, has their been any interaction between the two families?"

"I am glad you asked," Bernadine replied. "There is still tension in the older generation, but it seems to have faded away from the younger generation. Next month, there will be a wedding between one of my great grandchildren and a Giller girl, and both families will attend. It will be great if you can stay for the wedding and see for yourself what you accomplished." She gave him a kindly smile. "It will also help remind everyone of the repercussions if anyone breaks the truce."

"I cannot stay for a month, but I will stay for several days, making sure I am seen by as many people as possible. The word will soon spread that I am in town." He stood up. "I think I will go to the Giller house and see your counterpart."

"I am afraid that is not possible," she said. "Mary passed away five years ago."

"Do you think I should talk to Paul? He seemed to be the leader of the family."

"Yes," Bernadine agreed, "That is a good choice. Will I see you again before you leave?"

"No," Björn said. "After I see Paul, I will stay in town another day to be seen, then I will leave. I do not enjoy cities and avoid them whenever possible."

Björn stayed for two days, spending his time talking with both Paul Giller and Brian Gordo. They still harbored a bit of resentment, but admitted peace was better than the feud. Satisfied the truce was holding and likely to hold in the future, Björn left the city, feeling his presence showed his interest in permanent peace.

As nothing else demanded his immediate attention, he found Jago and the two of them set off once again, with no specific destination in mind. But after wandering about for a while, they returned to Gibbons' tavern.

CHAPTER NINE
THE REUNION

"I think you keep staying away longer each time. You have been gone nearly a year. The job must have been bigger than we expected," said Gibbons as his way of greeting.

"Yes, but I think it is resolved," Björn said.

Moving to his usual place behind the bar, Gibbons pulled out a pile of correspondence. With a flourish, he placed an ornate packet on the bar. "As curious as I was, I was afraid to open this one. I was not sure what you would do if you found it opened, but I was tempted. You were gone so long I was not certain you would ever return." Handing it to Björn, he said, "It came shortly after you left."

Björn took the packet and turned to walk to his table. " Bring me an ale, will you, Gibbons?"

"Oh, so we are going to celebrate, are we?"

"Gibbons, some day you are going to push my patience too far."

Sitting down, he slowly opened the packet. Using his knife to carefully slit the seal, he saw that it was Aleanna's ring that had made the impression. He unwound the string that had been held in place by the seal and opened the packet.

Gibbons brought him his ale, wisely saying nothing and returning to the bar. Taking a sip, Björn realized he was stalling because he was afraid of what the message might be but finally he pulled the letter from the packet. The message was short and simple. All it said was, "Please come, love, Aleanna."

He was dumbfounded. What did she mean by "Love?" He sat at the table without moving, but his mind raced. Was she in some kind of trouble? Was there some threat to her or to the kingdom? He realized he would never find out sitting there, so he rose to his feet and, leaving his ale and a gold piece on the table, he walked from the tavern without a word of farewell.

He whistled for Jago, and they moved out quickly. Instead of their customary fast trot, they ran. Björn realized it had been a long time since he and Jago had moved at such a rapid pace. Jago seemed to enjoy it and frequently leapt into the air, twisting his body and lashing out with his hind hooves, or turning his neck to bite into the air. Björn laughed at the horse's antics, knowing he would be feeling the same sense of excitement if it were not for his fear of Aleanna's situation.

At this pace, they arrived at Kallthom within two weeks. Close to Kallthom, Björn noticed a small lake that he remembered. Taking off his clothes and sliding into the cool water, he scrubbed his body vigorously. He perspired little, but he didn't want to smell like a pig farmer when he saw Aleanna. Dressing in a fresh shirt and pants, he stuffed his old clothes into his bag, then polished his boots before going on.

He strode toward the castle, so deep thought that he almost passed the old tavern where he had stopped the last time he was in Kallthom. Deciding to stop to learn what he could before meeting Aleanna, he opened the door and entered. He was the only patron, so he went to the bar and ordered an ale.

After the man brought his ale, Björn asked the barkeeper if he could answer a few questions and laid a gold piece on the bar. The man immediately reached for it, but Björn was faster.

"After you answer my questions, you may have the gold piece."

"Very well," he said, a little disgruntled.

"I have not been here for many years," Björn said. "I would like news of the kingdom."

"What kind of news, real news or gossip? I have little news but lots of gossip."

"Tell me the news first."

"How long have you been gone?"

"I have not been here for more than twenty years," Björn said. "What has happened during that time?"

"Well, it has been pretty quiet for the past twelve or thirteen years," the barkeeper started.

"How is the princess?" Björn interrupted.

"Do you mean the queen?" the man asked. "She is amazing. Surely you have you heard of what she did to Delph."

"No, I have not. What did she do?"

The bartender leaned on the bar with both elbows, a glass of ale at hand, as though he was going to tell a long story. "She is a warrior queen," he said proudly. "She decided to attack them and permanently remove them as a threat. But first, she organized a large army and captured as many of the roving bands as possible. The men who agreed to enter the army were accepted and trained with the other new soldiers. Those who would not swear allegiance to the queen were sent on their way." He took a swig of his ale. "She treated them like our own soldiers, spreading them throughout the army to keep them from getting together and plotting. When everything was ready, she attacked Delph.

"She split her army into three divisions against advice from her angry generals. One division attacked the Delph castle from the front, but she sent the other two groups to sneak over the low hills behind the castle to attack from the rear. Delph was prepared for a frontal attack, but not an assault from the rear, so it was a relatively easy victory. Then the queen made sure the defeated Delphs were treated better than they had been in Delph, thus assuring their loyalty. Yes, our queen is quite something."

The bartender started to leave, but Björn asked him to stay.

"Other customers have arrived, I must attend to them," the bartender said.

"Of course, but return and this is yours," said Björn, spinning the gold piece on the bar. "I have other questions to ask. The gold piece is yours when you return and answer them."

The bartender grumbled but hastened to fill the glasses and mugs of the waiting customers. As quickly as he could, he returned to Björn. "What else do you want to know?"

"What else is going on at the castle?"

"Well, the queen is no longer the ruler," the man said. "Last year, she turned that over to the prince when he became twenty-one. Now he is king of both Kallthom and Carigo, which he inherited when he came of age. His only problem was when a small army of dissidents attacked Carigo, but he took our army and routed them. Some say he will be as fine a leader as the queen was. He is twenty-two now, and it is said the queen is looking for a wife for him."

The barkeeper leaned close to Björn. "This part is gossip, but many say she is more interested in finding a husband for herself," he whispered confidentially. "She has had several suitors, but she would accept none. The gossip is that she has selected one and is only waiting for him to come." He leaned back and spoke normally again. "Other than that, there is little important news or gossip. Is there anything else in which you might be interested?"

"What about this supposed suitor for the queen?"

"Oh, I think that is merely gossip because she has never married. People say she is quite restless and complains about having little to do now that she no longer runs the kingdom."

Björn sipped his ale in silence. He was confused by what the man had told him, as it was not like Aleanna to be bored and restless. She always found something to do.

"Does she still run the legal system?" he asked.

"Yes, but that is running so smoothly that it takes little of her time."

Björn tossed the gold coin on the bar and continued to sip his ale. The barkeeper snatched the gold piece as if he were afraid Björn might change his mind and hurried off to take care of his other customers.

Björn had to admit he had some trepidation about going to the castle after all these years. He was still confused about why she walked away and left him standing alone. Finishing his ale, he stood motionless at the bar. The barkeeper started to refill his mug, but Björn shook his head, then turned and headed out the door. Jago was waiting patiently for him, and together they started for the castle.

As he walked, he continued to think about Aleanna. She must be in her early forties by now, and he wondered if she was still as beautiful as she had been when they returned from the fiasco at Carigo. Northlanders aged slowly, but he wondered what changes she would notice in him. He had added a few scars but thought he had changed little.

As he and Jago walked into the town surrounding the castle in Kallthom, his mind drifted back to his first visit so many years ago. He remembered how disappointed King Brewster had been when he had first seen Björn, and what the Northlander had to do to convince Brewster he was the man for the job.

Leaving Jago to graze in the courtyard, he was approaching the castle when the huge door swung open and Aleanna appeared. Despite the passage of time, she appeared little changed. She had matured and was even more beautiful than when he had last seen her.

For a moment, she stopped in mid-stride, then she ran to him, stopping a pace in front of him. Both of them remained motionless and without speaking.

Finally, Aleanna broke the silence. "You have not changed at all!" she exclaimed.

"You have," he replied softly. "You are even more beautiful than I remembered."

"I guess you have changed," she said, laughter in her voice. "Your eyesight has dimmed, but thank you." Taking his hand, she led him into the castle. "Come, there is someone you must meet." She continued holding his hand as she led him up the stairs. He followed her into what he remembered as the king's study.

Seated at the desk was a handsome young man who rose as they entered. Björn knew immediately that this was Aleanna's son. He was handsome in the same way that she was beautiful. His most striking feature was his wiry grey hair that was common only among Northlanders. He was taller than Björn and, although heavier, had the same slender build.

"Brewster, I want you to meet Björn."

Brewster extended his hand in greeting, saying, "I have heard so much about you and the trip Mother and you made to Carigo, and how you rescued her numerous times. I had the details memorized when I was still a young boy. It is such an honor to meet you."

"I told you that perhaps you would get to meet him some day. Is he the same as I described to you?"

"Not exactly," Brewster laughed. "He is even more dangerous-looking. I have not ever doubted that he accomplished all of the heroic things that you said he did, but seeing him in person certainly proves that he did. Those swords are even more intimidating that I expected. Mr. Björn, I hope you realize these are all compliments."

"Thank you, but my name is simply Björn."

"We will meet together again at dinner, Brewster, but now I must speak to Björn alone." She took his arm and led him into her sitting room.

"Now tell me, what have you been doing? Do you have a woman or are you married?" Her fingers dug into his arm and she looked at him anxiously.

"No, there has been no one after you."

She released his arm and, looking into his eyes, she said. "I have always regretted not telling you. I knew I had hurt you and was extremely sorry for it. I do not think I could have done anything else, but I should have confided in you. You had every right to know, but I was afraid to look at you." She lowered her head. "Walking away from you was the hardest thing I will ever do."

"I know that now," he said.

She raised her chin and looked directly at him. "What

do you think of Brewster?"

"He seems like a fine young man."

"Of course he is. Who is his father?" she asked. "Whose hair does he have?"

"Are you trying to tell me he is our son?"

"Yes, he is. I was afraid everyone would know by looking at the two of you together. That is why I had to send you away. When I heard my father had died, I realized I was the queen mother, and my son had to be of royal blood to become king." She looked at him, a silent plea in her eyes. "That is why I lied and told everyone the king of Carigo and I were married, and Brewster was his son."

"How were you so sure it would be a boy?"

"With you as the father, I knew it had to be a boy."

There was silence in the room for quite some time. Finally, Björn spoke. "Well, I finally know. What are we going to do?"

"You did not understand my note? I love you and have loved you ever since we parted. I no longer want to stay here in the kingdom. I want to leave and go with you."

"But you know the life I live is unsuitable for a woman," Björn said.

"Not for a woman who loves you as I do. I have been parted from you for too long, my love. I do not ever want to be separated from you again." She threw her arms around his neck, pulling him close.

"I have to admit I am confused. When do you wish to leave and where do you want to go?"

"I can go anywhere as long as I am with you. As far as when, as soon as we are married."

"We are to be married? I have never thought I would be married."

"Well, think about it now," she said. "What do you

think two people in love do?"

"I guess they get married, but I never thought about it, at least not for me."

"Surely Northlanders marry?"

"Of course they do. I never thought I would marry." He gazed at her lovingly. "What do we have to do to get married?"

"It will be a grand event," she gushed. "We will hold it outside in the courtyard to accommodate all the guests. The bishop will perform the ceremony, and Brewster can give the bride away. I will have a wedding dress made for me and a noble suit for you. I estimate it will take about a week to get all of that done, so we have no time to waste."

Björn visibly recoiled as she described the upcoming ceremony.

"What is the matter?" she asked anxiously.

"Do we have to have all that ceremony? We can have a small wedding," he said. "Surely there is some of that we can leave out."

She stood back from him, crossing her arms. "I am a middle-aged woman," she said indignantly, "and this is the only wedding I will ever have. Please do this for me. The people of the kingdom will be disappointed if they do not get to see their queen married. Please understand how important this is to me and to them," she pleaded. "I have dreamed of this for years, and I will not feel really married if we do not have a proper ceremony." She looked at Björn expectantly.

Björn didn't respond right away, and her heart started thumping. Finally, he smiled and said, "Of course I can do this for you; I was being selfish."

"Wonderful!" she exclaimed, throwing her arms around his neck again and squeezing him. "You do not have any idea how happy you have made me." Taking his arm, she led him to a sofa built into the wall. Sitting down with him next to her, she asked, "Are you happy we are together again?"

"Of course I am. I thought of you almost every day. I came back three times to see how you were doing," he confessed. Then he clapped her on the shoulder. "I understand you used the strategy we discussed to capture Delph. I learned about the great argument you had with your generals over splitting your force in order to attack Delph."

"Of course I remembered. It made great sense to me, but I had a very hard time getting it through the thick heads of my generals. They had never heard of it before, so they naturally were against it. Wait, you came back to Kallthom, but did not come to see me?"

"When you walked away, you said you could not see me so I took you at your word. I could not go against your wishes."

"It certainly was not my wish," she said, "It was responsibility and duty. My wish was always to be with you. You cannot imagine how much I have missed you all these years. It took almost a year for you to come after I sent you the letter, and I was afraid you were not going to come so I kept consoling myself with the thought that you were off on one of your jobs."

"I was, but as soon as I read your letter, Jago and I came on the run. We have never traveled that far so fast." He paused to stare at her for a long moment. "We stopped only an hour or two a day to eat and drink. I would have run straight through, but I knew it was best for us to stop."

"I was hoping that was what you would do, but I had given up believing. My hope diminished with every day. So you can imagine the ecstasy I felt when I finally saw you." She grasped his hands, imprisoning them in hers. "Now, tell me everything that has happened to you since you left," she said, snuggling close to him. "I want all the details."

"It was simply more of the same that I have always done, but there was one thing that was different, something I never encountered before." He told her the story of Gelda and how he had killed her, and that it was the only thing that had ever happened on one of his jobs that he regretted doing.

"Were you in love with her?"

"I liked her," he said, "but I certainly did not feel about her the way I feel for you. What I want to know is why she kept trying to kill me when she should have known it was beyond her skills."

Aleanna pursed her lips and then said, "I imagine she had spent all of her life proving she was as good as a man, and became obsessed. Maybe she knew she would not be able to kill you but, to keep her self-respect, she had to try."

"You are probably right. She spoke often about constantly having to prove she was as good as a man."

Aleanna looked up at him and appeared to be deep in thought. "When I first returned, I had a great deal to learn. Thank goodness I had such a good model in my father. The first problem I had was when the advisors challenged me. They thought they should rule as a council," she said sweetly, "and that a mere girl could not possibly rule adequately. I had them thrown in the dungeon for two weeks and then had them brought before me. I informed them I had no need for advisors on a permanent basis and that I would seek advice when I thought I needed it from those most qualified to give it. I told them it would most likely be different people at different times for different situations. And then," she said firmly, "I told them if they interfered I would have them imprisoned again, next time for life. Any time I had to make a decision, I thought about two people—you and my father—and asked myself what advice you would give me, then I followed it.

"One big event was when the sheep farmers rebelled. A disease had infected their flocks and killed many of the sheep. I had the soldiers kill and burn all the infected sheep. What caused the problem was when I had them kill unaffected sheep that were on the same farm as infected ones," she said. "I was stupid for not informing the farmers they would be paid for all the sheep destroyed, but I was so wrapped up in making sure we stopped the epidemic that I had not gotten around to making the announcement. Those farmers became almost uncontrollable in their rage; even the announcement did not stop their anger and their destruction. I finally had no choice but to call out the army.

"Those were the only times my authority was seriously challenged. Most of the time I was kept pretty busy. The legal system had fallen apart in my absence, so I had to get it back in order, then there were all the details of running the kingdom. You have no idea of how many details. The advisors had been delegated to take care of many of these things but, of course, now I had no one. I took one of the dukes I thought was capable, reliable and trustworthy and made him my prime minister. By the time he was familiar with the work, things went more smoothly for me.

"You know about war with Delph but, before we fought that war, we fought against all the roving bands. That took more time to accomplish than the war. They were not so hard to defeat," she said, "they were only hard to find. Once we had them, I gave them the choice of joining our army, and almost all of them did. Actually, I thought of you and your fierce independence and understood the ones who did not."

She pulled a tasseled rope, and he heard a bell ringing somewhere in the castle. Soon a servant entered the room, and she seemed shocked to see the queen and Björn sitting so close together.

"Etta," Aleanna said, "You are the first to know that Björn and I are to be married and you are in charge of organizing it."

Etta froze at the news, but quickly recovered. "Oh, congratulations, your Highness. The entire kingdom will be happy for you."

"Thank you, Etta. You are in charge of everything, but that does not mean you are to do everything yourself. You are in charge of all the castle staff and anyone else you need, and I will inform them of your authority. Now I think a week from tomorrow will be fine for the day. What do you think?"

"I think any day you pick will be fine, your Highness."

"You have heard of Björn, I think."

Etta blushed. "Yes, your Highness, the word is all over the castle."

"Indeed," said Aleanna. "What is the gossip?"

"How Mr. Björn was your bodyguard on your trip to and from Carigo, and that he saved your life many times."

"Is that all?"

Etta blushed again. "There is talk about he and Brewster having the same strange grey hair. Some say Mr. Björn is Brewster's father."

"And what do you think of that, Etta?"

Etta lowered her eyes and said, "Nothing, your Highness."

"Is there anything else you wish to say?" Aleanna asked.

"Some are saying they have been fooled, but others are saying it is none of their business. I think the latter is what most of the people feel. Remember, your Highness, the people love you and will never think badly of you. As for Mr. Björn, he is such a hero that no one will speak badly of him."

"So you do not think anything will happen to mar the ceremony?"

"No, your Highness, but your soldiers must surely be on hand just in case."

"Yes, they will," replied the queen. "Go now, spread the news and begin your work."

After the servant left the room, Björn asked, "What did you learn from all of that?"

"To keep the army handy just in case." She looked at him, a pleased look on her face. "Do you need anything? Are you hungry and need something to eat? After all your running, surely you need to rest." Then she waved her hand dismissively. "Never mind, I know you. You never get hungry and you never get tired, but if there is anything you want, tell me and I will see that you get it."

"The only thing I want is to stay here with you," he said. "We have a lot more to talk about."

"I know what I want to talk about. It is that woman Gelda," Aleanna said. "Tell me again how you met her and about the time you were together."

So Björn told her the entire story, leaving nothing out. Aleanna got visibly upset when he told her of Gelda's invitation to sleep with her. "Did you want to sleep with her?"

"Honestly, I was tempted. I was lonely and did not think I would never see you again, but I could not because of my memories of you. I felt it would be unfaithful, even though that was rather silly since I did not think you cared for me."

She hugged him. "That is beautiful, dear, but go on with the story."

When he had finished, it was late in the day. He would have finished sooner if it were not for being constantly interrupted by her questions.

Aleanna said they should get Brewster and the three of them would have some dinner. Taking Björn by the hand, she led him back to the study where Brewster was still hard at work.

"Come, dear," she said, "take a break and come to dinner with us." She rang the bell again and, when Etta responded, Aleanna announced they would be having dinner in the king's dining room. Then she led them to the small room where he had first dined with her father, his family and his retinue. Björn was pleased because the room was somewhat intimate and brought back good memories.

Etta soon appeared and set the table, with other servants on her heels carrying platters of food. Björn remembered the quantity, quality and variety of food served by Brewster's predecessor, noting it hat not diminished in any way.

Aleanna noted that Björn ate much more than she remembered and commented on it.

"We ate little on the trip here, and I must admit I am somewhat hungry. We only munched on some dried fruits and vegetables I had with me. Jago needed to eat, and since we did not have time for him to graze, I had to share the vegetables with him. We ran out of food about halfway here. Then we made only a few brief stops a day to eat some grass and what bulbs I could find," said Björn. "So, yes, I am rather hungry."

"You should have said something. Now I am angry at both of us; at you for not telling me and at me, for not realizing you would be hungry. But eat your fill now."

During dinner, Aleanna made sure Brewster learned about Björn. She knew the Northlander was reticent and humble, so she tried to draw him out with questions. Even so, there were some things he would not talk about, and she realized there was much they had talked about that was personal between the two of them. She felt very privileged that he had told her those things.

Björn kept trying to turn the conversation to Brewster, but Aleanna always shifted it back to Björn. By the time they had finished dining, the conversation seemed to be at an end.

Brewster excused himself, saying he had a full day ahead of him and must get to bed.

Aleanna and Brewster stood as well, and Brewster shook Björn's hand and kissed Aleanna on the cheek. "Good night to both of you," he said, "and Björn, it was an honor to meet you."

"The honor is mine," Björn said.

Brewster departed, and Aleanna took Björn's hand, saying, "Come, I will show to your room. It is our very best guest room, but I know it will be wasted on you. You would not care if I placed you in the stables or under one of the old oak trees in the courtyard." She smiled up at him. "But I want you to be civilized for once and stay in this room tonight."

She led him across the great room and to a large stairwell, where they ascended the ornate stairs and made their way to a large, intricately carved door. Opening the door, she showed him the room. Even Björn had to admit it was a beautiful room, but the centerpiece of the room was a huge four-poster bed covered with an intricately woven, beautiful canopy. He physically recoiled at the sight of the bed. "Surely you do not expect me to sleep in that!" he exclaimed.

Aleanna took his hand and squeezed it. "Please humor me, Björn. I guarantee you will be happy with the bed and now, good night." Stretching up and holding his shoulders, she kissed him firmly and for a long moment on the lips, then she glided to the door and passed through the doorway into the hallway.

It took at least two hours for all activity to cease and for the castle to become quiet. Aleanna spent the time sitting at her vanity brushing her hair and thinking. Björn stood inside the door of his room listening to all of the sounds. Then he heard the swishing of a woman's gown coming down the hallway to his room. The sound stopped and the door opened.

Aleanna slipped into the room and, stopping inside the doorway, asked, "Where are you? Remember, my eyes are not as good as yours in the dark. I see from the light coming in the window, that you are not in bed."

Hands came out of the darkness to catch her by the waist. She turned into the circle of his arms and kissed him passionately. Taking hold of his tunic, she pulled it over his head, letting it drop to the floor.

"Can you remember the first time I did that?" she whispered. "I can."

"I remember every detail of that evening and will never forget," Björn said softly. "You cannot imagine how many times I went over every moment in my mind."

"Me, too," she said.

She pushed him down on the bed and, kneeling, removed his boots. She made him take the weight off his body so she could remove his trousers then, slipping out of her robe and nightgown, she drew him up from the bed and held him close to her while she kissed him long and passionately. Starting at his shoulders, she kissed his body slowly, continuing to his feet. Slipping into the bed, she pulled him over on top of her. She decided he felt as good as she remembered and had dreamed of for twenty-three years. Holding him tightly, she slept better than she had since the last time they were together.

She awoke shortly before the castle did and, with a last kiss, she slid out of bed and donned her nightclothes.

"If you want me, I will be back tonight," she said, and she darted out the door before he could respond.

Returning to her room apparently unseen, Aleanna took her time bathing and preparing her appearance. She wondered when she had been this happy, and decided it must have been while she and Björn were returning from Carigo. But then she thought that this was a happier time because she had lost him, and now had him back. But she here she was dawdling when she could be with him.

Dressed for the day, she went in search of him. First, she went to his room but, as expected, he was gone. She found Etta and asked if she knew where he was. Etta didn't know but said she would check with the castle staff to see if anyone knew. When she returned, she told the queen that someone had seen him very early leaving the courtyard with his horse.

Mildly irritated, she ordered her horse prepared and, grabbing a small loaf of bread, ate it on her way to the stable where her grey mare was already saddled.

She guessed he would likely have gone the way the two of them had gone on their tour of the kingdom so many years ago. Mounting her mare, she recalled the trip to

Carigo and the loving mare she lost when she and Björn were captured, but her thoughts returned to the present when she found Björn and Jago.

"And where have you been?"

"Out for a stroll," he told her. "I did not know when you would be stirring, so Jago and I decided on a walk. Can you join us, or do you prefer to go back to the castle?"

Satisfied that he was not leaving, she told him they could go on together. She dismounted and walked beside him, asking if he noticed any changes since their first trip.

"I believe the village houses are in a better state of repair."

"I think the people are better off now," she said, happy to be with him again. "We have had a number of years of good weather and good crops, so people have more money. I am quite proud of them; they take such pride in their homes and their villages that they spend money on public buildings and homes first."

They continued walking and chatting until almost midday. "I hope you are hungry, as I am. I am not the girl I was back on our trip all those years ago so we must stop to eat, and I have close friends in that village," she said, pointing at a nearby hamlet. "We will stop there."

They entered the village, and immediately word spread that the queen was there. It seemed the entire village came running to greet her. It reminded Björn of the time years ago when the two of them had entered a similar hamlet.

After greeting the queen, the villagers began to cast sidewise glances at him.

Aleanna noticed. "I want you to meet my future husband, Björn," she announced proudly with a big smile on her face. "We will be married a week from tomorrow and all of you are invited. You are the first to know, and I would like for you to spread the word to the other villages."

The villagers clapped and cheered.

"I am sure some of you remember my trip to Carigo many years ago. Björn was my bodyguard. He has now returned after all this time."

The villagers bombarded her with many questions.

"Where has he been?"

"Where will the wedding be?"

"Should we send runners to the other villages?"

"Why did you wait all of these years to be married?"

"Are you going to stay and live in the kingdom?"

"I cannot answer all of your questions at once," Aleanna said cheerfully. "We are hungry. Erika, can you feed us?"

"Of course I can, your Highness." Erika moved toward her cottage, as the other villagers shouted their invitations.

Aleanna turned to the crowd. "After we eat, we will come out and I will attempt to answer all your questions," she told them, then they followed Erika into her cottage. The small home showed recent improvement and expansion. Aleanna clapped her hands and exclaimed about the changes.

"We have been able to make many improvements," Erika said. "Now we have separate bedrooms for the boys and the girls, we have an eating area separate from the kitchen and we enlarged our bedroom. We have also added some furniture."

"I am so happy for you, Erika. Times have indeed been good for you."

"We owe it all to you, your Highness," Erika said simply. "Come sit down." She went into the kitchen and in a few minutes returned with steaming platters. They had a fine meal, and Aleanna and Erika had an enjoyable time trading news and gossip. Björn sat patiently through it.

Finally, Aleanna got up and they said their good-byes, and Erika followed them outside where the rest of the village was still gathered.

Again questions rained down on Aleanna. She told her people that Björn was a mercenary and that he had been traveling and practicing his craft while she ran the affairs of the kingdom. "This is the first opportunity we have had to marry," she told them. "We have not decided on where we will live, but wedding will be in the castle courtyard."

There was a barrage of other questions that Aleanna tried to answer. Finally, she drew a halt to the questioning and saying goodbye, she and Björn left and started back to the castle.

On the way they talked about what plans they should make for after they were married.

"Will you still have responsibilities at the castle?" Björn asked.

"No, when we are married, I will have no responsibilities here," she answered. "Brewster has promised to keep the legal system in operation. That was my final responsibility. Now I am free to go where I want, and I want to go with you. I know you would not be happy caged up here and I prefer to get away as well. Traveling with you is the best that could happen to me since we first met."

"Traveling will be no problem," Björn said. "I have been almost everywhere, so I know the best places to take you. Of course, I will give up my mercenary work."

"You do not have to. I will travel with you and perhaps even help at times."

Björn shook his head. "I will not risk your life. I do not want anything to distract me from you, so I think it best that I retire. I have more than enough money to last us the rest of our lives. I spend little and save the rest except for what I give away."

"Okay, then it is settled. We will travel where we will."

CHAPTER TEN
THE WEDDING

The time flew by during the next week. Even though Aleanna had delegated everything to Etta, there were dozens of details only she could handle. The result was that the only time she and Björn had together was at night when Aleanna came to Björn's room.

The work went on at a furious pace. All day there was the noise of sawing, hammering and pounding outside the castle. A huge platform as tall as two men was erected next to the courtyard's outer wall, tall enough so that everyone would be able to see those on the platform. This was where the wedding would be held.

Aleanna's primary task was preparing her wedding dress. During her free time, she developed the ceremony with the bishop, deciding who would be on the platform as she didn't want to create hurt feelings. The only solution was to limit the wedding party to Brewster, Björn, and herself. The bishop would perform the ceremony.

It was still necessary to confer with Etta several times a day and with others as well, such as her generals. If the occasion arose that they were needed to maintain order, she wanted soldiers scattered conspicuously throughout the wedding crowd.

The days passed uneventfully for Björn except for the suit fitting. First they had to take all his measurements, which was most embarrassing for him, but he discovered his actual weight and height. The tailors cut a suit made of heavy paper and checked and rechecked them. Finally, they were sufficiently satisfied to commit the paper to cloth and try it on Björn. With only a few minor adjustments, they were satisfied. The suit was black, with black shoes made to match. Björn thought the shoes and suit were wearable, but he wasn't as sure about the shirt. It was white, with large ruffles on the cuffs that protruded from the sleeves of the coat. Ruffles also adorned the suit at the neck. Björn had seen dandies at various courts dressed in similar fashion and had always detested the style. Then he remembered that he was doing this for Aleanna.

Aleanna's nightly visits became even more enjoyable as they talked into the morning about the life they would have. She still insisted on traveling with him, but she was dubious about him giving up being a mercenary. She was afraid he would become bored and come to resent her for it.

His response was always the same. "It is worth giving up being a mercenary to be with you, Aleanna."

"Well," she said, "we can always change our minds."

She was surprised one night when Björn told her he was going to be gone for at least three days, starting the next day. She tried to find out where he was going and why, but he was very mysterious.

Aleanna was completely consumed with details of the wedding. She found that while Etta was quite competent, there were still many things that demanded her individual attention. First and foremost was the gown, a long flowing dress of soft yellow silk with a low-cut bodice decorated with gold beads. Around her hips she wore a soft leather girdle where a jeweled dagger rested.

Finally the day arrived. Björn had returned the night before, still mysterious. She stayed with him that night to be sure she was up early to get prepared. This time, she broke with precedent and had her maids prepare her. While it was luxurious to receive such pampering, she had to admit that she would not want it all the time. First they bathed her, then they dried her hair and to put it up. Normally she wore it down, but had decided to be more formal for the wedding. Her hair was upswept with soft ringlets trickling down the back, decorated with gold beads and tiny yellow rosebuds to match her gown.

Then they perfumed and oiled her, and put a bit of makeup on her face. Then came the gown, and, last of all came the haba skin ankle boots made from a small goat native to the high mountains. Haba was the softest leather they knew of.

When her ensemble was complete, she looked at her reflection in the mirrors on the four walls of the room. She was satisfied. She couldn't remember looking this attractive, and hoped Björn would be pleased.

They had nearly half an hour to wait for the ceremony. She had timed it that way, with barely enough time to be ready and not so much time that she became overly nervous; she was nervous enough the way it was. She stood because she didn't want to wrinkle the gown, and she didn't want to walk for the same reason. Finally, she had no choice and began to pace.

"Madame," her maids protested, "this is not good for your dress."

"I cannot help it," she said, traces of irritation in her tone. "I cannot stand still."

When it was almost time to go, the maids gave her one last careful look, reapplied her perfume and they were ready.

As they paraded down the hall and then the stairwell, she thought that she was leaving her home as a single woman, but would re-enter in a few hours as a married woman ready to leave her life-long home. A tear formed in the corner of one eye.

Etta, ever observant said, "Now, Madam, this is the happiest day of your life. You should not cry."

"That is exactly why I am crying, Etta," Aleanna said firmly.

"But, your Highness, you will ruin your makeup."

"Thank you, Etta." Aleanna gave the woman a grateful smile. "I promise I will control myself."

It was a big procession to the wedding platform. First came the palace guards in their bright red pants topped by black coats, Aleanna was next, and the ladies of the court followed dressed in their best finery. The group made its way down the stairs, across the courtyard to the gate, and finally to the steps going up to the platform. Brewster, dressed as king, held out his arm, and she took it.

The fields around the castle were packed. It seemed that the entire kingdom was there. All had been quite noisy until Aleanna appeared, then they grew silent, even those who couldn't see but could only guess what was happening. The moment she started to move up the steps, the people went wild with applauding, cheering and clapping.

Brewster escorted her up the stairs to where Björn and the bishop were waiting for them. As soon as she reached Björn's side, Brewster took her hand and placed it in the hand of the Northlander. Aleanna reached out and took his other hand, holding both tightly.

When they turned to face the people, the crowd became even louder. The cheering and applause went on until the bishop raised his hands for silence. Even then it took some time for quiet, but finally, it was almost silent. Björn and Aleanna hardly noticed. They were each staring into each other's eyes. Aleanna had a huge smile on her face, and Björn was smiling more than she had ever seen.

Aleanna thought of how she had dreamed of this day but never believed it possible. It had been so long in coming, and the past year of waiting had been unbearable. Björn had never thought anything like this could happen and was almost dumbfounded. Still holding hands, they turned to face the bishop. They were so focused on each other that several times he had to repeat himself when they needed to respond.

Finally, he came to the part where he asked, "Björn, do you take Aleanna to be your lawful wedded wife?" Holding both her hands and looking her in the eye, he said, "I do." Aleanna responded the same way.

Björn's heart jumped with joy; he couldn't imagine ever being this happy. He and Aleanna were actually going to spend the rest of their lives together.

With tears in her eyes, Aleanna thought of the year she had waited to hear back from him. Tears started flowing down her cheeks, and she caught Björn, holding him tightly. Rising on her toes, she put her cheek against his. He held her there and said, "Do not cry, my love."

"I must," she said. "I am so happy that I feel I am going to burst with happiness."

The people clapped and cheered even louder when Björn pulled a ring with a huge diamond out of his pocket and, holding Aleanna's hand in his, slipped the ring on her finger. Aleanna rose on her toes again and kissed him on the mouth. "Now I know where you were for those three days."

Björn smiled and, taking her hand, led her down the steps into the courtyard and from there into the castle. Aleanna stopped at the courtyard gate and give a final wave to her people and again they applauded and cheered madly.

As soon as they were in the castle, Aleanna grabbed Björn and gave him a long passionate kiss. Then, grabbing his arm, she led him upstairs to her sitting room, where she kissed him again. Then she stepped away. "We must be careful; we do not want to mess up the dress before we have to go out again."

There was a knock on the door, and Etta said, "Your Highness, they are ready for you in the courtyard." Aleanna crossed the room, Björn following, and said, "We are ready, Etta."

"No, your Highness, you are not. Let me fix your make-up. You have smudged it."

"I wonder how that happened," said Björn with a stoic face.

"Yes, I wonder," Aleanna said, honey dripping from her words.

Etta blushed but went to work on the queen's make-up. When she was satisfied, they exited the room, heading back to the courtyard. They waited at the bottom of the stairs to receive their guests; Björn shaking hands with people and Aleanna hugging everyone.

After they went through the receiving line, the villagers were guided outside the castle to where tables had been set with enormous amounts of food. The word had been sent out that dinner would be served immediately after the ceremony. Because many of the people had started their journeys the day before or even earlier, most of them were in need of a good meal, and it was a meal that would be remembered and talked about for years, with more food than any of the people had seen before. Aleanna knew she would become faint if she didn't eat beforehand and had done so. As eating wasn't that important to Björn, he had eaten a little, more to satisfy Aleanna than because he was hungry.

It was almost evening when all who came to pay their respects had gone through the line. Aleanna was exhausted. By the time the last person passed, she was holding onto Björn for support. He picked her up and carried her into the castle to her bedroom, where he turned her over to her servants to bathe her and prepare her for bed.

The servants informed Björn when she was ready, and he entered the bedroom. She was sitting up in bed and held out her arms to him. He went to her and, sitting on the bed next to her, he embraced her. She told him servants were bringing food and drink.

"Did you enjoy the ceremony, dearest?" she asked.

"Most of it," he answered. "But I could have done without the receiving line. I am not in the habit of shaking people's hands, and today was too much."

She snuggled against him. "You Northlanders are too reserved. I do not know how I ever convinced you to marry me."

"Oh, I came along willingly enough," he laughed. "I may have balked a little at the big wedding but I knew it was what you wanted. But tell me you would not have been disappointed if I had not gotten you that ring."

She held up her hand, showing off the exquisite ring. "I love it, but honestly, I never thought about it. How did you find such a stone? I imagine you got it at Yalta, which is the only place I know where they have such diamonds. But how did you get it on such short notice?"

"Jago and I ran all the way at our fastest. It took a day for the jeweler to mount the stone I selected in the ring I chose. And then," he said cheerfully, "we ran all of the way back so it took only three days."

"But how did you get a good jeweler to set the stone in only one day?"

"I persuaded him."

"Please do not tell me you threatened him."

"No, but I would have if he had not taken the extra gold I offered him. You need not worry, darling; he was more than happy with our bargain."

She cuddled against him again just as servants entered with their meal. Björn carried a small table from across the room and set it against the bed close enough for Aleanna to reach comfortably. The servants placed a chair for Björn across the table from his bride.

Aleanna ate ravenously for a bit, then stopped. "I am too tired to eat anymore," she announced.

Since Björn appeared to be finished, she asked the servants to remove the food. They did so quickly, then left the room at the queen's command.

"You should get some rest now," Björn said. "Would you like me to rub your back to relax you?"

"I would love it."

Björn rubbed her back gently until she fell asleep, and even continued long after she fell asleep. She sometimes moaned in her sleep while he was rubbing, but eventually he fell asleep for a few hours.

After he awoke, he became restless and got up and stood by the window looking out at the courtyard. He thought about tomorrow and how it would be the last day in the castle for Aleanna. It would be much happier for her than the last time when she left to marry the king of Carigo.

Aleanna awoke late, stretched, yawned and held out her arms to be held. Björn sat on the bed and held her.

"Oh, I feel so good!" Aleanna cooed. "Thank you for the back rub last night. You continued to rub me even after I went to sleep, I believe. I could tell in my sleep that you did. Now come here and let me repay you."

By the time they arose, the castle was in full operation. Aleanna said, "Let us get Etta to arrange for our breakfast to be served here. I do not want to go to all the trouble of getting dressed yet."

She pulled the cord for Etta, who arrived in moments, telling them she had been waiting for the summons.

"Yes, your Highness. I was sure you would be ready for breakfast. Where would you like to be served?"

"I think we will eat here, Etta."

Breakfast was served quickly, then Aleanna announced that she had to get dressed and make her preparations to leave.

Brewster stopped to see them and to say he had made sure he had this day free to talk to them. They decided the two men would talk while Aleanna went about her business in the castle.

Björn and Brewster walked around the courtyard, enjoying the sunny day.

"Mother told me right after you arrived that you were my father." He smiled at Björn. "Of course, I had figured it when I saw how much alike we looked. And when I thought about everything and the stories I had heard, I realized I shared natural physical abilities with you. I had always wondered why my abilities were so far beyond those of other men."

"Yes, I can see that you must have been curious, my son."

"Can you show me how you do the arrow trick?"

"Of course," Björn laughed. "Go get a bow and some arrows."

Brewster did as instructed, then stood some distance away, prepared to shoot. After raising the bow, he held it for a moment, then laid it on the ground.

"I am sorry, but I cannot do it."

"Well, let us get someone who can," Björn said.

Brewster turned to one of his soldiers and explained to the man what to do. Björn saw the man gesturing, obviously not in agreement with the order, but finally he picked up the bow and arrow and made a half-hearted attempt. Björn easily caught the arrow.

"Brewster, if you are not going to do better than that, it is hardly worth our time."

Chastised and slightly red in the face, Brewster took the bow, notched an arrow and let it fly toward Björn. With no apparent effort, Björn caught the arrow.

"So it is not merely a story," Brewster said. "Not that I disbelieved; it seemed too wild to be true. And your eyes were closed. How did you do it?"

Björn told Brewster the entire story and, when he had finished, Brewster peppered him with other questions that Björn answered as best he could.

"So that is how you came to be a mercenary and why you are so good at it. Will you tell me some of the adventures you have had?"

Björn related some stories of his escapades.

"Tell me of the trip you and mother made to Carigo," Brewster said.

"That is a long story," Björn said. "Are you sure you want to hear it?"

"Of course I do."

"Well, it is going take awhile and I am afraid you may become hungry, so we should return to the castle, get something to eat and make ourselves comfortable."

"Mother has told me that you are never hungry, tired or uncomfortable, but do not worry about me. Mother says I am like you. Still, it is getting dark so perhaps we had best do as you say, or Mother may be worried about us."

"I doubt she will worry, but we should go in."

They returned to the castle and Brewster ordered food be brought to them, telling a servant to inform his mother. Then he led the way to his study, where they sat on opposite sides of a table. Not long after, servants entered with platters of food and pitchers of milk and wine, and they began to eat. Aleanna arrived to join them for dinner and asked about their day.

"I very much enjoyed spending time with my father," Brewster said, "We know each other much better."

"What else did you do?" Aleanna asked.

"We talked, Mother. He told me about his early life and your trip to Carigo all those years ago."

"How about you, Björn? Did you get to know your son?"

"I did, but it was a difficult thing because he kept asking me so many questions, a trait I am certain he got from his mother."

Aleanna laughed. "I wish I had been there. I would have loved to hear you digging things out of your father. I am sure you noticed that he does not give up information about himself easily. As long as I have known him, I still keep learning new things. Please remember, my husband, that I must get to bed if we are to leave early in the morning."

"Do not rush," Björn said. "We can always leave the day after."

"Do that, Mother. I am enjoying visiting with my father.

We can use the time to get caught up."

"Very well," Aleanna said, "that will take some pressure off me. We will leave the day after tomorrow." She left the room.

"Now tell me everything and do not leave anything out."

"I am sure your mother has told you a great deal of the story, so I will give you the gist of it. It is quite long, so when you want details, please ask."

Björn began the story, beginning with when they left the castle with Rathe. Brewster was quite interested in the giant bipeds and asked a lot of questions, but he asked even more questions about the snow beast. When Björn glossed over his injuries, Brewster related that his mother had said that Björn was severely hurt.

"I was hurt several times on the trip, but never quite as badly as your mother thought."

Björn continued the story, telling Brewster of his mother's courage and acts of skill. Brewster wanted to know how the Northlander had escaped from the mine, as she had been vague on this.

"That was probably because we did not talk about it very much. We were too busy escaping and then we wanted to forget it. The truth is, I cut the manacles with my boot knife, then was able to rescue your mother so we could escape."

"How did you manage to cut the irons with only a knife?" Brewster asked.

"It was not just any knife, Brewster; it was this knife." Björn removed the knife from his boot. When Brewster saw the small knife, he was even more astounded. "It seems too small to do such damage!" he exclaimed.

"This is the strongest and sharpest steel I have ever seen," said Björn. "It comes exclusively from the

Northland. Do you have some steel or iron you are not concerned about getting marred? If so, try nicking it with this knife." He handed the knife to his son.

Brewster took it, trying it against a common-looking dagger he carried at his waist. "That is amazing," he said as Björn's knife cut through it like butter. "Mother told me the story of how you cut the blade off my grandfather's sword," Brewster said. "If your swords are made from the same material, I now see how you did it."

Aleanna came back into the room, telling Björn that she was off to bed. Björn commented that he was as well. Aleanna hugged Brewster and Björn said good night, then they departed for bed.

It wasn't long before Aleanna fell sound asleep. Björn tucked the covers around her, and she sighed contentedly. He stood by the bed for some time admiring her beauty. I am so fortunate to have her, he thought, then let himself out the door.

He strode down the hall and through the outside door. No one saw him, and he decided to take a different route than he had taken before and began walking down a road between houses.

Cries broke the stillness and Björn's wandering. He followed the noise and found four ruffians pummeling a man on the ground. Using his fists, his elbows and feet, Björn pounded the attackers to the ground, and they scrambled away from him before fleeing. When he helped the man to his feet, he saw he was badly hurt.

"Where can I take you?"

"My home is this way," the man said. "Thank you for getting those thugs off me. I am afraid you will have to help me, as I do not think I can walk by myself."

"Certainly," replied Björn, taking the man's arm. "Were

they trying to rob you or beat you?"

"They were trying to rob me, but did not get anything because I had nothing to steal. Normally I carry a large sum of money, but fortunately I was returning from a business trip and had left everything there."

The man directed Björn to a very nice small home he identified as his, and Björn helped him into the house. His wife jumped to her feet and came running toward them.

"Oh, my goodness, Oren. What has happened to you?"

"Some robbers attacked me. If not for the help of this man, they might have killed me. He dispatched the four men without using any weapons other than his hands and feet." He looked at Björn. "This is my wife Margaret. I am sorry, but I do not know your name."

"I am Björn," Björn said simply.

"How can we ever repay you?" Margaret asked, helping her husband to a sofa with Björn's help. "How badly are you hurt?" she asked Oren.

"I think I have some broken ribs and bruises," he told her.

A young man of about fourteen had entered the room. "Erin, please go get the doctor," Margaret told him.

Erin hurried out the door, and the woman turned back to her husband. "I have been telling you to get a bodyguard. Perhaps this man would take the job. He certainly appears to be both qualified and honest."

"You have convinced me," answered her husband. "Will you take the job?" he asked Björn. "I make trips about once a week that take two to three days. You will be very well paid for your work."

"I worry so much about him," Margaret pleaded, "and then something like this happens. Will you please take the job?"

At that moment, the village doctor entered with the young man. When he saw Björn, the physician said, "Mr. Björn, I am surprised to see you here."

"He saved Oren's life," Margaret gushed.

The doctor walked to Oren's side and started his examination. "Do you know who this man is?" he asked the family. "This is Björn, the man who married the queen today."

Margaret gasped and took a step back. "I was too far away to recognize him in those clothes," she said, "and the reception line was so long some of us decided not to go. We offered him a job as bodyguard to my husband. I am so embarrassed, sir."

"Do not be embarrassed," said Björn, "In the past, I have often served as a bodyguard. But since the queen and I are married, I have given up that kind of work. But thank you for the offer and the compliment."

The doctor looked up from his examination. "Oren has two broken ribs and some pretty bad bruises, but he will be fine."

"Thank you again for helping me," Oren said warmly.

Saying their good-byes, Björn and the doctor left the house and took leave of each other outside the home.

Björn continued his walk through the town. When he reached the outskirts, Jago fell into step beside him, and he continued his stroll into the countryside, again in deep thought. What would he and Aleanna do? There was no doubt they loved each other deeply, but could they adapt to their future lifestyle? Would Aleanna really be happy being a vagabond, or would she want to settle down at some point? What would he do if she did? He had been traveling ever since he left the Northland, and all of his training had prepared him to be a warrior. That was what he had been ever since leaving.

He had to admit it wasn not only for the money that he took on such dangerous jobs. It was the thrill, which he found much more important than money, even more important than helping people who, without him, had no hope. He knew losing that thrill would be a great loss to him, but when he compared that to Aleanna and the more than twenty years he had been without her, all those things were insignificant.

He was glad he had thought everything through. Of course Aleanna was the most important thing in his life now, just as she been since they met, even when he had given up hope of ever seeing her again. He felt quite content and came out of his reverie totally committed to trying to make his beloved as happy as possible.

Looking up, he was startled to see that the sun was up and he was miles from the castle. He hoped Aleanna was still asleep so she wouldn't worry about where he was. He started back to the castle at a fast run, Jago galloping beside him. The sun was high in the sky when he reached the castle, and he hurried to Aleanna's room. Thankfully, she was still asleep, and even though he entered the room in his typical silent fashion, Aleanna still began to stir and soon was awake. He moved to sit on the bed and took her hand.

She sat up and kissed him passionately. "Where did you spend the night, my love? I know you did not stay in our room."

"You are getting to know me too well, Aleanna. I could not sleep so I went for a long walk with Jago."

"Well, I hope you are not planning to keep on with that practice when we are sleeping together," she said. "It would disturb me to awaken and find you gone."

"Then I have a reason to stay, although I question if you really want someone beside you who is wide awake. But, as I recall, it did not seem to bother you on our trip from Carigo."

"You are right; I guess it did not then and I suppose it will not now." She hugged him tightly. "What is important is that you are here."

"I promise I will not do it again."

"You had better not." She gave him another kiss, untangled herself from him and the bedclothes, and slipped out of bed. After she dressed, she took his arm and said, "Let us get some breakfast."

As they left, they met Etta, who had evidently had been waiting for them.

"I will have breakfast served right away, your Highness. It will only take a few minutes." She hurried off.

"Björn, I am certainly going to miss her, unless you will wait on me in this fashion."

"I will and more so, your Highness." He bowed deeply.

"I did not believe it possible, but I do think you are developing a sense of humor."

"I would not go that far," he chuckled.

They entered the small dining room, and found that Etta already had placed the breads and jellies and jams on the table. She returned shortly with two other servants bearing plates of eggs, ham and bacon.

"I believe we have to get away before I become fat!" Björn said.

"I doubt that you would ever get fat," Aleanna said, "but I am was sure I will lose weight on the trail. I will enjoy becoming lean again."

"How are your preparations coming along, my love?"

"I will complete my work well before the end of the day,

and then I can spend time with you and Brewster if you wish."

"I would like that very much," he said, leaning down to kiss her. They departed after making plans for lunch.

Björn found Brewster in the king's study.

"Please come in, Father," Brewster said. "Can I get you something?"

"No, no, I am fine," Björn said.

"Then perhaps I shall take a break and you can continue the story of you and my mother."

Björn renewed the tale from the point they had ended the day before. "I escaped from the mine, but I had to release the other prisoners as well because of how we were fettered. I tried to convince them to help me, but they were so frightened they scurried this way and that, like rats. Still, as I sought to find your mother in the castle, I literally bumped into her in a castle hallway, and we made our escape."

Pausing, he asked Brewster if he could have a drink from the pitcher of water sitting on a sidebar. Brewster got up and poured his father a glass of water, then sat down again. Björn took a drink, then started to gloss over the part about the prime minister, but Brewster insisted that he tell him everything.

"Are you sure you want all the details?" Björn asked. "It is not a pleasant story."

"I understand," Brewster said, "but Mother never told me what happened."

"That is because I never told her the entire story," Björn said, "but I will tell you since you are so insistent," and he gave his son with all the gory details.

"He got exactly what he deserved," commented Brewster.

"No, not nearly as much. I could have made it much worse." Björn continued with the story, and was finishing when Aleanna slipped into the room.

Brewster jumped up and hugged Aleanna. "Mother, we have just gotten to the part where the two of you parted after arriving in Kallthom. Why did the two of you separate?"

After a long hesitation, she told him that part of the story.

"You mean you cared more for the kingdom than you did for Björn?"

"No," she said, "but I knew Björn could take care of himself, and I was not sure what would become of the kingdom. Besides, what would we have done with an infant on the trail?" she teased. Getting serious again, she went on. "It was difficult enough being separated from your father, let alone having to worry about letting Kallthom deteriorate after it had taken years for our family to build. So now you have the entire story, Brewster. I want you to know that I missed your father every single day he was gone. Are you satisfied?"

"Yes, Mother, I am happy to have everything tied together for me. I very much appreciate that you shared it with me. What a story I will have to tell my children and my grandchildren! I will not forget a single detail."

He pulled the cord to summon the servants and ordered lunch. Brewster had more questions and after lunch, Aleanna announced she had a bit more work to do and she would be ready. "We can definitely leave first thing in the morning."

Brewster asked Björn if he would like to go for a ride. Björn nodded, and the king ordered two horses prepared for them. Taking Jago, they cantered slowly over the countryside, talking as they rode.

Brewster told his father of the most recent changes in Kallthom, but said that most of the changes had been made in Delph and Carigo. In fact, he spent more time in those two places than he did in Kallthom. Björn asked if any changes had been made in the operation of the mine at Carigo.

"I am sorry," Brewster said. "I should have known you would want to know about that. We no longer keep any convicts underground for more than four hours at a time. They are given one fifteen-minute break in that time and all the water they need. Instead of being starved, they are now fed decent meals. When any of the convicts are too ill to work, the supervisor finds something else for them to do. Based on your experience there, I thought you would want to know they are now treated humanely. The men who work for pay work the same hours but are paid decent wages.

"Mother brought men from Kallthom to be in leadership positions in both Delph and Carigo, wanting leaders who understood her philosophy to be in charge. She had everything organized so well that it was easy for me to step in. I have continued what she started."

Brewster halted, and waved his arms as if to encompass the kingdom. "Even here in Kallthom, she made many changes, like giving the nomadic tribes the option of either staying here or resuming their roving. A few stayed, but most kept their nomadic ways. They come back to trade and visit several times a year. There has not been a single problem in all this time from them."

He turned his horse back toward the castle, and Björn did the same, Jago bringing up the rear. Brewster continued to relate the things they had accomplished and of their plans for the future. "I wish that I could go over every project in detail with Mother before she leaves."

"I am sure your mother has prepared you for this day. I thought she said you worked alongside her in each of the projects, and if that is so, I am confident she did all she could to prepare you for your responsibilities. Knowing your mother as I do, I am confident she would not be leaving if she did not think you were ready."

Brewster grinned broadly and said, "I am sure you are correct and, if you are not, she will be back to check on me on a regular basis."

Björn agreed. As dusk approached, they arrived back at the castle, handing off their mounts to stable hands. Then they walked into the castle.

One of the servants immediately notified Aleanna, who caught up with them before they finished washing. "You were certainly gone a long time! Brewster, I was wondering if your father was getting you into his bad habit of staying out all night."

"No, Mother, I did not notice the time."

"You may not have, but your father did," she retorted. "He always knows the time. Now let us go in for dinner.

Later that evening, when they had gone to bed, Aleanna embraced and kissed Björn. She told him this would be one of the rare times when they would have a bed to sleep in, so they should make the best of it.

The next morning when she awoke, Aleanna was astonished to find Björn beside her in bed. She hugged him tightly and then asked what he was doing still in bed.

"I am trying to be a good husband," he said. "I know how important it is for you to have me beside you when you wake up, so here I am. I am afraid that Jago will have to do the guarding on the trail. I enjoyed being close to you in the night so much that it will easily become a very nice habit."

"Did you really enjoy it?"

"Yes, I did. It is much better than standing and looking out the window, or being on the trail and staying up all night."

They rose, and Aleanna said she was going to take a bath, as this might the last time for a while that she would have the opportunity to bathe in a tub. She pulled the cord and Etta appeared.

"Etta, I am going to spoil myself this morning. Will you please get the girls and help me bathe?"

"Of course, Madame." She turned to leave.

"Oh, and Etta, get some food for Björn. Otherwise he will not eat." She shot Björn an impish look. "Now, Björn, stay right here and eat your breakfast."

He did as he was told when the food arrived, knowing it was best to eat to store up energy for the trail. He ate quickly and when finished said, "I will be with Brewster. Come and get me there when you finish."

He found Brewster in his room.

"Good morning, Father," Brewster said, then asked where they were going on their trip.

"I have no idea," Björn responded. "When we are ready to leave, I will ask your mother which direction she wants to go, and that is where we will go."

They continued talking until Aleanna arrived. She hugged Brewster. "Goodbye for now," she said wistfully.

Brewster shook hands with Björn and then, to Björn's surprise, hugged him as well.

When they went down the stairs, all the servants were gathered to tell them goodbye. Most of them were weeping or at the least had damp eyes. Aleanna had to hug each one. While this was going on, Björn went to the stable to get Jago. As he did not like to see crying, he stayed there until Aleanna was finished.

They left the castle, Aleanna riding her mare with Björn and Jago trotting beside them. When they came to a high hill overlooking the castle, Aleanna turned for a final look at the only home she had ever known. A few tears tumbled down her cheeks, but after a few minutes, she dried her eyes. She swung around, looking in the direction they were headed, and smiled at Björn. "Someday," she said, "we shall return."

THE END

CPSIA information can be obtained at www.ICGtesting.com
Printed in the USA
LVOW060050280911

248156LV00004B/1/P